DOING TIME
IN CALIFORNIA

DOING TIME

IN CALIFORNIA

DWIGHT JESMER

atmosphere press

PROLOGUE

"Forgive me, Father, for I have sinned. My last confession was, well, I don't remember. It's been a while. I've done a lot of sinning, and I don't quite remember the way this goes."

"Why don't you just pick a place and start, and I'll guide you through it."

The priest's voice was calming, not judgmental the way some priests' tones took in my past, voices of hypocrisy and intolerance which helped drive me away from the church.

"Well, I guess it started when I was a child, before I even entered school. My dad would go away on business trips, and when my mom wanted some peace, she would tell me she was calling the orphanage to come take me back. I ran and hid under the bed in sheer terror, so fearful of being taken from my family and ending up alone."

"Excuse me, um, I'm sorry to hear that. I know I said to pick a place and start, but could you bring it a little further up to date? I have a funeral in an hour."

"Oh, sorry. It's just kind of relevant, but okay. I guess I hit rock bottom about ten years ago. I was at a Christmas party, and a girl that I thought I loved told me she'd been married to my best friend's brother for six months, and uh, I just kind of lost it."

"You didn't know she was married?"

"No. I had been out of the loop for a while. I had moved down to L.A. to be an actor, went to the cattle calls, suffered the rejection, you know, same old story. I was just another bartender, just another dreamer getting crushed down in the city of angels. I don't blame L.A. for my descent into darkness. I chose it freely. It just seemed like the natural flow of my life, so I simply let go and drifted along with it."

"And it led you to rock bottom?"

"Yeah."

"And just where is that, exactly?"

"Huh?"

"I believe you were getting to your sins."

The priest's voice sounded bemused by my beating around the bush.

"Yes, rock bottom. Well, I found myself drunk, naked, and limp in a massage parlor where a woman with fake boobs was sticking her finger up my butt, trying to get me erect."

"Oh." The priest's voice changed, maybe blindsided, possibly surprised.

"That's not the worst of it, Father. Two days before that, I killed my grandfather. I don't deserve to live."

"Oh."

ONE

I was bending down to pick up a used condom when I heard the hawk's cry. I looked up and saw it coasting on the thermals, never flapping its wings, just riding the waves of heat like it was surfing. Now that was freedom. I threw the evidence of someone's good time in my plastic garbage bag and continued up the road. At least Mother Nature was taking its course, and someone was having fun.

This was the first really hot day of the summer, and the trash along the road was particularly putrid. My hands were sweating inside rubber gloves, but I was glad to have some protection between my skin and the human condition I had to pick up. My penance was cleaning up after the "law-abiding" citizens. It probably saved my life.

After the condom came a cigarette butt, a common find, many times hurled from cars by ignorant fools not realizing it's a Molotov Cocktail to the dried grass on hills like this one on Marsh Creek Road. Last summer, when I arrived at the detention center here in the shadows of Mount Diablo, the ground along this hill was scorched earth. From the road down to the creek, all life was taken by fire, and everything was black, collateral damage to the vice of smoking. A woman driving to the Marsh Creek Springs to plan her daughter's reception tossed her butt without thought of the consequences.

Now life was coming back, and little bits of grass, like green peach fuzz, rose toward the sun. I wish the dead trees provided some shade. I could climb down the hill, cross the creek, and rest in the shade of a living tree on the other side, but that might blow everything. That's the last thing I wanted. A confrontation of any kind, be it guard or fellow inmate, would ruin my plan, and there was no need for that. For Christ's sake, it's minimum security! All I had to do was play it cool, and this time tomorrow, I'd be playing golf.

I often visualized the hills and valleys along Marsh Creek Road as a golf course, with the detention center as the country club. It seems to me the real estate would be better used making money off the rich rather than taking time away from minor offenders of society's rules. Of course, the local ranchers might disagree. They must love the splendid isolation, located as they are between the heat and dust of the San Joaquin Valley and the cold and fog of San Francisco Bay.

The nearest golf course is in Clayton, a few miles west over the hills. My mind is on the course in Stockton, about thirty miles east, where the Angelina's Golf Tournament will tee off tomorrow at noon. I'm part of a foursome that hasn't missed the tournament in the last ten years. We were in a punk band in high school, Stillborn and the Afterbirths. I came up with the name. Do you think I needed some attention? They are three great guys, two of whom don't even know I've been locked up (it's a guy thing). I'm not going to let a little thing like prison get in the way of what has become an enjoyable tradition in my life. Besides, it's just the inspiration they'd want from their front man.

In fact, it was just a couple of weeks after last year's

tournament that I drove my Ford Fiesta across the lawn and into the statue in front of Saint Mary's School. I have no idea what I was doing driving by the school, but it pretty much ended my career as a Catholic School teacher. Luckily, it happened during the summer, so I didn't have to face the kids. I never wanted to be a role model; I needed a job, and it turned out I had a gift for teaching. My students loved me, their parents loved me, and even their pets loved me. Only Michelle didn't, and that bummed me out.

When Michelle left teaching, I went into my "red" period—red wine, red meat, and red eyes. The last thing I remembered was Michelle ignoring me at Frank's party, the next thing I knew, paramedics were trying to pry me out of the car. I had been pinned down by the statue of the Virgin Mary, which had broken off and fallen during the collision.

Mary's marble bosom was separated from my lips by the shattered windshield. I remember feeling guilty by being slightly aroused by the statue, the rain falling like tears down the virgin's face, bleeding through the cracks in the wind-shield, dropping on my lips like beats from her sacred heart. Small shards cut into my chest and face, the pain keeping me from passing out. That or the voice from the paramedic who kept telling me that everything was going to be okay.

I survived, was prosecuted for my crime, and was found guilty by a judge. I should have gone with a jury, but hindsight is twenty-twenty. The judge said that since I'm a role model, I had to set an example, so he sentenced me to one year at the Marsh Creek Detention Center. I gave out detentions in school, so I suppose turnabout is fair play.

My whole life would be different if that one human being chose to love me. I would never have crashed; we'd be together, and life would be sweet.

Why Michelle? Because she inspired me. She saw ways to be a good human being, which helped me see things I could do to follow her lead.

During my first-year teaching with her, she would always spend our lunch break inside her classroom with some of her students. Granted, it's not a best practice to be alone with students in your room and the door closed, but I found her trustworthy. Unfortunately, people started to talk. I overheard gossip whispered during dismissal duty until finally, she was brought before the principal by parents and questioned about it.

Turns out some of her students couldn't afford lunch, and out of her own pocket Michelle bought supplies and made them sandwiches every day. She didn't want them to be humiliated and teased by the other students, so she kept it quiet.

That is Michelle. She saw a need and did what she could to help. She didn't turn a blind eye to the problem. Because of her, I started playing Elvis Presley's "In the Ghetto" in class and challenged my students not to be blind to their world nor to turn their heads and look away. Each student had to do a service project during their fourth quarter in religion, and many people were helped. I would never have come up with that without Michelle's inspiration.

My best time with her was when she was taking the eighth graders on a weeklong field trip to Washington D.C. I was the only male teacher in the school, so I got to go along as a chaperone. I was, literally, a man among boys confidently leading them to the National Gallery to see Thomas Cole's The Voyage of Life. After giving a brief talk on each of the four paintings, Childhood, Youth, Manhood, and Old Age, I stood back and watched the kids eagerly explore each brilliant canvas.

Michelle came over, so excited to see her jaded students' genuine interest in what we were doing. She gave me a quick squeeze from behind that jolted my equilibrium and burned the memory into my brain, proving that any moment can indeed be powerful. I wanted more.

That whole week I was the center of her attention, well, among adults. It was glorious. After the kids' curfew, we'd get together in her room and talk. She introduced me to *Dalva* by Jim Harrison, and I played her *Union* by Toni Childs, and occasionally we'd have to apprehend teens looking for late-night adventures that weren't in the curriculum. It was hard to get angry because I was in my early twenties, and those kids' libidos weren't stronger than mine. There was definitely sexual tension between Michelle and me. It's just that she wouldn't do anything that she thought set a bad example to the students, so it smoldered for years.

"Hey, dumb ass!"

Back to reality. It was Glebe, a rather portly, small-time embezzler with a balding head and double chin. He was caught skimming from a county contract given by the Environmental Protection Agency to study strip mining's effect on the water system. "Everyone's buying bottled water anyway" was his excuse. He had an ex-wife and two kids that he paid the bills for and only saw every other weekend, and that was before jail. Poor kids.

"You walked right by that," he said, pointing to a yellow sweatshirt in the middle of the road.

I walked out and got it. It had been run over a few times, but other than that was in good shape. It had the name Liszt handwritten in black marker across the front of it.

"What the hell is Liszt? Is that a beer?" Glebe asks.

"I believe he was a classical composer."

"Oh yeah? What songs would I know?"

"I have no idea. I couldn't tell you a thing he did."

"He ain't no Beethoven, or the M-guy. What's his name?"

"Mozart?"

"Yeah, Mozart. I'm not into that old stuff. The blues are as far back as I go. Stevie Ray, man, what a fucking tragedy!"

The new guys talked too much. They were still insecure, still fearing all the frightening images of prison that have been fed to us since childhood and not yet realizing the different reality of doing time in minimum security. You could drop the soap and not have to worry! We were living proof of white privilege.

I nodded my head to him, threw the sweatshirt over my shoulder, and continued up my side of the road, leaving Glebe, who was going into an air guitar solo. I could use this sweatshirt later and wanted to get as far away from Glebe before stuffing it down my pants.

My thoughts drifted back to Michelle. Had I ever really loved her? I mean, sure, she inspired me. I sincerely wanted to be a better human being every time I saw her, but is that love, or is it as silly as saying I loved her eyes, which I did! Yes, they were vibrant and beautiful, but so are stained glass windows, and you can only see that from the inside. Was there something worth worshiping in her, or was everything I thought I saw just a projection reflected off those lovely eyes? What did I know of love, and what difference did it make? She married Ron.

Ron, Frank's older brother, and the wild drummer in our band. It was just a phase he grew out of when he left for the Air Force Academy to learn how to fly like their father, who went MIA during a mission before I knew them. Ron was gone for nine years with school and his commitment to the Air Force. He didn't meet Michelle until I moved down to L.A. to become a star.

That was another of my questionable choices to gain the attention I always seem to need, which dates back to hiding under the bed from my mother's calls to the orphanage. After Ron left, the band broke up, and my mantra became Bob Dylan's line, "when you ain't got nothing, you've got nothing to lose." Seems like that only brought me more of nothing.

Ron came home with a job flying executives from the Spanos family empire. He met Michelle through Frank. Frank and I met Michelle when we were undergrads at the University of San Francisco. Michelle was an education major and started teaching right after graduation. I needed a job and taught with her for three years before deciding I would impress her more if I were a Hollywood star. Ron didn't try to impress her.

Ron's a good guy, hardworking, and stable. He could provide for her. I don't blame Michelle for marrying him or Ron for marrying her. They're good together. It just hurt. It's not logical; simply emotional pain.

I was glad to have this year removed from society because it had been good for me. I had lost weight, got in pretty good shape, and learned some things. Left to myself, I would battle the ever-charging waves of the seven deadly sins that constantly crashed over me, thrusting me along at their merciless power, pushing me ever down, squeezing me between metaphorical rocks and hard places, until finally, powerless, I lost control. It was a wipeout.

The guard's whistle brought me back to the present moment. I tied my garbage bag, threw it over my shoulder, and walked down the hill to the waiting van. I tossed the bag in the back with the others and climbed in. The van headed west toward the Marsh Creek Detention Center. I whistled the theme to *The Bridge on the River Kwai*, and others joined me. We turned a corner and went down another hill, following the path of the creek.

"Ahoy! There's a party at the Springs!" one of the inmates cried out as if he was a pirate on lookout in the crow's nest. Everyone leaned to the driver's side to get a better look.

"Any babes?"

"It's a wedding reception," said Glebe. "There's got to be ladies."

There were a lot of cars parked at the Marsh Creek Springs, including a limo with a "Just Married" sign on the back. From the speeding van, you could just make out groups of dressed-up people on the grounds.

This was not good news.

The Springs is about a quarter of a mile east down the creek from the Detention Center. Most days, it was empty. I don't understand how they stay in business. But every other lunar full moon or so, it was busy, and then the place rocked. You could hear it from the barracks, which reminded me that prisoners on Alcatraz back in the day used to say the worst thing about being in prison there was that you could hear all the people across the water in San Francisco having fun. They were constantly reminded of what was taken away from them by their actions.

This reception was directly on my escape route.

I quickly thought about ways around it as the van turned and headed down the gravel road to the detention center. Across the creek was the firing range for the sheriffs in Contra Costa County, and as the van crossed the bridge over Marsh Creek and headed up the hill to let us out, I figured there was no choice but to stick to my plan and hope for the best.

The van stopped in front of the gate leading into the barracks. We got out and took the garbage bags to the dumpsters before heading inside the fence. I told the guards I had to water the trees by the creek and walked back down the hill.

I got the hose out of the shed and began watering the baby sycamores, which were planted after the original trees here, black oaks, died from sudden oak death disease (a fungus related to the pathogen Phytophthora ramorum infestans, the nasty cousin that was responsible for the great potato famine in Ireland in which a million people starved). I learned about it in the horticulture class I was taking, a class I took so I'd have access to these trees and the job of watering them.

When I finished, I rolled up and put away the hose, then headed over to the bridge, lowered myself into the trickling water of the creek, and started my escape by simply walking away.

"Super Freak" by Rick James was blasting from speakers at the reception while gunshots echo from the firing range in the other direction. I had at least an hour before I'd be discovered missing, so I headed east toward the joyous sounds coming from the Marsh Creek Springs.

I stopped at a bend in the creek where I could sit and be out of view from both directions. Did I really want to do this? Those are real bullets they're firing, and I'm sitting within range. I only had three more weeks on my sentence. The smart person would just finish their time and golf when they're free. But where's the story in that? This is one of those decisions that I tend to make from under the bed where my insecurity was born. I have to do something to get love and attention because I never felt I was worthy of it as a kid. (I know, waaaah said the whiner.)

I want to play in Angelina's with my guys! I deserve a twenty-four-hour pass because I've been a good prisoner. I completed AA, learned horticulture, and never once caused trouble. By the grace of God, nobody got hurt from my crime, so hadn't justice been served? Having your freedom taken from you is no day at the beach. It's no matinee at the movies, no afternoon in the park, no meals of your own choosing, no evenings of live music, no stroll down the links, no women enjoying the sun, no sitting on your board waiting for the next set.

I just sat there listening to the sound of people I'd recognize trying to better their aim with lethal weapons, while downstream, Rick James was fading into Sly and the Family Stone, and people I didn't know were celebrating the sacrament of marriage. I calmed my mind and focused on my breathing.

I could hear the whispering and murmurs from the water flowing east down Marsh Creek. Its headlands were just west of here between the detention center and Mount Diablo and just beginning its thirty-mile journey to the Sacramento-San Joaquin River Delta. From there, it ran into San Francisco Bay and then surged under the Golden Gate Bridge, absorbed into the Pacific Ocean, the journey back to the source complete.

I said a quick prayer, asking for God's guidance. "Divine love fills my soul and cleanses my mind. Divine love goes before me, making straight and perfect my path. Divine love dissolves everything unlike itself."

Downstream, people were laughing and singing and enjoying life. Up creek Contra Costa sheriffs were good shots getting better. This is the critical decision point. Wait three weeks and miss a good time with close friends, which we could do later, but not at Angelina's, or live in the moment. Damn the torpedoes and give them a story, a greatest hit for future golf outings. I've made some choices in my past that blew up in my face: the band, acting, Mavericks, and Kauai. No one died, well, except for my grandfather. I prayed for God to give me a sign, and you know what? I believe in God. I believe He'll lead me to what He wants.

Now, I don't want to get all Hemingway on you, but once again, I heard a hawk's cry, and when I looked up and found it, it was catching a wave heading east. Toward Stockton. Toward Angelina's. Toward Michelle.

Once again, the hawk shrieked with pleasure. It was a good enough sign for me. I got off my rear and started moving, staying low in the creek, following the hawk's lead. I pulled the sweatshirt out of my pants and put it on. It was way too hot for a sweatshirt, but I hoped the yellow would balance out the prison orange and maybe fool people.

***

I got as far as the bridge at Marsh Creek Springs before I was busted. She came down to the creek from the other side of the bridge, and I froze and watched her light a joint and inhale deeply. She had on what I would imagine was a bridesmaid's dress the color of a bruise, her hair was up in a style I bet her close friends wouldn't recognize, and too much makeup was dripping down sweat streams, coloring what looked like could be a cute face out of this heat. It seemed like she was trying to make the most of her situation as she slowly blew out the smoke before opening her eyes and seeing me.

I smiled and waved, "hi."

"You're not a cop!" she said.

"No!"

She looked me over. "Are you from that prison?"

"Well, it's really a detention center, minimum security, nonviolent offenders."

"What are you doing here?" she asked.

"Uh, I'm trying to escape." What was I going to do, lie to her?

"Really?"

"Yeah."

"What are you in for?"

"DUI."

"Really." She took another hit from the joint, then offered it to me. "How long have you been in jail for that?"

"Almost a year." It had been a while, and I needed to keep moving, so I waved it off. "I'd better not."

She slowly exhaled. "So, what's it like in there? Were you raped?"

"No. It's minimum security."

"So why Liszt?"

I looked down at my sweatshirt. "I just found it today and was hoping it might act as a disguise. At least make people look twice before realizing I was a convict."

"Do you know anything about him?"

"Not much. I know he was a classical composer."

"He was much more than that! You should read his diaries."

"You've read them?"

"Yes. I'm a music major at Cal."

"Good school. You must be smart."

"I'm smart enough to know you're not going to get far wearing that outfit. You've got to do something with those pants."

I again look down at my prison-issue orange pants. They shout convict as loud as the bruised dress screams bridesmaid.

"You can make them shorts!" She lifted her bridesmaid dress, stepped out of her heels, and walked across the water to me. She handed me the joint, opened her purse, and pulled out her keys, which had a little Swiss army knife attached to the ring. She flipped open the blade, grabbed my pants leg just above my knee, and tore into it. Once she got a hole, she ripped the pants until I had one leg in shorts. She pulled the excess pants down, and I stepped out of it. She looked up at me and smiled, her face a blend of colors from her makeup. I guess this is a good time to mention she's Asian because I was reminded of a Kabuki dancer, a girl before women were banned in 1629. The history teacher of my nature is always on, and this young lady has my attention.

"Nice job. You know maybe you shouldn't help me. You could get in trouble."

She started on the second leg. "Wasting time is one of the worst faults in the world. Life is short, every moment is precious: yet we live as if life will never end." She nodded at my sweatshirt. "He said that."

"Liszt?"

"When he was fifteen!" She finished with my second pants leg. I stepped out of it, and she folded both edges until they were even. Her hands brushed against my now bare thighs and brought up an embarrassing natural reaction. She noticed, then looked up at me, still smiling. "So, you haven't had sex in a year?"

I laugh nervously; the truth hurts. "Unfortunately, that's true."

She finished with my pants, took the joint from my hand, and inhaled. "Do you want to have sex with me?"

***

Now, I had been in jail for almost a full year. Despite the smeared make-up, this young lady was attractive and had a glassy twinkle in her eyes. She held my gaze, exhaled, and moved toward me. Stevie Wonder started singing "Higher Ground."

"How old are you?" I asked.

"Old enough," she leaned up and kissed me, her mouth and tongue tasting like good green buds and cabernet grapes from California dirt. I went with it, licking her in, grateful for this lovely creation of God's. I held her tighter. After a year of absolutely no human contact, unless you count my right hand, you can imagine how thankful I was for the gift of human touch, contact, and sensory overload. If Jesus was celibate, it's because of his divine nature; the human part of him couldn't resist the human sense of touch, that's why the whole Mary Magdalene controversy won't go away. Her hand found me, my, uh, you know, and it was responding. Now, I'll be honest, I'm not the most endowed specimen of the human race, but with this young lady's help, I was, in the words of the late, great Warren Zevon, "a credit to my gender."

She undid my pants, dropped to her knees, and pulled them down. She put me in her mouth. Okay. I'm a sinner. I didn't even know this girl's name, and she's giving me one of the top moments of my life! She has the unbridled enthusiasm of a fan, and I'm the home team. If that's a sin, then I'm guilty, damn it. Everything was rising, including my soul, and I'm happy and praise God for life.

She swallowed what she could and then led me over to the creek, where my little swimmers took a high dive down toward the water. She moved upstream and cleansed her mouth. She then rinsed me gently, pulled up my new shorts, and gave me a smile to remember.

"Welcome back."

TWO

We're driving east on Highway 4. Red-winged blackbirds zoom across the levee road, swooping from the water of the Delta over to fields of alfalfa, asparagus, and corn. Tractors work up the dirt, hiding the Sierra Nevada Mountains on the far side of the valley. I'm contemplating how God works in mysterious ways. Less than an hour ago, I was a prisoner. Now I'm free. Sure, an escaped convict, but I think a jury of my peers would show me some compassion. I should have gone with a jury the first time.

Because of my leap of faith, I've already had oral sex, and God love her! Her name is Rachel Wong, a grad student at Cal who said I showed up at just the right time to save her from "terminal boredom." (Wong is Chinese, so the Kabuki reference is totally incorrect because Kabuki theater was Japanese.) Anyway, I was her "perfect stranger." She offered to drive me anywhere as long as she could be back to Berkeley by Tuesday's class, using me as an excuse to get away from her sister's reception and end her weekend on a high note. As she was smuggling me to her car, past the friends and relatives gathered to celebrate her older sister's wedding, she told me the only reason to get married was alimony. It saddened me to see someone so young and full of life this cynical. It took me years longer.

But then there are moments like this, when you wonder if you are indeed being led by a higher power, and one, it seems, that likes golf. Fireworks and brats will be consumed tonight at Harley's. Michelle, and her husband, Ron, will be there. Ron's little brother and my best friend, Frank, will also be there. A Stillborn and the Afterbirths reunion, with special guest Rachel. Tomorrow we'll tee off for our tenth Angelina's. Those twenty-four hours with my friends are worth whatever time I might get for breaking out.

"Look at those; they look like breasts." Rachel takes the joint out of her mouth and points to Rough and Ready Island. "My mom's first implant looked kind of like one of those and cost twenty-eight hundred dollars. My mom wanted a nipple, but that was another twenty-eight hundred, and we didn't have it. Of course, her insurance wouldn't cover it. Nipples are cosmetic."

I could see Stockton's "boobs" on the horizon. I don't know what they hold, but there are two storage buildings on Rough and Ready Island that look like massive, man-made mammary glands, welcoming all into the town's bosom. You can't get more inviting than that. Though they also didn't have nipples.

"Cancer destroyed their marriage, and our family slowly decayed. It was like COVID all over again, being so careful, so close to tragedy. My dad was a dick about it. He didn't mean to be. It just killed the physical attraction. My mom suffered."

"I'm sorry about your mom."

"Thanks. I hope I die before I get old."

"So did Pete Townshend, but he changed his mind the

older he got. I thought their last album should have been called *Who's Left* because it was just him and Daltrey."

Rachel takes her eyes off the road and stares at me. Her face looks much younger without the make-up in the soft light of the sun fading behind Mount Diablo. "What are you talking about?"

"The Who. 'I hope I die before I get old...' *My Generation?*"

"Oh yeah. My dad listens to them. You are old."

Ouch. That hurt. But, compared to her, I most definitely am "old school." I grew up with classic rock and punk, then lived long enough for alternative to become mainstream only to be engulfed by hip hop and rap.

"I could see my dad breaking out to play golf."

She's coming out swinging.

"Course, I couldn't see him doing something stupid enough to go to jail."

Her mouth cuts. How could the mouth so skilled in pleasure also cause so much pain? She's probably conscious of her ability to give pleasure and mindless to the wounds she makes. Or is she? What kind of person puts a complete stranger's penis in her mouth, an escaped convict no less? What if I was a serial killer?

What if she is? What do I really know about her?

"I think we're going to make it!" She gives me a joyous smile. She's definitely cute and has already been quite a blessing. She's given me oral sex, but I've yet to see skin. Good God, I'm a sick pervert! All I wanted to do was golf with some friends, but now I can't get my mind off sex. I'd like to see and touch Rachel's breasts. Michelle had nice breasts. They fluctuated based on her weight, but she was young, sometimes big, and mostly firm.

I remember sleeping with them in my hands one night in San Francisco. We'd had a date, a fun one, and when we got back to her apartment, it was clear that I'd had too much to drink, so she invited me to stay the night on her living room floor. It was one of those rare nights when the temperature was close to freezing, and it was cold on that floor with only a thin blanket to warm me. I was like a baby seal adrift on the frigid bay; club me and put me out of my misery!

Around four o'clock in the morning, I couldn't take it anymore and went into Michelle's room, got under the comforter on her bed, and put my ice-cold feet between hers for warmth. Her feet rubbed mine, and the friction brought the circulation back. Everything about me started to thaw. I had a deep, restful sleep and woke up with my hands cradling her breasts. Of course, with that, all hell broke loose.

"So, where to from here? We're coming up to I-5."

"Go north."

We drive under the freeway, then make a left at the light onto the ramp. Rachel steps on it, and we rise up to join the traffic on I-5. I feel like I'm catching a wave; such is the adrenaline rush of merging onto a major freeway for the first time in almost a year. Rachel handles it with ease. She glides in behind a white SUV and in front of a truck hauling Sierra Nevada Pale Ale. That's a truck I'd like to hijack right about now.

It feels great to be back on I-5, even if it's only for a couple of miles. I've traveled this road from Tijuana, Mexico, all the way up to Vancouver, British Columbia. I love road trips, and I-5 has been a major artery for many of mine.

The freeway is invigorating. All these people driving all this weight at enormous speeds, and you have no idea what's on any driver's mind. We're being passed by a blue Volvo station wagon going eighty. There are two kids strapped into car seats behind the driver, and in the rear, two other kids are hitting each other. They might be two brothers fighting, and the driver could be their mother, who has just zoned out on them. Five complicated lives whizzing past us on the way to the rest of their lives. I could have slammed into them the night of my accident and killed them all. Yet, here is Rachel, stoned since I met her, driving with skill, focus, and ease. We glide up and over the port of Stockton, downtown off to the east, the main channel heading west.

"Take the upcoming Pershing exit."

"Look at the size of that ship! How'd that get all the way here?" Rachel has an enthusiastic curiosity.

"I think Stockton is the furthest inland deep-water port in the country, maybe the world. They built part of the latest Bay Bridge and shipped it to San Francisco from here."

"How would you like to sail under the Golden Gate Bridge after being at sea for months and have to bypass San Francisco for here?"

"Hey, Stockton's not that bad."

"It's not San Francisco."

"No. It's not the Marsh Creek Detention Center either."

Rachel takes the Pershing exit, slowing down and descending away from the freeway, dropping down to Pershing Avenue, heading north. It's like pulling out of a wave and getting back down on your board, the power surging away from you so you can relax.

"Okay, what's this guy's name again?"

"Frank."

"And what's the connection?"

"We've been friends since high school."

"Is he a criminal too?"

"Funny girl. Take the first left after the park."

We're passing the playground at Victory Park. A Hispanic man is selling mangoes on a stick to the migrant kids who are playing on the slide near where Michelle and I committed adultery. Well, I guess Michelle actually committed adultery; I coveted my neighbor's wife. Still, we broke two of the Ten Commandments.

"A left here?"

"What?"

"Take this street?"

"Yes."

She slows down, lets a couple of cars go by, then hooks a left onto Argonne. It seems to me she cuts it a little close in front of the oncoming truck, and I think its driver agrees with me. I give him a wave, motioning that I agree with him, and he nods as we drive our separate ways. The last thing I need is to be broadsided this close to golfing again.

The park is alive with families cooking, eating, and playing. Michelle and my sins started on an evening like this, only it was a Wednesday when bands play free concerts, and the neighborhood comes together to celebrate old-time Americana.

We started with cocktails in Frank's backyard. Frank's brother Ron, Michelle's husband, had to leave early to fly one of the Spanos executives somewhere. Michelle and I were teachers on summer break, and Frank worked his own hours, so we were partying. After the concert in the park, we came back to the backyard, and Frank barbecued his teriyaki chicken and sweet corn in the husks, with fresh artichokes as the appetizer. Tequila flowed. The birth of a harvest moon rose over the trees, and when I walked Michelle out to her car after the feast, I suggested we walk back to the park to look for satellites. I told myself it was so she could sober up before driving home, but that was the first sin of the night because it was a lie.

We laid on our backs by the slide and looked up into God's great heaven. There's nothing like staring into that vast darkness, knowing that the light we see travels across the silent space from far-off and long-dead stars. It makes me feel small and my sins insignificant. Michelle softly snored, and it brought me a moment of great joy to share that place and time with her under the immense and boundless sky. I savored the moment, and after a while, I spotted a satellite going north and nudged her awake. She got excited, then leaned over and kissed me.

I was kissing Michelle!

It was a dream come true. Years in the making, and in sight of that satellite and the heavenly stars beyond, I couldn't care less about my fellow man. I was selfish. I knew her first and loved her before Ron even met her. I'd been praying for and visualizing this for years! It seemed like an answered prayer. So, even though she was now Ron's wife, I coveted and consumed and committed a sin that goes back to David and Bathsheba, and, like theirs, which has stood the test of time, my soul has a permanent stain, like a sanbenito with painted devils and flames I wear every day, or a tattoo across my face that I see every time I look in a mirror. It wounds and diminishes me.

"Where to?"

"Right on Yale."

"Oh, that's good. When my mom asks me who I disappeared with, I can tell her it was a guy from Yale and not be lying."

Rachel is fun. There's no doubt about that. I should stay focused on the present moment. "Take a left on Lucerne."

"Who lives here again?"

"Frank. It was his grandparents' place. The first time I stayed here was after surfing Mavericks. Frank's grandfather was already dead—he built the house—but his grandmother was still alive and a saint. She let us stay here after Frank got out of the hospital and never told his mother."

"What were you, gay lovers?"

"No!" The residual homophobia kicks in.

"Then what happened?"

"It was one of my bright ideas to surf Mavericks. We were young and stupid and thought more of our abilities than they deserved. It was foolish and an ugly morning. We almost died."

"Young, dumb, and full of cum, huh?"

"Yeah."

"Well, you obviously survived."

"It was an act of God." I see Frank's house coming up on the left. His truck isn't there. "Pull into that driveway. He's not home, so go all the way up to his boat."

She maneuvers her car all the way up to his boat, an eighteen-foot Glastron resting on its trailer. She turns to me and smiles. "Now what?"

"We wait."

She grabs her purse and pulls out her phone. "I've got to tweet about this."

"What? No, you can't do that!"

"Why not?"

"Uh, the police?"

"They don't follow me."

"The NSA does. You can't be posting anything about my escape. I'll get caught, and you'll get in trouble for helping me."

"I'll say you kidnapped me! You tied me up and put something in my mouth so I couldn't scream," she says this with a devilish grin that opens my mind to the dark side.

"No."

"No social media?"

"How about after I turn myself in?"

"How about we take a selfie that I can post on my Instagram Story before you turn yourself in."

"You'll get in trouble."

"Trouble's overrated. Come on, my friends won't believe me otherwise."

"No."

She frowns, then quickly smiles. "Okay."

Good God, social media makes me feel old! I open the door and get out. Frank's rose bushes under his kitchen windows are blooming, and I lean down to inhale their sweet fragrance. I remember the old saying, so I stop and enjoy the moment. I have to hand it to Frank; he's got a green thumb, and they smell great.

Of course, Frank plants them for a dual purpose, sure to add beauty but also to protect his windows with their thorns. I found that out one day when I tried to break into his house my first year out of college. He was supposed to drive me to a job interview but got distracted by a Greek girl on a bike. I was going to take his spare keys and borrow his car, but was locked out. I slipped trying to climb in the side window and cut up my face landing in his rose bushes. I missed the interview and didn't get the job. Michelle took pity on me and got me an interview at her school, and the rest is history.

I lead Rachel to the backyard gate, reach over and unlatch it, and hold it open for her. We walk into the backyard and scare away the sparrows that are feeding in the birdfeeder that Frank hung from the tree next to the "office," a separate little cabin that his grandfather built for his grandchildren to stay in when they visited. Between the gate and the office is Frank's outdoor bar. I walk over to the mini refrigerator under a sign that reads, "Life is uncertain. Drink the good wine first!"

"Would you like something to drink?"

"Sure."

I open the fridge. "Chardonnay or beer?"

"Any red?"

"I'm sure he's got some inside, but none out here."

"I'll take a beer."

"Coors Light or Sierra Nevada?"

"Light."

I grab a silver can and take a Sierra for myself.

"Is that surfboard from your day at Mavericks?" Rachel's pointing to Frank's board, which he has mounted on his back fence between two strands of flowering Mandeville.

"Yeah. He never surfed again. That's his reminder of how lucky he is to be alive."

I lead Rachel over to the two beach chairs that Frank has on his back porch. I sit down, grab the opener between the chairs, and pop open my first beer in what seems like an eternity. God, it tastes good! I have been without this sweet nectar for far too long. I take another gulp and savor it with great delight.

A breeze blows in from the Delta, swaying the tops of the trees and cooling things down. The sparrows return to finish eating. It's so peaceful. This is what life is about, the simple pleasures. I'm more aware of that since I lost them in jail.

"Cheers," Rachel offers me her can to toast. I touch it with my bottle and gladly take another sip. Life is good.

"So, where do you think your friend is?"

"He might already be at Harley's, but it's a bit early."

"You want to use my phone and call him?"

"No. I really don't want there to be any trace that you were involved with me."

"You think the police know about me?"

"They might. I would think they know I'm missing by now, and your wedding party was the closest group of people to the detention center, so they might have been questioned. It's not that I'm a high-profile criminal or anything, but I can't help but be a little paranoid."

"Dude, what are you going to do after golf?"

"That's a good question. Maybe I'm not the brightest, but I figure I'll just turn myself in and face the consequences."

How bad could it be? I'm not hurting anyone; I am playing golf, for Christ's sake! Okay, I might hit someone with an errant shot. But as bad as my game is, it hasn't happened yet, and I like my chances.

"You'll definitely get more time, and I bet they move you out of minimum security. You could end up some bad man's girlfriend."

What the fuck? I hadn't thought of that.

"Well, thank you, that's a pleasant thought. Are you trying to bring me down?"

"No."

"Well, you're starting to."

"I'm sorry."

"I mean, come on, it's twenty-four hours! I've been locked up for almost an entire year. I'm free in three weeks, anyway. This is just a preview, a twenty-four-hour pass. Fireworks tonight, golf tomorrow, then I turn myself in. Everyone deserves a get out of jail free card every once in a while. Maybe I'll set a precedent and help reform the legal system. Besides, it's off to a great start, and that's because of you. You're supposed to keep me up, not bring me down."

"Keep you up, huh?" She smiles at my weak innuendo. It's enough to get my blood flowing. "I'd love to get out of this stupid dress. Should we do it right here in your friend's yard? What will his neighbors think? As loud as I'm going to be, they might call the cops."

This girl is killing me. I mean, she's got me fluffed and ready. But she's right; we can't do it out here. "All right, give me your phone."

She reaches into her purse and hands me her phone. I dial Frank's number. He answers. "You should never pick up from a number you don't know," I say.

"Who the fuck are you?"

Okay, mistake, never start with a flippant comment. "Hey, how are you? I'm sitting in your backyard. What time are we going over to Harley's?"

"Kimo?"

"Yes!"

"Where are you?"

"I'm sitting in your backyard, and it's as peaceful as ever. Your grandfather would be proud."

"Did you get released early?"

"We'll talk when you get here. And when will that be?"

"I'm at work."

"It's the Sunday before Angelina's, Frank. I know you'll be at Harley's after dark. Could you please stop by your house and pick me up on the way?"

"We're not playing this year, Kimo."

"What?"

"Look, you weren't supposed to make it. Ron can't make it, and Harley and I didn't want to play without you guys, so we pulled out."

"Well, call Harley and have him call Spike and get us back in. Why can't Ron play?"

"Look, I'll leave work and come home. I have a feeling you should get off the phone anyway, they can be traced. I'll be home in twenty."

"Frank!" There's more desperation in my voice than I intended.

"What?"

"Do you have a hidden key or something so we can wait inside?"

"I thought you liked my backyard. We?"

"What?"

"You said so we can wait inside."

"Yes, Rachel and me. I'll introduce you when you get here."

"Okay. There's a spare key to the office on the ankle strap of my board. That's the best I can do until I get home."

"Great! See you soon." I end the call and hand the phone back to Rachel. "Okay, we've got about twenty minutes. Unfortunately for you, that's probably more time than we need." I get up and walk across the lawn to the surfboard.

"Kimo?"

"Yes?"

"That's your name?"

"Yeah."

"What is that, Hawaiian?"

"Yeah, it's James in English."

"So, are you from Hawaii?"

"My grandparents lived there, and my mom lives there now." I reach around to the back of the board and feel for the key. I grab it and hold it up for Rachel to see.

"What is that?"

"Hopefully, it's the key to the best twenty minutes of our lives."

***

The bible teaches that the body is the temple of the soul, so I joyfully go on a pilgrimage, worshiping the wonders of the female form. She tastes like salt from seawater, and I drink from her like a thirsty false prophet at an oasis, tumbling in from too many lost days in the desert. I finish quickly, but you must remember, we only had twenty minutes. I had been in jail for a long time, and she's a vision. Imagine Balboa first seeing the Pacific. Imagine skin touching skin, warm, wet, and wondrous. Imagine the frustration of hearing Frank's truck coming up his driveway.

THREE

Frank is in work clothes, which for him means blue jeans and a green work shirt. He looks worried, but then Frank is a worrier.

"My man!" I walk up and hug him. There's nothing better than hugging a true friend.

"What the fuck are you doing here, Kimo? Are you a fucking idiot?"

Okay. When Frank starts tossing the F-bombs, it's because he's bothered by something, and obviously, Frank is bothered. I think it must be me. "I'm here to play in Angelina's, Frank. That's all."

"We're not playing this year, Kimo."

"Why not?"

Before he can answer, Rachel comes out of the office wearing one of Frank's shirts. A woman in a man's dress shirt is always sexy, and Rachel looks hot. I've known Frank for almost twenty years and know what he's thinking because I'm thinking the same thing. He looks at me and can't help but smile.

"Holy smokes. Rachel, I presume?"

She sticks out her hand and answers before me. "Yes, and it's nice to meet you, Frank. Kimo has said such nice things about you."

He takes her hand, looks over his shirt, and glances back at me. "That's my shirt."

"Yes, and it smells great. I hope you don't mind. All I had was my bridesmaid dress."

Frank blushes as he looks back at her and shakes her hand. "I don't mind. In fact, it's never looked better."

"Aren't you sweet?"

So, it seems to me that Rachel is flirting with Frank. It's a little early for jealousy, so maybe it's just my basic insecurity, but I don't like it one bit. I need to change the subject fast. "So how come Ron isn't playing?"

Frank gives me a haunted look that scares me. "What are you doing here?"

"It's Angelina's, Frank. I didn't want to miss it. Look, I know it's stupid of me, but if I get back Tuesday morning, what's the harm? If I must do more time, then so be it. I miss having fun with my friends."

He shakes his head and then looks back at Rachel. "Would you like something to drink?"

"Do you have any red wine?"

"I have a Tempranillo from a small winery in Winters..."

"Winters? I've been there!" exclaims Rachel. "Cute little town in the middle of nowhere with a great Main Street?"

"Yes!"

"Which Winery?"

"Berryessa Gap?"

"I was at Berryessa Brewery just outside of town."

"Berryessa Gap's winery is right there. Their main tasting room is downtown on Main Street."

"Cool. Okay, I'm up for trying that!" She smiles at Frank

and her smile is contagious. "I can't believe we've both been to Winters. Kimo, have you been there?"

"No," I'm feeling left out.

"Rachel, Berryessa Gap has a paella cook-off at the winery in the Fall," Frank says. "If you're interested, maybe we could go."

Uh, excuse me? Frank's already asking her out. Am I not visible?

"Sounds fun," Rachel coos. "We'll have to keep in touch."

Really? I want to yell, "Hello, I'm a human being standing right here!" but instead, I just keep my silence and take a deep breath.

"Great. Anyway, I just put in a wine cellar. Kimo, you haven't even seen it." He looks at me and can tell I'm agitated. "Do you want to see it?"

I hesitate while my eyes shoot imaginary poisoned darts from Borneo at him. "Sure, Frank."

He ignores my lethal look, unlocks the back door, and leads us straight across the landing to a descending staircase instead of heading right and into the kitchen.

"Watch your step. These stairs are original, and people were smaller back then."

We follow him down into the cool darkness of the basement. He reaches up and pulls a string, and we have light. The room is dominated by a huge, black, cast-iron water heater that Frank's grandfather built the house around. Frank opens a small glass door and grabs a bottle off of one of the shelves.

"I put it where my grandmother made beer during the prohibition."

"Your grandmother made beer during the prohibition? Wasn't that illegal?" Rachel asks.

"Celebrating life has been in Frank's DNA for generations. Tell her about their parties."

Frank smiles. "Upstairs in the living room, my grandparents used to roll back the carpet, invite some friends over, drink her homemade beer, and dance to my grandfather playing the piano."

"Fantastic!" exclaims Rachel. "Do you still have the piano?"

"No. My brother has it."

"Speaking of your brother, why isn't Ron playing tomorrow?" I ask.

Frank looks at me; he's actually struggling to hold back tears. Something's not right. "What?"

His eyes deaden as he holds my look. He tries to talk, but his lips quiver, and a sliver of snot runs down his nose.

"What is it?"

"Michelle."

Uh oh. "What about Michelle?"

"She's dying."

I never got hit by Muhammad Ali, but I imagine it feels like this. My knees literally buckle. I'm dazed. Rachel looks at me with trepidation.

"Who's Michelle?" she asks.

Frank tells her, "My brother's wife."

My mind is reeling. I'm lightheaded and off-balance. It reminds me of the waves at Mavericks that punished us, hammering us again and again, keeping us under long after I'd lost my breath. I'd never been so scared and spent until now. "Come on, Frank, I just saw her last summer."

"I know, Kimo. It's been unbelievable. You remember she went in to have a cyst removed right before Angelina's last year?"

"Yeah."

"Well, they found she had stage four cancer."

"Stage four?" asks Rachel, the blood draining from her face.

Frank looks at her and tears up. "Yes."

This is hard to swallow. I mean, this is complete bullshit! Cancer? Can you get a bigger cliché? I don't know if I should believe Frank or punch him in the face. It's not the least bit funny, and obviously, he's not kidding. I'm getting hot, even though the basement is much cooler than the outside. It's stuffy down here and smells like the old, musty boxes stacked under the stairs, leftovers from Frank's grandparents' lives. I need to escape and get some fresh air, so I climb out of the basement and into the fading light of the backyard.

The sparrows that have returned scatter once again at my appearance. I take a deep breath. This is not right. This is not part of the plan. How can I concentrate on golf now?

Exhale, just keep breathing.

"Are you all right?" Rachel has followed me out.

Her look of concern warms my heart. Am I all right? No. This can't be happening. It can't be true. I just saw Michelle last summer, and she was fine.

Frank comes out with three bottles in his hands. "Kimo, I brought you up a couple of Cabs. We need to drink."

"Thanks." Is drinking the answer? Until I come up with a better idea, it will do. "Rachel, do you have any more Bob Marley?" I put my fingers to my lips and inhale.

"There's a reference even my age understands! Let me get my purse. I think I left it on the dryer." She gives me a smile, and the way she grabs my arm and squeezes reminds me of Michelle in D.C. Rachel heads into the office.

"Bro, why don't you put on some music?" Frank suggests, while opening the bottles to let them breathe.

Music, now there's a blessing. Music would be good. "Okay," I say.

I follow Rachel into the office, and as soon as I enter, the smell of our sexual encounter greets me.

"We need to open a window and air this place out," Rachel says as she comes from the laundry room and shows me a little golden canister with a label on it.

I nod my agreement and inhale deeply the aroma of life. I

pass her and walk through the little bathroom into the laundry room to open the back door. I touch the dryer where we finished our twenty minutes of bliss. She'd sat down and turned it on as I took her standing up. The heat and vibration of the dryer acted like a metronome, keeping me in rhythm and from getting too fired up. I didn't need the help, but I also didn't want it to be like a blistering two-minute punk anthem. I wanted our session to have majestic rises, and stomach-in-your-throat rollercoaster falls, like an early Van Morrison or Waterboys tune.

I'm sure I would have had performance anxiety if I had known that Rachel was looking for cascading arpeggios and acciaccaturas leading to a crescendo brought on by a virtuoso, Liszt-like performance of one of his Symphonic Poems. Luckily, the performance was hers, and I the grateful audience, even though it was the name on the sweatshirt she was playing to.

"Can you roll?" Rachel asks, snapping me back to the moment.

"Frank can."

"Okay."

She leaves me alone in the office to deliver the goods to Frank. I notice her walk right by my golf bag and clubs. I didn't notice them earlier when I had a lust for Rachel on my mind, but now they reach out to me like a lighthouse. The last time I saw them, Michelle was fine.

I say a quick prayer for her and ask God what the hell is going on? This is turning into a nightmare. Maybe this was a colossally stupid idea like God cares if I play golf, and I think a hawk is His messenger. I'm a complete idiot. Good God, I belong in prison because I'm a menace to society! Maybe I should ask Frank to drive me back right now before anyone gets hurt.

"Kimo, have you seen this? Get out here!"

God help me. I shut the back door and walk out of the office into the twilight. Frank and Rachel are sitting in the beach chairs with their glasses of wine. Frank tosses me Rachel's canister.

"Read that."

"California Healthcare Collective. Medicinal Cannabis. For medical use only. Not for resale. Type, Bubble Funk. Weight 3.5 grams. Keep out of reach of children."

Frank has a huge smile on his face. "Is this a great country or what?" He starts singing, "Get the funk outta my face, get that funk outta my face." He turns to Rachel, "That's the Average White Band, young lady."

"Actually, Frank, that's the Brothers Johnson."

He looks back at me in shock. "Are you sure? What about Wild Cherry?"

"They did 'Play That Funky Music White Boy.'"

Rachel takes the canister out of my hand. "I don't think you guys need any of this."

Frank takes her wine glass hostage. "I know I need it. It's been a long year, and that would do me a world of good. I'll trade you."

He holds her wine glass out and smiles. She exchanges the canister for the glass. Frank gives me a triumphant smile, puts the canister down, and hands me a glass. He pours Cabernet Sauvignon into it and then raises his glass to toast. "Once again, welcome to my backyard."

We all touch glasses and drink. It tastes good, like Rachel's mouth. Kissing her was just the vaunt courier; now I have the spiritual drink, made from human hands. It makes me think of Jesus, and I praise him in silence and ask for his guidance.

"Now, if you don't mind, I'd like to roll a doobie," Frank says.

Rachel again smiles at Frank. "Be my guest. The papers are in there."

Frank opens the canister, takes a smell, grins, and goes to work. "It's been a while since I rolled one, but it's got to be like riding a bike."

I walk to the center of the yard, take a deep breath, and think of Michelle. "So, what is it, breast cancer?"

"No."

"Colon?"

Frank's licking the papers and shakes his head.

"Ovarian?" asks Rachel.

"No." He puts the joint to his lips and lights it.

"Lung?" I ask as he inhales. He shakes his head again. "Brain? Pancreatic? What?"

He puts up his finger while passing the joint to Rachel. She takes it and asks, "leukemia?"

Frank exhales, "Bile duct."

"Bile duct?"

Frank starts coughing. "It's rare, and it's a killer. Like Michelle says, it's not one of the popular cancers."

Rachel brings me the joint without taking a hit. "What's your relationship with Michelle?"

"What's my relationship with Michelle?" I take the joint and inhale deeply.

"Obsession, stalking, delusion," is Frank's answer.

I start laughing and coughing.

"Ashes to ashes, dust to dust, my what the ash does to us," Frank recites dramatically.

Rachel asks, "What's that?"

"Kimo came up with that bit of poetry while we were in a band in high school. You okay, big man?"

I nod and inhale again. It echoes the taste of Rachel's mouth.

"So, what is your relationship with her?"

I look into Rachel's eyes, then turn away before exhaling, "I love her."

Rachel takes the joint and puts it in her mouth, the mouth that tastes great and is skilled at oral sex. "Then you'd better go see her while you have the chance."

I ponder this. The truth is I thought I would see her while I was here, tonight, in fact, at Harley's for brats and fireworks. I pictured her happy to see me and rushing to give me a hug. I fantasized that while the night sky was exploding in colors and noise, I would catch her smiling at me while in Ron's arms, and I would lay my head down on the grass above the thirteenth green and remember the starlight and satellite from our night long ago.

"Don't Bogart that bad boy, darling."

I'm brought back to the moment and watch Rachel happily take the joint over to Frank. I think about Ron's feelings for the first time. "How's your brother doing?"

"How the fuck do you think he's doing?"

"I can't imagine it's good. I'm having a hard time processing it, and I just found out. He's been dealing with it from the beginning, and I'm just asking how he's holding up."

"Sorry. He's not good. I think it's killing him as well. The worst thing he's dealing with right now is that Michelle wants to be cremated and have Ron take her ashes and spread them under the Golden Gate Bridge." He takes a hit and holds it out for me before looking at Rachel. "My brother took her there on his boat to propose to her."

"Seriously? That's romantic."

"Yeah. The problem is we have a cemetery that's been in the family for generations, and Ron has a special place picked out to bury her, you know, so he has someplace to visit her after she's gone."

"It's her body."

"True, but this isn't an anti-feminist argument about what she can do with her body. She'll be dead. We are spiritual entities in human bodies; her soul will be gone. We want to think the key thing is remembering what she left behind."

"But that's just bones."

"If that's all that's left of her time on earth, we think they're worthy of respect and remembrance. Our father's jet was shot down in Afghanistan, and he went MIA, so not having his body resting at peace here is hard on Ron. I was so young when he died that I barely even remember him, so it's not that big a deal to me. But it is to Ron."

"Does Michelle realize that?" I ask.

"Yes. But like Rachel's instinct, Michelle sees it through a feminist lens and wants to do what she wants to do with her body."

"You make it sound like she's being selfish," Rachel says.

"I don't mean to be. It's just that death is the family business, and we have our way of looking at it."

"Which is why they celebrate life so well!" I take another hit. The pot is starting to shrink and heighten my focus. My tolerance for alcohol is low after being sober for the past year, so I'm already feeling the beer and wine and dope. My thoughts swirl: freedom, stupidity, death, sex, choices, consequences, delusions, love, pleasure, suffering, life, lies, desolation, time. I close my eyes and take a deep breath. I taught my students that God is Absolute Harmony, Boundless Love, Infinite Intelligence, and Supreme Wisdom, and I ask for it to flow through me now.

"Kimo, are you okay?"

I open my eyes and see Frank and Rachel looking back at me.

"I don't feel so good. It's been a long day, and I could use a shower," I answer.

"When was the last time you had something to eat?" Frank asks.

"Breakfast this morning."

"I've got the munchies!" Rachel quickly adds. "Can you cook, Frank?"

"Oh, I can cook. What are you in the mood for?"

Rachel just gives one of her smiles, "Surprise me."

"Well then, I need to feed you both. Kimo, we're not going to Harley's. The last time we talked, we decided we weren't playing, so the Angelina's pregame meal was called off. Why don't you go take a shower, and Rachel and I will go to the store and find something to cook."

"Sounds good. Do you think you could pick me up a pair of shorts or something I can golf in tomorrow?"

"Bro, you've lost weight. You can probably fit into something of mine. If not, we can handle that in the morning. Just get into the shower and relax. You look red."

I nod and go inside. I walk through the kitchen and head for the bathroom. I turn on the water and take off my clothes. I'm tired, and I stink. I look in the mirror and see bloodshot eyes staring back from my sunburned face. Who the fuck are you?

I step into the shower and get a shock from the cold water that stirs me awake. I move away from the streaming water until it warms up, then I step back in and let it run all over my dirty body. I open my mouth and let the shower send its force into action, like a water cannon blasting away the germs, massaging my gums and tongue, and, unfortunately, cleansing the taste of Rachel right out of my mouth.

I lean down and let the water baptize my head, then soothe my neck and shoulders. Imagine how nice it is not to be in a communal shower with a bunch of other guys. It is so comforting that I feel like I could be back in the womb, peaceful, pacifying, liquescent. I sit down in the tub and surrender to the flow.

"Kimo?"

It's Frank's voice. There's a knock on the door, and I hear it open, and then the shower curtain is pulled back, and Frank looks in and is surprised to see me sitting down. "Are you okay?"

"I'm getting there."

"We'll be back in a few. Anything you want?"

"I'm sure whatever you get will be fine."

He gives me a serious look. "It's good to see you, bro. We'll figure out Angelina's."

I nod. "Why didn't you tell me about Michelle?"

A look of frustration crosses his face. "What could you do? Look, you asked me not to tell anyone you were in jail, and she asked me not to tell you about her condition. She tried to tell you at the party, but you know how that ended. You both put me in the middle, and I didn't like keeping your secrets from each other."

"She knew at the party?"

"Uh-huh."

That's why she was acting so strange toward me! I got jealous and angry and took myself out of her life when she needed me most. What an ass.

"Is he okay?" I hear Rachel ask. The other side of the shower curtain parts, and she looks in. "Mmm, that looks comfortable. I need a shower."

"You can take one while I'm cooking dinner," Frank quickly replies. "Kimo, you relax, and we'll be back soon."

I nod again, and Frank's head disappears. Rachel smiles, then closes the shower curtain, only to reappear above me where Franks was. She leans down and kisses my forehead. "I hope you feel better."

"Thanks." She leaves. I close my eyes and focus on the sensation of the water cascading down on me and pray that it revives me so I know what I should do.

***

Frank and Rachel are still away when I finally get out of the shower. I feel much better. I go into Frank's bedroom and find a pair of shorts that I can squeeze into, then take a Hawaiian shirt out of his closet and find a pair of flip flops that he hasn't used yet. I finally feel like I'm no longer a convict. I head for the refrigerator, take out a bottle of water, and decide to go for a walk.

I know my destination. I walk west on Lucerne to Buena Vista and head north a couple of blocks to the Smith Canal. I wonder how Frank's grandparents would feel about the way the neighborhood has changed. There's a new store on the corner that Frank says is selling black market cigarettes and attracting the wrong crowd. A dark SUV drives up to the curb in front of the store, its sound system blaring so the entire block can hear Jay Z rap about, "ninety-nine problems, but a bitch ain't one." The bass is up so high that I actually vibrate as I pass it. Now, I have no problem with whatever someone wants to listen to, but does everyone have to hear it? And feel it? I guess I am getting old.

I climb up the road to the south side of the canal and walk west a couple of hundred yards until I reach my objective. Across the canal and over the bank is Ron and Michelle's house. Their master bedroom is on the second floor, which rises above the bank and is in clear view from where I stand. I know this sounds creepy like I'm a pervert or a stalker, but I'm not. I just want to be close and, yes, maybe even catch a glimpse of Michelle.

Unfortunately, the bedroom is dark. Maybe they're downstairs or in their backyard, which has a beautiful swimming pool but is out of sight from this side of the canal. I can see the stairs that lead from their backyard down the bank to their dock, where Ron's boat, a 1987 Carver 36' Aft Cabin named *It's All Good*, is moored. Ron was always an optimist and named his boat, the one he proposed to Michelle on, accordingly. I'm curious if he's still optimistic about life after what he's gone through this last year. I see two large swans resting on deck and wonder if Michelle still feeds them.

Suddenly the skies light up! Muffled sounds of explosions follow the sparkling streaks of color. The fireworks in Brookside, the gated community where Harley lives and where we normally have our pre-tournament meal, have begun. I didn't know you could see them from here, but the pyrotechnics reflecting off the water from the canal are beautiful, like an Impressionist painting. The swans must disagree because they dive off the dock and swim for cover.

A light goes on in Michelle and Ron's bedroom, and my heart tumbles. The curtains are closed, but I see a spectral shadow move away from the light, which must be a lamp, and cross to the other side. My guess is that Ron's helping Michelle out of bed. The shadow drifts to what I remember was their bay window. The room goes dark, and I feel they must be watching the fireworks.

I do as well, but mostly I'm looking at their house illuminated by the iridescent bursts, which gives their home a colorful, ephemeral loveliness, a paradox to what must be happening inside. What must they be thinking? Is this the last time Michelle will see fireworks? What, if anything, can I do? This whole situation is completely messed up. Tears fall freely down my face. How can this be? It's not right.

People start coming to view the show, and I don't want to be part of a crowd. I ask God to bless Michelle and Ron, then turn and walk away. I'm empty. When I get to where Buena Vista turns south and goes down the bank, I glance upward into the measureless darkness and spot a forlorn satellite heading north. I immediately remember my night in Victory Park with Michelle. I don't know if it's a sign or symbolic of my life, but I do know that every time I see a satellite in the night skies over Stockton, I'll think of Michelle.

Who am I kidding? She'll haunt my every waking moment.

FOUR

The smell of ribs smoking on the grill welcomes me back to Frank's backyard. It reminds me I'm still alive, and I remember Jim Harrison always said, "eat or die." I walk over and inhale the aromatic smoke before heading inside and finding Frank in the kitchen. "Smells good out there," I tell him.

"You're back! We thought maybe you went and turned yourself in. That's applewood smoking those bad boys. I started with a rub of sea salt, coarse black pepper, cayenne pepper, and garlic, and now I'm reducing my glaze, made with a mixture of brown sugar—'how come you taste so good,'—Jack Daniels, apple cider vinegar, a little ketchup, a little Worcestershire, and my secret ingredient, Cholula hot sauce. Yeah, baby, this is going to be an orgiastic eruption of flavor in your mouth!"

"Speaking of which, where's Rachel?"

"She's taking a shower. Holy smokes, dude, she's a keeper. Did you know she's a concert pianist? I think I'm in love. Do you mind if I ask her out once you go back to jail?"

I snap. "First your brother, and now you? What am I, the Rominger boys' pimp? Can't you find your own girls? Do you always have to steal mine?" I guess I'm a little angry, but he's a bit cavalier with his attitude about me going back to jail and him being free to pursue Rachel. Of course, I'm definitely going to have to go back to jail, and it probably will be longer than three weeks. Damn it, what the hell was I thinking? How could I be so stupid?

"Ron didn't steal Michelle from you, asshole! You went off looking for fame and fortune, going to be a big Hollywood star! You left! Ron moved back. They met and fell in love, and got married. You're too immature and self-centered to be married anyway!" He's stirring his glaze so hard it shoots up and burns his skin. "Fuck!" He turns off the burner.

"Karma's a bitch."

"Fuck you!" He pours the glaze into some Tupperware and takes it to the refrigerator. He comes back with a couple of bags of chocolate chips, one milk chocolate, and the other white. "Your primary relationship is between you and your ego, and all other relationships become intrusions. I don't know who I was reading, but they said marriage is about letting go of your ego, allowing the grace of participating in another life! That's a religious exercise, which is why it's a sacrament."

"Wow, you read a book?"

"Again, fuck you. You couldn't have handled this last year with Michelle. Thank God she has my brother." Frank sets up a double boiler and starts to melt the chocolate.

"I just came from your brother's place."

He stops and looks at me. "You went to their house?"

"No, I just looked from this side of the canal."

"Observing from the shadows, huh? That's creepy. Did you see them?"

"No. But I could see the fireworks from Brookside."

"Really?" He's genuinely surprised.

"Yeah." I grab a chair from the dining room, bring it into the kitchen and sit. "You know I thought I'd see her tonight at Harley's."

"Maybe it's better that you don't see her. At least you'll only have the memory of her healthy. Since your relationship with her is mostly fantasy anyway, you won't have that reality intruding on it."

I look at Frank and fight back tears. I want my friends to be honest with me, but damn, to be so misunderstood hurts. "My love for her is real. Not conventional maybe, mostly platonic perhaps, unrequited, okay, but still love. She affects my soul, and that's true love."

Frank walks over to get some wax paper from the drawer by the sink and notices me wiping my eyes. "Look, I'm sorry," he says. "You just have no idea how hard this year has been."

"Well, mine hasn't been easy either, which is why I made the stupid decision to come here and play golf with who I thought were my friends."

"Kimo, you know I'm your friend, but you're not really grounded in reality right now. There are more important things than golf."

"Blasphemy! If anything, this year has taught me the importance of time with friends! And what better way to spend that time than out in nature, swinging a club at your problems?"

Frank smiles. "You're an idiot. Now, can I trust you with a knife to help dice up some vegetables for the salad and appetizer? I don't want that knife in my back."

I get up and grab a knife from the block. "What do you want me to do?"

"Well, I'm making ribs in your honor, and I'm melting some chocolate to dip strawberries into for dessert, and then I'll make coleslaw to go with dinner, and for an appetizer, we'll stuff these mini peppers with mozzarella and put them on the grill. There's going to be a lot of hands-on, finger-licking, melted gooey fun in this meal."

"Oh, I see. It's okay for you to stab me in the back trying to woo Rachel away from me with a sensuous dinner, but I can't shove this into your kidneys. You'd never last in jail."

"Speaking of that, do you like being butt fucked now?"

"Not as much as your mother does."

"Hey! No mother jokes!"

"Boys!" Rachel is standing outside the bathroom in a towel. "Can't we all just get along?"

I look at Frank. "Is she quoting Rodney King?"

I turn back to Rachel, who is stunning, and we stand there ogling like two preteen boys discovering lingerie ads in the Sunday paper for the first time. Do we ever really grow up? I again look over to Frank. "What can I help you with, my man?"

He slowly takes his eyes off Rachel and looks at me with one of those joyful Frank smiles. "It would be great if you could dice some red pepper and carrots for the slaw, my fine fellow."

We both look back at Rachel. "Everything's good here. We both look forward to you joining us, right, Frank?"

"Oh, most definitely."

"Okay, that's better." She turns and walks back into the bathroom, leaving us with an uncovered view of her lovely derriere and some kind of tattoo just below her neck that I notice for the first time.

Frank looks at me after the bathroom door closes. "Ho-ly smokes."

"Yeah, that about sums it up."

"Well, Kimo, if you hadn't made that stupid decision of yours, I would never have had that pleasurable moment, so I sincerely thank you, my friend."

"I do what I can."

"And you've had sex with her?"

"I have."

"Proof that there is a God."

"Amen, brother."

Frank takes a deep breath and shudders. "Okay, what do you say we make a meal worthy of her?"

"Pass the peppers."

***

Frank has set up the table in the backyard, covering it with a colorful cotton tablecloth of sunflowers and matching napkins. Tiki torches light up the surfboard, and candles on the table make shadows play across Rachel's lovely face. I'd like to chase them with my tongue.

She takes a bite of an orange pepper, and some cheese oozes out of her mouth and down her lip. "Oh, my," she says with her mouth full. "Frank, this is delicious!"

Frank reaches over with his napkin and wipes her clean. "Let me get that for you."

This is pissing me off. Not the food, which is a beautiful thing. Frank put some garlic salt inside the peppers I gutted and cleaned out before he added the mozzarella, then he brushed them with a local olive oil before putting them on the grill. The roasted sweetness of the pepper combined with the garlic salt and chewy goodness of the cheese is indeed a mouthful of joyous freedom. I'm looking forward to the ribs, coleslaw, and chocolate-covered strawberries. But this completely overt flirting between Frank and Rachel is killing me. Have they no shame? Then again, shame can be a wasted emotion. There's nothing disgraceful about them being attracted to each other. Rachel has this sexual energy, this life force, a gravitational wave that pulls you in. I decide to let the anger go and enjoy the meal.

"You know, I helped," I say. "I mean, if it weren't for me doing the hard labor, you'd have a mouth full of seeds."

"Well, thank you, Kimo. You've given me a great day!" Rachel's acknowledgment lifts me up.

"A toast to Kimo, whose decision to go his own way has brought pleasure to his friends, both new and old! May you not pay too steep a price for your misguided choice." Frank raises his glass.

I raise mine to meet theirs. When Rachel joined us after her shower, we switched beverages to Frank's Mojos, a legacy from the Gillis Beach Volleyball Tournament that Frank plays in down in Playa Del Rey every summer. He makes them with dark rum and orange, peach, and mango juices. They're quite tasty, and once again, my head swims in a current of alcohol. It feels great to be alive and free.

Rachel continues, "I mean, this has turned into an amazing Sunday for me. I really wasn't looking forward to my sister's wedding and watching my mother and father avoid each other as they circled through the crowd dredged up all the bitterness and pain my mom's cancer brought to our family. Then I met Liszt here under the bridge, and he swept me away from the agony like an angel and brought me here to this wonderful meal with two great guys. I'm like Dorothy in the land of Oz. Thank you."

She raises her glass, and again the three touch.

Frank looks at me in amazement. "That's the first time I've heard Kimo called an angel, but I have to agree. Today I mowed the plot where my brother wants to bury Michelle and tended the rose bushes, and it was depressing to think that she'd take that sanctuary away from him. When you die, you either go to a better place or not, depending on what you believe in and what's the actual truth. But a gravesite is for those left behind, a place they can go and find some solace and feel close to the departed. I was pissed at Michelle because the whole, 'it's my body, and I'll do what I want with it' argument just seems selfish to me at this point. Then you call, Kimo, and I transferred that anger to you, but you're a great friend, and you're back in my backyard, and you brought Rachel." He looks at her. "And you're a blessing."

This is a lovefest! It's San Francisco in the sixties, and damn it, that's the way it should be. I need to spread some. "Here's to the chef! Frank, God love you. This meal is a blessing."

"Yes, to Frank," Rachel again puts her glass in. We touch glasses and take another drink.

After all these toasts, our glasses are empty. "I'll refill those," Frank says as he gets up and reaches for our empties. "Kimo, I asked you before, but you got sidetracked, so would you please put some music on? I know you've got CDs you left back there."

"I can do that. In fact, do you still have my *Portrait of a Damaged Family* CD? Miracle Legion's 'You're My Blessing' would be perfect right now." I get up and head for the office. I hear Rachel say, "what can I do?"

"You, my dear, can sit there and illuminate my backyard, and Kimo, I have no idea what CDs you left back there," Frank says as he heads into the house. I walk back into the office. The aroma from earlier is gone, which is sad—everything passes too quickly. I walk to the far wall where Frank has his outdoor stereo components and look through his CDs, searching for the ones I've left with him. I find *Drenched* but can't find *Portrait of a Damaged Family*. I do come across *This is The Sea* by The Waterboys and decide to go with that. I power it on, take a look at Mike Scott's hair on the cover as I take the disc out and slip it into the player. Roddy Lorimer's trumpet starts blowing on the opening track, "Don't Bang the Drum," and I feel like a matador as I head outside.

Kevin Wilkinson's drums and Mike Scott's guitars kick in

as Frank comes outside with liquid reinforcements. "I remember this, Son Volt?"

"Waterboys."

"I knew it was one of those bands you liked."

"I like the yelps, sounds like a climax," says Rachel as she takes her drink from Frank. Frank looks at me and just shakes his head. "He also sounds like Dylan," she adds.

"Good girl, I'm impressed."

"My dad listens to him."

Here we go again.

"Bob Dylan can't sing," Frank shares his opinion. "Everybody sings his songs better."

"Blasphemy!" I snarl.

"Didn't The Waterboys cover Dylan?" Frank asks.

"Yes, they did a great 'Girl from the North Country,' and when Karl Wallinger left and formed World Party, they did a great 'All I Really Want to Do.' But Dylan's were good too."

"I didn't know World Party was made by a Waterboy. You're an encyclopedia of musical information."

"And you're cute. You should be a YouTube reactor." Rachel smiles. It's infectious.

"Yeah! You could call it Jailhouse Rock!"

"It's illegal to do social media in jail," I say.

Frank laughs. "So, when did legality stop you?"

"I like the sax in this song," Rachel adds. "Who plays the saxophone?"

"That would be Anthony Thistlethwaite. He eventually left and joined the Saw Doctors."

"See! Who knows this shit?" exclaims Frank.

"I don't know anything about Liszt."

"Maybe we could start a channel where I teach you classical music, and you teach me rock."

"You could call it Classic Rock!" Frank's proud of himself.

"Or I could just play him for you sometime. You'd like him."

"Count me in!" Frank can see he's losing her focus and wants it back. "I'll get the piano back from Ron after Michelle..."

He looks at me and stops. The elephant has arrived in the backyard.

"I don't mean it the way it sounded." Frank starts up again, "Ron has a meeting tomorrow morning with hospice care, so she's on my mind. I just meant that the piano was always in this house until Ron got married and Michelle wanted to learn to play the piano. I'd much rather have Michelle live a long time and never get the piano back, even if she can't play a lick, and don't kid yourself, she can't."

We both give Frank a smile at his attempt to bring back some humor, but as "Don't Bang the Drum" fades away the song, and the mood, change.

The rest of the dinner has more of an undertow than a flow. The ribs are fantastic, but the thought that Michelle might have had her last solid meal, or a meal of any kind that didn't make her sick, makes every bite a mixed blessing. After The Waterboys, Frank wanted to change the mood, so he put on David and David's *Boomtown*, knowing that it was one of our favorites in L.A. But the musical tales of romance and drugs in Los Angeles didn't take me back to our time there; instead, they reminded me of Toni Child's counterpoint CD *Union*, the female perspective of her relationship with David Ricketts, one of the Davids, who played on and produced *Union*. Those two CDs were a punch, counterpunch of a tempestuous relationship. I gave Michelle my copy of *Union* when we were in D.C. She loved it so much that she never gave it back.

And now she's close to dying. So much misery happens to us all that I try to focus on Warren Zevon's final advice to "enjoy every sandwich." Frank put little chunks of apple in his coleslaw, which I normally wouldn't like, but they underscore the applewood taste of the ribs brilliantly.

"So, when are you going to see Michelle?" Rachel smiles reassuringly as she asks.

"Frank thinks maybe I shouldn't see her."

"What do you think?"

I think I'm scared. I can't even begin to picture her sick, much less dying. "I don't know. I guess I could go in the morning before Angelina's."

"I think this is the real reason you broke out."

"I broke out to play in Angelina's!"

"'Life is what happens when you're busy making other plans.' John Lennon. My mom was a huge Beatles fan, and then loved solo John and George, and early Paul, and early Ringo too. During chemo she'd listen to *Ram* by Paul and Linda McCartney, which I loved, and George's *Concert for Bangladesh* CD. By the way, Billy Preston is unbelievably good at that show, on CD and DVD, and of course, John Lennon's *Greatest Hits* CD was a regular at her treatments."

"Michelle likes to listen to the Cure, R.E.M., which she says you got her into, Kimo, the Smiths, she still has her sense of humor, Death Cab for Cutie, and World Party, which she also gives you credit for making her aware of. Kimo, you know what? I apologize because you do have to see Michelle. She needs to see you before she dies."

"I'll drive you in the morning." Rachel squeezes my shoulder as she says this.

"Okay," I say.

I'm going to see Michelle.

I have an empty feeling at my core, and it scares me. "I'm going to skip dessert, Frank, and hit the sack. It's going to be a big day tomorrow, and today has been big, and I need my beauty sleep. We're playing golf tomorrow, right, Frank?"

"I'll call Spike tonight, bro."

We get up and hug, not just a man hug, but a full-on hug between friends, until Frank hides the obvious with a sarcastic, "I love you, man!"

"It's great to be here, Frank."

"It's great to have you. The sheets in the guest room are clean, but you'll have to move a bunch of boxes off the bed. Wait, I'll do it."

"No. I can do it, Frank. Do you have an extra toothbrush I could use?"

"Believe it or not, I got you one when we went shopping. It's on the sink in the bathroom."

"Well, God love you, my man."

"I do what I can. You'll want to turn the fan on and keep it on all night."

"Okay." I turn and lean down to hug Rachel. "Thank you for a great day."

"I'll be in after dessert."

"You do what you want."

"I do, and I'll be in after dessert. That doesn't mean I won't thank Frank for the meal."

She smiles, and I look at Frank, and we share a smile. What can I say? She does what she wants.

I leave them in the backyard and go inside the house. My first stop is the bathroom and brushing my teeth. Then I go to the next room over. I take the boxes off the bed in Frank's guest room and set them next to the open window. I'm dead tired. It's been a long, though invigorating day. I take off my clothes, remove the comforter and set it on the boxes, then lay down on the sheets. It's still hot, so I remember to get up and turn on the fan to blow some of this hot air around. I get back down on the bed and lay still.

I can hear Rachel giggling outside, and I'm sure Frank is getting a stiff one because I am just thinking about what we did today. You just never know, do you? And then there's Michelle. I just can't get my head around her dying. Is she the real reason why I broke out? Is there something I can do to help her? I need to get myself mentally prepared to face whatever tomorrow brings. I start a relaxation technique I used in my classroom with the kids, whispering, "My ankles are relaxed. My calves are relaxed. My legs are relaxed. My spine is relaxed. My shoulders are relaxed. My neck is relaxed. My heart and lungs are relaxed. My brain is relaxed. My whole body is completely relaxed. God's river of peace flows through me."

I thank God for this day, ask Him to forgive my sins, and then pray for Michelle and Ron, and the souls of the departed, especially my grandmother and grandfather.

Please forgive me, Grandpa.

FIVE

I wake up with an erection. When I was younger, it was par for the course to wake up with morning wood, but the older I get, and being in jail for a year, make it an uncommon occurrence. Of course, waking up with my hands cradling Rachel's breasts and spooning with her naked next to me gives my penis all the incentive it needs to grow and try to find some space between her butt cheeks.

"You're not sticking that in my ass," mumbles a half-asleep Rachel.

"I'm not trying to. It's just happy and rising on its own and looking for a little room." Okay, maybe the thought did cross my mind; she's got a lovely rear end.

"Mmm." Unfortunately, she moves her butt away.

I don't remember Rachel coming to bed last night, but I sure am thankful to wake up next to her. I start kissing her neck and moving down her spine with my mouth. I trace her tattoo with my tongue. It is a tree with its leaves blowing away on one side. I wonder if it's symbolic of how cancer destroyed her family tree. I'll have to ask her about it, but now I just want to continue my journey. When I get to the small of her back, she rolls over and grabs my head, and leads me to where she wants me.

"Gently, I'm a little sore from yesterday."

I'm not quite sure how to take that. Let's face it; it couldn't be from our twenty minutes in the office. Just what the hell happened after I went to bed last night? I smell my way forward, and there's nothing offensive, so life is short. She smells fine, and no disrespect intended to Wheaties, but this is the breakfast of champions. I dive in.

"Frank told me you saved his life at Mavericks."

"I'm a little focused at the moment," I say with my mouth full.

"He made a point of... right there! Mmm, yes!"

I think of Graham Parker's song "You Hit the Spot" and thank God for the start to this day.

***

Frank is all smiles when I get out of the shower and join him in the kitchen. "Kimo, I want to thank you."

"For what?"

"I want to thank you for dropping in out of the blue and bringing a little joy back into my life. More than a little joy, you've brought some real fun back! Spike is thrilled we're going to play this year."

"Beautiful!"

"I'm meeting Ron at the gravesite and going with him to his hospice meeting. You can come with me and take my car to go see Michelle, but remember to be at Angelina's by noon."

"I can't take your car. I don't have my license with me."

"That's funny; I think that's the least of your crimes. Did

Rachel tell you about her call?"

"No. What call?"

"Where is she, anyway?"

"She's still in bed. She said she was pretty worn out after last night."

Frank smiles.

"I know you had sex with her."

Frank explodes. "She's unbelievable! She's like this hot-shot pilot that flies a dam buster and blows away all inhibitions!" He leans over and whispers. "She let me pack the poop chute. I know you've been in jail, but I've only seen that in porn!"

Damn it! Who is this chick giving me this 'you're not sticking that in my ass' bull when Frank's already been there? What the fuck? Is she a slut? "Look, just because I've been in jail doesn't mean I know anything about being fucked in the ass. Did you ever consider you were just exercising your homosexual tendencies?"

Immediately Frank's defenses go up. "No, I didn't."

"Well, it's something to consider."

"No, it's not! It might be kinky, but it's not immoral. Well, I don't know, some people may see it that way, all right, it might be immoral, but it doesn't mean I'm gay! And like they said on 'Seinfeld,' not that there's anything wrong with that."

"You're the one that brought it up."

"Do you want to know about the damn phone call?"

"Sure. What?"

"It was Rachel's mother. They'd been questioned by the police at the reception. The police wanted Rachel to call them."

"Okay. That was bound to happen. When is she going to call them?"

"She did."

"She did?" Cue the defibrillator.

"Yeah, last night, and she was brilliant. She told the police she left the reception because of how depressed she got watching her parents avoid each other and how she was happy for her sister but felt like her sister settled for less because of the pain she'd witnessed being the oldest and trying to hold the family together, and she talked about how superficial everyone is about looks and how she's going to get the most out of hers while she has them because you never know when you'll get sick and lose a breast, or your hair, or your desire. She was looking at me the whole time she was talking, and when she hung up, we went at it. She told me you guys used her last condom, and she's not on birth control, so she asked me to stick it in her rear. So, I did."

"Do you think she's out of control?"

"Kimo, she was cold-blooded and completely relaxed."

"Are you using a Graham Parker lyric on me?"

"'Empty Lives,' my man."

"I was thinking of him earlier. Huh." So, what's with Rachel? What demons is she trying to slay with sex? Sex with one stranger in twenty-four hours is one thing, but two? And anal? I'm going to have to get to know her a bit better and take a deeper dive into her world.

"Rachel's so fucking Zen! Every moment to her is precious!" Frank interrupts my train of thought.

"I would say every moment with her is precious!"

"That's because she knows every moment is precious."

"Look, I'm never this deep before breakfast."

"What can I make you?"

"You know what I'd love after not having one in a year?"

Frank smiles and starts singing, "Star-bucks..."

I answer, singing, "Nothing but Star-bucks..."

"Saving the day! Life's only a musical if you make it one."

"God love Bill Murray."

"Amen, brother."

***

What is the life expectancy of a dragonfly?

Twenty-four hours, five days, three weeks, two months.

So, we're standing in Starbucks, and this question is written on a little chalkboard. While I'm waiting for my Venti, no-whip, mocha, I'm thinking that whatever the answer to the question is, it sucks. I feel sorry for dragonflies. No matter what the answer is, they don't get enough time. Speaking of time, I just can't wait to taste a mocha again. Actually, I've waited for almost a year, which I guess is generations of dragonflies, but now that I've ordered, I can't wait! These people standing around looking at their phones just take this sweet beverage for granted, and that's their right. That is freedom, but I can't wait!

From behind me, a voice says, "Mr. Jones?"

Oh no.

"Mr. Jones, it's me, Wilfredo, from St. Mary's."

This is brutal. What the hell is Wilfredo Muzo doing in a Starbucks in Stockton? I look over and notice how much he's grown since he was in my classroom. He's taller and not as chubby and looks like he's got a little hair growing on his chin.

"Wilfredo, how are you?"

"I passed into the seventh grade!"

"It's amazing what happens when you do your homework, huh?"

"Remember that day when you pounded my head into the desk for Mrs. Oiler?"

I smile at the memory.

The principal, Mrs. Oiler, came to my class to observe me. It's a yearly review in the life of a teacher, and I had one of my girls, girls being more reliable in fifth grade, keep watch at the top of the stairs so she could let me know when the principal was on her way up. A couple of years earlier, I had a student who believed professional wrestling was real, and I had to teach him the truth, so I acted like I was slamming my head into the turnbuckle, grabbing the back of my head and slamming my face into my desk, sealing the illusion by hitting the desk with my front hand, so it sounded like my head was actually hitting the wood. What can I say? It was a hit with the kids, so I added it to my teaching repertoire. So, when Mrs. Oiler got to the door, I grabbed Wilfredo by his head and pretended to slam it onto his desk.

She nearly had a coronary and asked me what I thought I was doing, and I said I was knocking some sense into him. The class cracked up, and Mrs. Oiler realized we were putting her on. I have to hand it to her; she had a sense of humor that most in the administration don't have.

"That was my favorite day of school ever, Mr. Jones! My sister was so upset you left before she could have you. Dad, look, it's Mr. Jones! We're on our way to our cabin in Arnold for the Fourth. It's so good to see you. Why did you leave us?"

I want to tell him the truth; that I got drunk and crashed, and I want to ask him if there was a new statue of Mary in front of the school, but I don't. "I had some things come up that I had to deal with, Wilfredo."

"You were my best teacher, Mr. Jones. You knocked some sense into me!" He smiles and laughs.

"Hello, Mr. Jones."

I turn and shake Mr. Muzo's hand. "Hello, Mr. Muzo. How are you?"

"We're good."

He knows the truth. I can tell.

"You've been missed at St. Mary's. Jessa cried when she found out you weren't going to be her teacher."

"Where is Jessa?"

"She's already in Arnold with Mrs. Muzo."

"Tell them both I said hello."

"We will. Wilfredo, do you have your Frappuccino?"

"Yep."

"Then say goodbye to Mr. Jones because we've got to get back on the road."

"I hope you come back to school, Mr. Jones."

"Well, you never know, Wilfredo. What did I always tell you?"

"That God works in mysterious ways."

"That's right. It was good seeing you, Wilfredo. Good luck in seventh grade."

"Thank you, Mr. Jones!" He starts slurping up some of his Frappuccino.

"Good luck, Mr. Jones." Mr. Muzo again shakes my hand.

"Thank you, Mr. Muzo."

They leave just as Frank comes up with our drinks. "Do you know those people?"

"That was one of my students and his father."

"What? What are they doing here?"

"They're on their way to Arnold, and the kid wanted a Frappuccino."

"What are the odds? Uh oh, the father's coming back."

I turn and see Mr. Muzo walking toward me. He's got a newspaper in his hand, which he gives to me when he arrives.

"Page four, Mr. Jones. I don't know what trouble you're in, but I wish you peace, and may God bless you." He turns and leaves.

I look at the paper, the *Contra Costa Times*. I open to page four and see an article below the fold about James Jones, me, escaping from the Marsh Creek Detention Center. Thank God there's no picture! I hand the paper to Frank and take a sip of my mocha. It is a brilliant, simple pleasure, and I savor the taste.

"Uh oh. Do you think he'll call the police?"

"No. Why would he give me this if he was going to turn me in?"

"We should check out the *Record* and see if they have anything."

"The *Record?*"

"Stockton's paper. Let's hope you're not in it."

"Hey, thanks for the drink. What'd you get for Rachel?"

"I got her a latte."

"She'll like that."

We walk out of Starbucks, and Frank slips some coins into the newspaper stand to get the *Record*. He hands it to me as we get into Frank's truck. I take another sip of my mocha and look for a story about my escape. Chocolate and coffee are a lovely blend of flavors on my tongue. It's weird to be enjoying that taste again while flipping through a paper looking for stories about myself.

And how weird is it to run into a former student like that? He had passed year after year, then had a rude awakening in my class when he found out that he'd have to do some work to pass or he'd be back with me another year. It took a lot of meetings with his parents and the administration because it's hard to flunk a student, even if it's the best thing for the child. It doesn't make the school look good, so you need an extensive paper trail.

No one wants a kid to flunk, but there must be standards, and it's important for a student to reach them. Otherwise they might end up like poor Wilfredo when I first got him. He had no expectations of himself after he kept moving up, no matter how little he worked. I found that if you asked a lot from the kids, and asked them to ask a lot of themselves, you would get a lot in return. If you don't ask much from them, then that's exactly what you'll get. It was a hard change and a difficult year for Wilfredo, but look at him now, going into seventh grade with some confidence because he learned that self-esteem can't be given, only earned, and he earned it in fifth grade. We had fun, but we sure worked hard as well. Saint Ignatius said, "laugh and grow strong," and that was pretty much the inspiration for my teaching philosophy. High expectations, discipline, and consequences, balanced with humor and fun, are my philosophy of education.

I used to give CDs that I burned for Christmas and end-of-the-year presents to my students. The Christmas CD was made up of seasonal songs that I liked, such as "Do They Know it's Christmas" by Band Aid, "A Christmas Song" by Jethro Tull, and "Father Christmas" by the Kinks. Then, the end of the year CD was made up of songs we listened to in class; I had certain staples every year and then filled in with whatever was organic to each class. "On My Way to Heaven" by The Waterboys opened every end of the year CD because we would start each year with it, along with "Spirit," and its refrain "What spirit is man can be." I challenged every class to live up to that. I always ended the CD with a Waterboys tune as well, the live version of "Saints and Angels."

Michelle took me to my first Waterboys concert on my thirtieth birthday at the Warfield in San Francisco. We were attracted to each other, but she had a boyfriend away at grad school, and I was an old man of thirty! Karl Wallinger was no longer with the band, and for some reason, Steve Wickham had left the tour, but Mike and Anto were still together, and Mike brought Roddy and the horns back to replace Steve's fiddle. The show was awesome, but the goodnight kiss was on the cheek, and that pretty much summed things up. The best Waterboys show I ever saw was just after 9/11 when they played "The Pan Within" and "The Return of Pan" back-to-back, and for an encore, played "Don't Bang the Drum" and "This is the Sea." Like the Scots say, it was brilliant!

"Anything?" Frank's worried.

"Not yet."

"Maybe you shouldn't take my car. I mean, if you got caught, then I'd be busted for aiding a fugitive. With all that's going on, I really don't need that right now. You know what? Maybe we shouldn't play Angelina's. I mean, do you really want to be out in public?"

Here we go. I've got to get him calmed down. Yes, he has valid points, but I've come too far to turn back now. In a few hours, we'll be playing golf! It's time to change the subject. "Rachel told me the thing she liked about you was how stable you were under the pressure of Michelle's illness and my escape. She said you were a rock that others could count on."

He takes his eyes off the road and looks at me inquisitively. "Okay. What's your point?"

"My point? I don't know that this isn't Russia. The KGB isn't going to bust into your house and take you away to a gulag for golfing with me. Seriously, Frank, what's the worst that can happen?"

"Uh, someone gets shot?"

I laugh, "This is America! White guys don't get shot by the police! If I get caught, I go back to jail without playing golf. You can always say you had no idea I escaped. Plausible deniability, didn't you learn anything from the Reagan Administration?"

"Don't bash Reagan. You know I'm not political, but I liked him."

"I'm not bashing him; I'm just trying to tell you that you shouldn't be worried."

"I'll decide what I'll worry about."

"Fine, just don't show that side of yourself around Rachel. It's not attractive. You should live more like a dragonfly."

"What the hell does that mean?"

"It means life is short. Didn't you see that in Starbucks?"

He flips me his middle finger as we drive south on Pershing up and over the Smith Canal. A mile or so west of here is Michelle and Ron's house. I take another sip of my mocha and relish it. It really is the simple things. We take a right on Harding and head back toward Frank's house. He seems to be deep in thought, probably deciding how to act when we get back in Rachel's presence.

Frank finally speaks. "I suppose I have to pay for Angelina's."

"I'll pay you back when I get out of jail. I don't think it would be wise to access my account at this time. I'm good for it."

"How are you good for it? There's no telling when you'll get out, and even when you do, what are you going to do? Who's going to hire you?"

"Why don't you hire me? You've got no problem hiring illegal aliens. I can cut the grass at the cemetery."

"All my workers are documented, asshole."

"You know I don't care if they are or not. This is America, Frank, the land of second chances. I'll find something. If there's one thing I learned from the Clinton administration, it's that you have to be able to compartmentalize. The thing we need to do is focus on the here and now, and that means Angelina's my man. Let's take it one hole, one swing, and one drink at a time and worry about the future later!"

"But your 'here and now' is a fantasy! You have no money! You have no job! You have no bills! You're a fucking fugitive from jail! There are people with guns looking for you at this very moment, and I bet they aren't happy about it!"

"It's not for everybody, but those are the cards I've been dealt."

"Bullshit! Those are the cards you played! You were dealt a fine hand; white, American, male, that's a Royal Flush!" He swings into his driveway and pulls in behind Rachel's car. "What about Michelle?"

"Rachel said she'd take me, so you don't have to worry about your truck."

We sit there; the tension, like humidity, makes the atmosphere in the cab oppressive.

"Look, I just don't need trouble right now," he says.

"I understand, and I'm sorry that I've brought you trouble."

The gate to the backyard swings open, and Rachel walks out in skintight black exercise shorts and an orange San Francisco Giants t-shirt. Frank looks over at me and can't help but smile. "Holy smokes, she's wearing another one of my shirts."

"Speaking of the trouble I brought, I'm sorry that I've caused you more wash."

"You kidding me? I'll never wash those shirts again."

"Don't forget to give her the latte you bought for her." I open the door and get out of the truck and step into the fresh air. "Good morning, beautiful."

"Where'd you guys go?"

Frank gets out and hands her the latte. "Kimo was in Starbucks withdrawals, and I thought you might want a latte."

"Oh, aren't you sweet, Frank?" She kisses him on his cheek, then takes a sip from the latte. "Oh, that's good. Thank you."

"Kimo made the news."

"What?"

"Only in the *Contra Costa Times*. It didn't rate making the local paper."

"I got a call from the police last night."

"Frank told me. He said you were great."

"This is getting exciting!" she says.

"I'm glad you're having fun."

Frank moves to the gate. "Let's sit in the backyard; I'd hate for a cop to drive by and put an end to all the fun."

We move to the backyard and sit in the shade of the privet tree. A hummingbird scats away from the feeder but quickly returns for its morning drink.

"So, you need to see Michelle before you get caught."

"And play golf," I remind them.

"Sure, whatever, but Michelle has to be a priority."

"She is. Would you mind driving me over to her house?"

"I told you I would."

"Frank is meeting his brother and going with him to his hospice meeting."

"Oh. That's good. You're going with him, sometimes in meetings like those you need more ears because some things you hear just stop you from concentrating on anything else."

Frank and I go silent as reality again makes its presence felt.

"Can I make you some breakfast, Rachel?"

"I've already had some leftovers from last night. Nothing like chocolate-covered strawberries for breakfast. They're so good, Frank!"

"What about you, big man?"

"This mocha is a beautiful thing. I'll wait for my hot dog and chili at Angelina's."

"So, what are your plans, Rachel? You're welcome to join us for steaks and ravioli after the tournament. Angelina's is so well thought-out because they let wives and girlfriends eat for free, so those golfers who might overindulge during the round have designated drivers to take us home."

"Are you planning to overindulge?"

"It's been our M.O. over the years."

"We usually come in dead last," I add. "But no one has more fun than we do!"

"I have class in the morning."

"What time?" Frank asks.

"Ten."

"What class is it?" I ask.

"Ethnomusicology."

"Say what?" Frank says.

"It's basically an anthropological look at music. Right now, we're studying Colin Turnbull's study of the Mbuti pygmies of Zaire."

"I studied the munchkin lollipop kids of the *Wizard of Oz*," Frank jokes.

"That's the lollipop guild, Frank," I say.

"What you talkin' 'bout, Willis?"

"They're not the lollipop kids. They're the lollipop guild."

He starts singing, "We are the lollipop kids, the lollipop kids, the lollipop kids."

Rachel starts laughing, which only encourages Frank to continue. He gets up and adds the dance to the song, putting his hands in his pockets as he sways back and forth.

"That makes no sense!" I say, which forces me to stand up, stick my hands in my pockets, and sing to Rachel. "We represent the lollipop guild, the lollipop guild, the lollipop guild, and in the name of the lollipop guild, we welcome you to munchkin land." I clasp my hands and move them from shoulder to shoulder as I move backward, only to trip over the leg of my chair, knocking my mocha to the ground, where thankfully, the lid keeps it from spilling too much, that is before I drop on it like Dorothy's house crashing on Oz. The cup explodes violently, sending my precious mocha flying across the backyard. "No!"

"Kimo!" Rachel screams as she comes over to check on me.

"You okay, bro?" Frank kneels next to me.

I take inventory. My back's a little sore, and though I'm a bit shaken up by how quickly a disaster can strike, I feel all right. Luckily, I took judo as a child and learned how to fall because if I had landed differently, this could have immediately ended my golf outing. "I guess I'm not in Kansas anymore."

After realizing I'm okay, they burst into laughter.

"Are you okay?" Rachel's look of concern is so heartwarming.

"I'm okay, just a little embarrassed."

"You should have stuck with the lollipop kids," Frank teases.

"I better get you to Michelle before a catastrophe strikes," Rachel says with that sparkle in her smile.

"What do you call the loss of my mocha?"

SIX

We are sitting in Rachel's car outside of Michelle and Ron's house. It looks different from this side of Smith Canal, somewhat foreboding. I haven't felt this nervous and queasy since my trial. Rachel reaches over and takes my hand. "It's going to be fine. I'll wait here and take you to the golf course when you're done."

I nod my head. "Thanks."

I could throw up. Instead, I take a deep breath and ask God for strength by silently repeating the prayer, "God loves, governs, guides, and directs me in all ways." I get out of the car. My legs are a bit shaky as I walk up to the front door. I take another deep breath and push the doorbell button. I can hear the bells ring inside the house and think of the lines from John Donne's Meditation XVII "...never send to know for whom the bell tolls; it tolls for thee." Of course, that reminds me of Hemingway's *For Whom the Bell Tolls,* and while I wait for the door to be opened, I think of Robert Jordan and Maria's doomed love during the Spanish Civil War.

And wait.

Finally, I knock. I turn and look at Rachel in the car, and she motions for me to go in. I'm sweating. I sniff my armpits, and they're okay, so I wipe my hands on my shorts and grab the doorknob. The door's unlocked, and I step inside. "Hello?" It's gloomy inside the house because the curtains are all closed, keeping the sunlight out. "Michelle?"

"Up here."

It's her!

Her voice is weak, but it's definitely Michelle. I walk by a picture of her and Ron on their wedding day before I start up into the darkness at the top of the stairs. I can feel my heartbeat in my ears, pounding like drums, and I feel like a galley slave rowing to their rhythm and chained to my oar, unable to flee even if the ship sinks. I get to the top floor and walk into the master bedroom and see...

...Oh my God.

I immediately flash to a scandal when Michelle was teaching eighth grade. In history class, she showed pictures of starving prisoners during the liberation at Auschwitz. A couple of parents revolted, saying Michelle had traumatized their children. I didn't think much of their argument at the time, but Michelle looks like she could be in that picture, and I'm traumatized.

What's left of Michelle is sitting in a La-Z-Boy chair next to the bed. I try to be strong, but tears build, and I can't stop their flow. I'm sure I'm of no comfort to her. She's just a skull, no eyebrows, no eyelashes, just a wisp of hair, but mostly veins, looking like roots from a tree that have been exposed by erosion, little purple streams zigzagging along the topography of her bald head carrying the disease and cure that are killing her. Her haunted eyes, sunken and surrounded by bruises, have a phosphorescence and narcotic glaze. Her skin looks shriveled around a strong jaw that wasn't as noticeable when her face was normal; it's like my bike seat when I remove the cushion, hard and angular. Her nightgown hangs limply on skeletal shoulders that could be mistaken for a fragile plastic hanger. I can't believe a body could ravage itself so thoroughly in such a short time, and I can't hide my horror.

"Where the fuck have you been?" she says with more anger than I've ever seen, and I've never heard her drop the f-bomb.

"I've been in jail."

"So have I."

I walk over and kiss her warm forehead. "Michelle, I'm so sorry."

She reaches out and takes my hand with her boney fingers. "I'm glad you came."

This is unbelievable. Michelle is literally skin and bones, practically a skeleton; cancer, a sanguinary beast, waged a scorched earth campaign against her body, relentlessly laying to waste all she once was. I feel not only for her but for Ron, powerless against this annihilation. I can't imagine what it must have been like to watch her suffer on a daily basis. I'm devastated.

Why? What good does this do anybody, God? If You created everything, why cancer? What purpose does it serve in the Master's plan? Jesus only suffered for a day, and He knew He was God and would be resurrected. I look around and notice all the cards, mostly handmade by kids she once taught. What lesson does this teach them, Lord? I mean, isn't this Hell, and what did she do to deserve this? A woman that sacrificed so much of her time for her students, who knew and appreciated and loved her for it, dies like this? What's the point? What good comes from this?

I get to my knees and look into Michelle's eyes. "I'm so sorry."

"I'm scared, Kimo."

I kiss her fingers. "So am I." I move to the front of the chair, lift her blanket, and find her feet. I start with the one closest to me, but there's not much meat left on her foot to massage, and what's left is chapped and dry. I grab the lotion that's on the nightstand, pour some on her foot, and get started. I start with her ankle, rubbing the lotion slowly over the arteries and veins that protrude above the skin.

"That feels good." She closes her eyes and lays her head back. I continue with the top of the foot, long strokes, gentle squeezes, and then move to what used to be the ball of her foot, but now is basically bone. I tenderly rub and massage the bones. Michelle casually turns her head and throws up a clear liquid on her sleeve. "Sorry."

I start to get up to find a towel.

"No, don't stop! Please. It can wait. It's normal."

I sit back down and start on the next foot.

"Thank you," she says as she again closes her eyes and leans back. I try to infuse some healthy energy into her through my touch. Inch by inch, I press and knead her foot, working the lotion into dry cracks and split skin. I pray for the healing power of God to flow through me. I wish I knew more about massaging feet so I could do her the most good. I seem to remember that in reflexology, the entire body was connected to different places on the foot, but since I have no idea what is where I just take my time and thoroughly caress them both. Michelle starts to snore softly. That's what I love about her. She feels comfortable enough in my presence to sleep deeply.

I look at her and just can't believe this is the same human being that snored next to me in Victory Park the night of the satellite and sins. The last time I saw her, she was vibrant, even though I now know she knew she had cancer. How did I misread the situation so horribly at Frank's party? I feel sick about all the time I've wasted because I got jealous and stupid. It's not that I could have changed the outcome, but I could have been around to help. I could have had more moments like this, just trying to comfort her in silence. I could have taken her to chemo, done research, maybe found the best doctor, something, anything, other than the nothing that I did do.

Time passes, and I'm happy that she can rest peacefully. Finally, Michelle wakes up and stares at me. "Kimo."

"Michelle." I'm not sure she remembers my arrival.

"That feels good." She notices the mess on her sleeve. "The pool would feel good. Would you help me to the pool?"

"Sure." I get up and help her out of the La-Z-Boy. She's as frail as a newly orphaned bird that's fallen out of the nest.

"My bathing suit is in the bathroom." She takes a deep breath as if it took all her energy to stand up and speak. I don't know if I should leave her and get the suit or lead her to the bathroom. Once again, she throws up. It's not much and just slides down her chin. "Sorry, but dignity is the first thing this disease takes."

I lift her nightgown and wipe her face, then kiss her on her cheek. "You're still beautiful."

"You've been in jail too long." She smiles. "What did you do?"

"DUI."

"Frank's party?"

"Yep."

"You were fucked up. I should have told you about my diagnosis sooner. You would have felt sorry for me instead of yourself and would never have left the party."

"Yeah, it's your fault." We share a smile, but there's despair in her eyes. "So, your bathing suit?"

"Put me on the bed, and could you get it out of the bathroom?"

"Of course."

I guide her over to the bed and help her sit. Then I walk across the room and into the bathroom. The counter is full of drug canisters, at least fifteen different prescriptions with multiple syllable words. Her bathing suit is hanging on the shower rod. I grab it and head back to the bed where Michelle is trying to take her nightgown off, but it's stuck on her head. I help her take it off, and she sits there naked.

"Well, you finally got me with my clothes off. Is it everything you dreamed of?"

Her emaciated body is a stark reminder of how shallow physical attraction is. What's left of her breasts are just bags of sagging flesh on an otherwise concave chest. Her legs are like a heron, long and scrawny, no longer able to carry her weight. Her knees look like golf balls resting on tees—all right, they're closer in size to baseballs in a kid's t-ball, but golf is on my mind. Besides, this gaunt and undernourished body is still Michelle, and I still love her. I hand her the bathing suit. "If you want to skinny dip, it's fine by me."

Michelle looks funny, like a child trying on mommy's big girl swimsuit. I help her rearrange the bathing suit, then carry her downstairs and outside.

It's already hot. I wade into the shallow end of the pool with her. The water is cold and refreshing. I have one hand on the small of her back, the other between her shoulder blades, and I let Michelle float. She closes her eyes and seems to release her pain into the surrounding water.

"I'm having my ashes spread under the Golden Gate," she says without opening her eyes.

"Frank told me. He said Ron's not happy about it."

"It's my body."

What's left of her body barely registers as weight in my hands. "I feel sorry for Ron."

She opens her eyes and looks at me. "Why?"

"He's had to endure your sickness, and when you're gone, he'll have no place to go be with you."

"I won't be anywhere. I want him to move on."

I don't want to argue with her, so I remain silent.

But I can't. "You know about his dad, right?"

"Yes. So?"

"Look, I've known him a long time, but I never knew his dad. I know that his family has a history with their cemetery. They respect the departed. And they know what those left behind need."

"Oh yeah? And what's that?"

"I don't know. Did you ever ask your husband that question?"

"No, and it doesn't matter," she continues, "I was happiest when Ron proposed to me on his boat under the bridge. If there is anything after death, I want to start my journey to whatever is next from there."

"It seems to me your soul would leave your body at death, not where your ashes are scattered."

Michelle looks like she's seriously considering what I just said. "I never thought about that."

And just what is next, I wonder. The afterlife is a worrisome mystery when you lack faith, and it seems as if Michelle can read my thoughts.

"Do you think there is a hell?"

"I don't know what I believe anymore. It was much easier when I was a kid."

"I have a hard time sleeping, and sometimes in the middle of the night, when Ron's finally fallen asleep, I worry that I'll go to hell."

"Please, Michelle. I don't believe in a Jesus or a God that would condemn you to eternal damnation. You're not going to hell; if anything, you've been there for the last few months."

"I've sinned!" she argues.

"I'm sure of that, but kill anybody?"

"No."

"Are you sorry for your sins?"

"Yes."

"You're not going to hell." I wonder if she's thinking about our night in Victory Park. Could she be carrying around guilt from our sin? I'm not sorry that it happened. When Michelle is gone, I'll treasure that memory until I die and meet my maker, and if He sends me to hell, it won't be for that. It's up to Him. "Are you thinking about us?"

"No. I made peace with that a long time ago. Ron was very understanding."

"You told Ron?" Oh no.

"Of course, he's my husband."

"How'd he take it?"

"He was hurt. But he eventually forgave me."

"Has he forgiven me?"

"Have you asked him?"

"No."

Damn it; I thought this was just between Michelle and me. I never thought it would get out. It had absolutely nothing to do with Ron except for timing; it wasn't done against him, it was a dream come true! I prayed for it! God knows the flesh is weak, and my spirit was willing, so when it's my time to be judged, He's got some explaining to do because I can't count how many times I've asked Him to lead me away from temptation. Wasn't He listening? Wasn't He watching over me?

"Ron thinks that's why no one ever sees you anymore, that you feel guilty."

I hear that. Oh, if they only knew. "Well, actually, I was found guilty and sent to prison, just not for that. It doesn't mean I'm not carrying around a ton of guilt, but we are Catholic, or at least I used to be. Why do you think you're going to hell?"

She tries to turn herself over but can't. "Hold on to my hands and let me go under the water."

I change my grip on her and reach for her hands. I turn her over, and she takes a deep breath, and I let her slip under the surface. The air bubbles rise from her mouth and ascend, only to make little pops as the air escapes back into the atmosphere. Pretty soon, there are no more bubbles, and Michelle hasn't come up for air. I panic and jerk her head up. She spits out water in my face. "Ouch!"

"I'm sorry! Are you okay?"

"No, I'm not fucking okay! I'm dying!" She starts to cry. "And I'm ready." She looks me straight in the eyes. "Help me. I've never told anybody about Kauai."

Kauai! She's bringing that up? I knew it would come back to haunt me, not that it ever goes away. But I can't believe she's bringing that up. All my secrets are being exposed, and I feel a malignant shame permeating from my core. "You promised me you'd never talk about that."

"I need your help, Kimo."

I shake my head. "Michelle, you can't ask that of me."

"Please," she pleads. "I've asked Ron, but he won't."

"Because he loves you!"

"You say you do too, but you're both selfish with your love! I'm begging for an act of love!"

I'm numb.

"You help me, and I'll let Ron bury me wherever he wants. Just hold me under."

I look at her in disbelief. I guess dying makes you desperate. God, why didn't I just stay in jail and finish my time?

"Now you know why I think I'm going to hell," Michelle says.

Yeah, and I'll be there too.

Suddenly, there's music! Chords on a piano are coming from inside the house. It's dramatic and powerful. Then the tempo changes, and the music gets lighter, keys go up and down the scales, until finally, it goes into a playful echo. Da-da, da-da, da-da-da, on and on, the notes fly out of the house, over the pool, up the bank, and out over Smith Canal. Bling, bling, bling, da da da dum. The tempo increases and gets sprightlier and more joyful. Michelle looks confused. "What's that?"

"Let's go see."

It's Rachel.

She's playing the old family piano in the living room. I later learn it's Liszt's "Hungarian Rhapsody #2 in C-Sharp Minor," but at the moment, I just watch her fingers frolic across the keyboard. Rachel looks over, gives us a luminous smile, and continues her performance. The sound she makes is enchanting and transcendent, and Michelle seems transformed by the music with a look of ebullience on her face. I am filled with joy at having Michelle in my arms while watching Rachel's rapturous recital. It's amazing what humans can do and what an effect it can have on others. When she finishes, Michelle is in tears. Rachel notices, but I can't read the expression on her face.

"That was beautiful," Michelle says. "It's been a long time since music filled this house. Who are you?"

Rachel comes back from wherever she was, gets up, and takes Michelle's hand. "Hi, Michelle, I'm Rachel. Kimo and Frank have said such nice things about you. I'm very happy to meet you. Do you need a towel?"

Michelle and I realize that we're both wet and dripping on the hardwood floor. I remember there was a towel hanging next to Michelle's bathing suit upstairs. "Michelle's towel is upstairs in the bathroom."

"I'll get it," Rachel replies as she heads for the stairs.

"You look like you forgot about your pain," I comment.

Michelle looks at me as if she just realized the truth. "You can put me down," Michelle tells me. I do but continue to hold her up. "It will return," she says fearfully. When Rachel gets to the top of the stairs, Michelle looks at me and asks, "Who is she?"

"Rachel? I met her yesterday. She helped me escape from jail."

"Escape?"

"Yeah."

"You broke out to come see me? That's so sweet."

"Well, actually, I didn't know about you." Michelle looks hurt. "But I came as soon as I found out!"

"Then why?"

"Why what?"

"Why break out?"

I smile and say, "Angelina's." Uh oh, that's not a good look on her face.

"Angelina's!" Michelle shouts. "You broke out of jail for Angelina's? You're a dumb ass!"

Rachel comes back down the stairs with Michelle's towel and cautiously approaches us. "Here you go." She offers the towel to Michelle.

"You helped him escape to play in that stupid golf tournament?"

Rachel tries to diffuse the tension with her smile. "Hey, I just helped him for the fun of it. I didn't know about golf, or you, or him for that matter." She gently tucks the towel over Michelle's shoulders; the tenderness catches Michelle by surprise.

"Thank you." Her voice softens. "You have a beautiful talent on the piano."

"Thanks. Do you want me to play some more for you?"

"You don't have to do that."

"I won't if you're more comfortable with silence, but if it will help give you a little cheer, I'd be happy to play for you."

Michelle starts to cry. "Thank you. I'd love that. Let me put on a dry nightgown."

"I'll help you," Rachel says. She takes Michelle away from me, leads her over to the couch, and helps her lay down.

"Um, Rachel," I hesitate to continue, but I'm not comfortable with the way things went with Michelle in the pool, and, well, I've got to get to the course.

"I know. You can take my car."

Michelle looks shocked. "You're leaving?"

"He'll be back," Rachel assures her. She looks at me, "Won't you." It's not a question. She looks back at Michelle. "Where's a dry nightgown?"

What is with Rachel? Why is she doing this? Why does she care about any of us? I thought she had to get back to Berkeley for class.

"There's one in the dryer. The laundry room is off the kitchen," Michelle answers.

Rachel starts to walk toward the kitchen, then veers over toward me. "Here are my keys." Rachel reaches into her pocket and offers them to me.

"I'm not sure I should take your car. If something happens, you could get in trouble. Besides, I haven't driven in a while, and, uh, I'm not sure it's a good idea." In fact, I haven't driven since my accident, and I'm more than a bit scared. "Besides, we'll be in no condition to drive afterward."

"Good, then you can stay," says Michelle. "I want you to stay, Kimo. I don't have much time."

Her eyes have never seemed so clear, so purposeful. It hurts. What should I do?

"Let him go, Michelle," Rachel interrupts. "We'll spend the afternoon enjoying music, and then I'll give you a manicure and a pedicure, you know, girl stuff. Then he'll be back later to see you."

Michelle looks at me, "Promise?"

"I promise." I feel terrible. Am I lying? This wasn't in the plan. What the hell should I do?

"And you'll help me?" she adds.

Fuck! I reluctantly nod my head.

She looks relieved and lies back down. "Okay. Have fun. I'll see you in a few hours. It's great seeing you, Kimo."

"You too, Michelle. I'll see you later." God willing.

"I'll take a cab to the course and pick you up. What's it called?" Rachel thinks of everything.

"Oak Moore," replies Michelle. "Ron can drive you there."

"Perfect!" exclaims Rachel.

Perfect? This is far from perfect! Now I have to face Ron, knowing he knows about my dream night in Victory Park with his wife, and I've just said yes to my dying friend's last, unbearable request. This is turning into my worst nightmare. All I wanted to do was play golf!

"Don't you have a class?" I softly ask Rachel, hoping for an escape.

There's a momentary eclipse of the light in her eyes as she quietly answers. "You have no idea what this means to me. My playing actually affected her."

"You have a gift."

"Believe me, it's not a gift. I put in a lot of time, but to actually see it move another human being in her condition is the gift."

Rachel reaches into her pocket, pulls out some money, and then slips it into my hand as she kisses me on the cheek. "Pick up some condoms if you can," she whispers into my ear before taking a quick nibble of my lobe. "I'm proud of you. You're making Michelle happy."

Great. Well, there you go. I'm getting aroused again like a schoolboy after his first slow dance, and I don't want Michelle to notice, so I quickly walk out the front door. There are definitely pros and cons to being free. God help me.

SEVEN

God damn it!

I'm golfing again. Nature, weather, friends, endless possibilities, a good walk, and, upon reflection, most joys of life.

But my drive is slicing over the trees, out of bounds, across a road, and into a dirt field. Fuck! My first swing that counts in over a year, and it's a fucking loser! I broke out for this? My warm-up swings were fine. But when the horn went off for the shotgun start, I stepped up to lead us off, then thought of Michelle's skeletal face at the top of my backswing, and after that, I don't know what the fuck I did, but there it fucking goes! One swing, one fucking lost ball.

"Just a little outside," Harley says, imitating Bob Uecker in one of those baseball movies. "You lifted your head. And you were trying to kill it."

"Thanks, Harley, that's insightful," I say as I pick up my damn tee and try to hide in plain sight.

"That's okay, bro," consoles Frank.

"I believe what you were trying to do is this," Harley puts his ball on a tee, addresses it, deliberately swings his arms up in a slow motion, then hesitates at the top of his swing before bringing it down smoothly and following through. That baby sails off the tee and flies long and straight down the fairway before landing and running further into the sun. "You've just got to gently kiss the ball, Kimo. Let the club do the work."

Harley is the best and brightest of our group, but after a few drinks, his game deteriorates rapidly, so he fits right in with our foursome. His dad was a used car salesman that raised his son to be streetwise and confident. He taught him to smile at everyone and treat them the way you'd want to be treated. Harley is the most successful of us all. He grabs his cigar off the custom-made stand that he plants into the ground so he doesn't have to bend over and pick up his cigars. He then lifts the stand and puts it into his bag next to his irons. "Are you sure you don't want one, Kimo? They're Montecristos."

"You know what, Harley, why not? It couldn't hurt." He reaches into one of the pockets of his golf bag and pulls out a traveling humidor. He flips it open and offers it to me. I grab an illegal import from Cuba. Harley offers me the clippers, and I slice off the end. He flicks open his lighter, and there is fire. I suck on the island tobacco and inhale. Soon, I have the sweet taste of success in my mouth. It is good.

Frank is next on the tee. He came to golf later in life and swings like he's playing baseball, but he can hit it straight, if not far. He's great at the bump and run and can sink putts, and he doesn't take his stogie out of his mouth while swinging, so doesn't need a custom stand.

"So, are things all right with you, Kimo?" Harley asks sincerely.

"Well, to be perfectly honest with you, Harley, I've been in jail this last year."

He cracks up. It's a big, heartfelt laugh, right in the middle of Frank's swing. Frank tops the ball, and it rolls just past what would be the ladies' tee, but because there are only nine holes on the course, we play each hole twice, so it is our thirteenth tee. He turns and looks at Harley. "Thanks, asshole."

"Sorry, Frank, you can take a mulligan, but you know we're going to use my drive, anyway." He turns back to me. "Are you serious?"

"Yeah."

"Frank, did you know he was in the slammer?"

"Yeah, he told me not to tell anybody."

Harley starts laughing again, "Kimo, you're a bad mother..."

"Watch yo mouth!" Frank and I play along with the theme from *Shaft*.

"I'm talking about Kimo!" Harley shouts.

"And we can dig it!" We scream.

"What were you in for? Mug one of your students for his lunch money?"

"D.U.I."

"A Catholic school has a problem with that? Did they forget Jesus's first miracle was with wine? And his mother made him do it! When did you get out?"

"Yesterday."

"Yesterday? Well, the golf gods were smiling on you to have your release date the day before Angelina's."

"Yeah, well, my actual release date is in three weeks. I'm, uh, kind of taking a weekend pass."

"That's cool. I didn't know the prison system was that progressive."

"It's a new program," I lie.

Frank walks by on the way to put his driver in his bag. "He broke out yesterday so he could play with us today."

"What? Get out of here! Kimo, you're fucking Paul Newman in *Cool Hand Luke!* That calls for a drink. Where are the cart girls when you need them?" Harley looks around for the girls in the drink cart, but they're nowhere to be seen. "You guys go ahead and hit. I'll drive back to the clubhouse for some drinks. You're a superhero, Kimo! Greyhounds for all?"

"I'll stick with beer," Frank answers.

"Man up, Frank, and have an adult beverage," Harley teases as he drives his cart away.

"Fuck you. Kimo, you want to drive?"

That reminds me of the drive over here in Rachel's car. A police car pulled up behind me at a red light. I felt like that guy in the movie *Midnight Express*, my heart thumping—ba boomp, ba boomp. I thought for sure they were going to stop me and send me back to jail. But then, maybe I didn't deserve to golf after all. I had to remind myself that I wasn't doing anything wrong and just focus on driving. I started singing the refrain of a Kinks song, "Paranoia the destroyer," while they followed me. Finally, they turned off, and I could calm down. Needless to say, I didn't dare stop for condoms. "You go ahead and drive, Frank."

He scoots over, I get in, and off we go. I lean over and pick up Frank's ball as we pass the ladies' tee. I feel some pain in my lower back where I fell earlier. Frank steers us down the fairway of the fourth hole, our traditional starting hole, keeping us in the shade of the valley oaks, redwoods, and Monterey Pines, as it's good and hot in the sun.

"How's Ron?" I ask.

Frank shakes his head. "Not good. The hospice nurse who visited the house on Friday said Michelle's down to days, not weeks. What'd you think when you saw her?"

I don't want to think about that memory. Too late, the depression creeps in. "It's brutal."

"Yeah. The nurse wants to start her on a morphine drip. Michelle will be able to control the dosage herself. Hopefully, she can be pain free until she passes."

"I think that's how Sigmund Freud died, but I'm pretty

sure that was considered euthanasia."

"Yutes in Asia? What yutes, your honor?" Frank's acting like Joe Pesci in *My Cousin Vinny*.

"The two yutes in question?"

"What a great movie!" Frank exclaims.

"Yeah."

"Who was the babe in that movie?"

"I don't know. I can see her, but I can't remember her name."

"Me neither. I remember she was funny and cute."

"Yeah. She was kind of like Michelle, except for the Jersey accent."

"And before the cancer."

I look over at Frank. "Obviously before the cancer. I just can't get the way she looks now out of my head."

We roll out of the shade and to Harley's ball; he hit a nice drive. The hole doglegs left, so we're set up nicely for our second shot. We get out of the cart and put a tee next to Harley's ball to mark where we'll shoot from. Frank pulls out his three-wood. "Look, you took a big chance coming here, and you got us to play, except for Ron, so what do you say we just focus on enjoying Angelina's, and we can talk about reality later?"

"So, we should be more dragonfly?"

Frank smiles. "Yes, let's be more dragonfly."

"Sounds good to me. How far is it to the green?"

"I don't know, but I'm hitting my three-wood." He looks back toward the clubhouse. "Should we wait for Harley?"

"No, ready golf, my man. We don't want to keep those guys waiting on the tee."

"You're right." Frank drops his ball next to the tee and takes a couple of practice swings. He addresses his ball, focuses, and swings. He makes good contact, and the ball flies off to the right and is short of the raised green.

"Not bad. We can play that if no one gets on." All right, let's focus on golf. This is why I'm here. I get a couple of balls out of my bag, put one in my pocket, and toss the other one next to Harley's ball. I'm thinking of using my utility club, a Mizuno CLK with 20-degree loft and a titanium crown. It also has a cool blue shaft and was a gift from one of my students, so it has sentimental value as well as practicality. This student's dad took us to the first round of the U.S. Open at the Olympic Club in San Francisco, which was amazing to see the pros play in a major.

I stand behind my ball and visualize my shot. I see my ball rise high into the air and land right on the green. Okay, let's make it happen. I move to the side of my ball and take a nice easy practice swing, remembering what Harley said about letting the club do the work. I address my ball, inhale deeply through my nose, calmly exhale as I start my backswing, and let her flow.

Are you fucking kidding me?

Damn it! I dig a divot behind the ball, don't make clean contact, and send it low and straight for maybe all of seventy yards. What the fuck. This game sucks!

"You need to relax, Kimo!" yells Harley as he drives up and parks behind our cart. "And I've got just the remedy." He gets out and hands Frank and me plastic cups with a golden liquid. He goes back to the cart and comes out with a plastic cup of his own. "A toast to my missing partner, with just what he would have wanted, tequila from the lowest shelf. To Ron," he raises his cup, and we join him.

"Ron," I say.

"My big brother."

"And his wife," I add.

We down the shots. It's a bit nasty, but for a good cause.

Harley walks back to the cart again. "Now Frank, you can go back to drinking that piss water you call a beer, and Kimo, here's a Greyhound for you," he hands me a different plastic cup, "and one for me." He takes a gulp before putting it in the cup holder of his cart. He moves to the back of the cart and pulls out his cigar holder and a two iron. He shoves the holder into the ground, sets his cigar on it, and then looks at me and smiles. "You've got to lighten up and have some fun." He turns and quickly swings at his ball. The shot soars but ultimately lands in the front left bunker. He looks back and smiles. "It's all good. That's a beach party. And you're all invited."

He's got a great attitude. I need to adjust mine and start having fun.

"Frank, where'd you go? Your shot had to be better than Kimo's and mine."

"We can use mine," Frank says as he steps on the gas and starts for his ball.

"Hey! What about me?" I scream after him. He turns around to look and slows down.

"You can ride with me, Kimo."

I look over at Harley. "Of course. What am I thinking?"

"Whatever it is, it's too much. Go ahead, Franko. We'll follow you." Harley grabs his cigar and puts the holder and club back in his bag. "Frank's so excited because we haven't used a shot of his this early in years."

"You're riding him pretty hard."

"If I don't, he'll crumble. This has been a tough year." We get in the cart, and Harley drives toward my ball. "It's hard to watch people you love suffer. He's taking it hard. He needs to get laid."

I smile and keep Frank and Rachel's rendezvous secret. "What about you, Harley? How's your family?"

"Obviously, they're driving me to drink," he jokes. "My wife is still beautiful and does a great job with our kids, but has no limits on spending my money. The kids are pains in the ass, the selfish little fuckers, but they keep me young, and I love 'em. Last week Mia complimented me on my tie and said she loved the way it went with my hair. It was a silver fucking tie, and she was being sincere! Come on, man!" He starts singing. "Kids, huh? What are they good for? Absolutely, nothing. Say it again!"

Harley is a funny guy. I bend down and scoop up my ball as we drive to the bunker where Harley gets out. "You can take it from here." He grabs a rake and heads into the sand for his ball, where he stops and turns around. "Look, Kimo, I know we don't stay in touch as much as we'd like, but if you ever need anything, all you need to do is ask."

"Thanks, Harley." I drive around the green to where Frank is parked. His ball is at the foot of the mound that protects the green. For most people, it's not a hard up and down, but we're not most people. We're hacks, and this is going to test our skills.

"You going to chip it in?" I ask as I pull up behind his cart.

"Of course. Don't even get out of the cart." He takes a few practice swings. "I'm going to hit it into the hill, deaden the speed, and have it roll down to the pin." He swings, and the ball hits into the slope and stays there. "Would you believe you're going to chip it in?" Frank says in his best Maxwell Smart imitation.

I get out of the cart, walk over to my bag, and pull out my pitching wedge. It feels good in my hands. I love my irons; Wilson Staff Ci6s with graphite shafts. I got them at a golf convention at the Cow Palace. I hurt my shoulder during our blunder at Mavericks, and the graphite shafts are much easier on my swing. I take a few practice swings and try to visualize my shot. I'm going to try to land it on the green and let it roll down and in.

Okay, I put my feet so the ball is behind them in my stance, take a nice easy swing, keep my eye on the ball, and voila. My ball actually does what I visualized, to a certain extent. Unfortunately, I must have had my clubface closed because rather than heading for the pin, it is a little to the left and rolls a little further past the hole than I wanted, but still, it's an uphill putt from there for a legitimate par opportunity.

"That's not bad, bro!" says Frank. He comes over and gives me a high five.

"Nice shot," agrees Harley as he walks across the green after getting his ball from the trap. "Where are we hitting from?"

Frank points to the tee. Harley plants his cigar holder just off the green before walking down the hill and dropping his ball at the tee. He gets out a loft wedge, takes some full swings for practice, then walks up and hits an amazing shot. If I had taken that swing, the ball would be fifty yards away, but his ball goes straight up, lands at the top of the green, and rolls down to the hole, just missing it by half an inch, and unfortunately rolls past it about twenty feet.

"Oh!" We all scream as it barely slides by. Harley's grin lets us know he thought it was falling in. "We've got a better putt from your ball, Kimo."

I walk over to my ball, stick a tee in the ground next to it, and then start to read the putt. "Just straight in?"

"If it breaks, it will be toward the water," says Frank.

"What water?" I ask.

"The water hazard, Frank?" Harley asks in disbelief.

"No, the Delta."

"The Delta's going to have an effect on my shot?"

"Isn't that what they always say? It breaks to the water. What the hell do I know? So maybe the Delta won't affect your shot, but that Greyhound might."

"This is true." I look at the putt again. It seems straight up. I get in position over my ball, slowly take my putter back, and bring it softly forward. My ball is straight on path but stops a full foot short of the hole.

"You got to hit the ball, Alice," teases Frank.

"Knock it in so we know we have bogey, then Frank and I can take shots at the par and not leave ours short," commands Harley.

I step up and sink my putt for bogey.

"Okay, Frank, work your magic, so I don't have to play with my putter." Harley walks over and gets his cigar off his stand. "Besides, I'm thirsty, and my drink is back at the cart."

Frank lines up with his putter and does what he does best. It rolls in for a par.

"Nice putt, Frank," I say as I give him a high five.

"Good putt, Frankie. Okay, we saved par but let's get under it this next hole," Harley says as he too comes over and high fives Frank. We leave the green and head for our drinks. Harley puts his cigar stand and wedge back in his bag, then pulls a silver flask out of another of its pockets. "Gentlemen, it's great to be spending this Monday golfing with you, away from work, away from responsibilities, away from the pain and suffering of this last year, but let's take a moment and remember those poor bastards who can't be playing with us today!" He takes a healthy swig from his flask before passing it to Frank.

"To the poor bastards!" Frank takes a drink and then hands me the flask.

"And to us lucky bastards!" I say as I take the flask from Frank. It's good. Single malt whisky from Scotland. "Mmm, that's good, Harley. Single malt?"

"Yeah, Macallan, eighteen years old."

"Just like my women," Frank chimes in.

"In your wet dreams, Frankie. I got it this spring when my dad and I went to play St. Andrews."

"You played St. Andrews?"

"Not the old course, but the Jubilee and Castle Courses. Then we went to the Highlands for distilleries and to play a round at Dufftown. The front nine is all uphill. My dad was a champ. The six pillars of Macallan were his ten command-ments."

"What are they?"

"A spiritual home and a peerless spirit are the only ones I remember."

"Sounds good to me." I take another swallow before handing the flask back.

Harley takes it and offers it again to Frank. "No, I'll get my piss water at the next tee."

"Suit yourself," Harley says before downing another wee dram.

Frank gets in our cart and drives away. Harley offers me another belt. "I'll have some later." He puts it back in its place on his golf bag, and we follow Frank to the fifth tee.

We have to drive back down the cart path about a hundred yards, and when we come upon the tee, we're about sixty feet down range and blinded by bushes. One year when we made the turn, an errant drive flew into our cart and ricocheted around, hitting a drink right out of my hand before bouncing out. Still, despite that casualty, and the danger, we continue to take the turn at full speed, making a mad dash to the tree on this side of the tee box where safety and a blue tub loaded with liquid refreshments await.

When we pull up, the last of the foursome in front of us is walking off the tee, and Frank is out of his cart, grabbing another light beer from the blue tub. They're giving each other shit. I recognize most of the regulars, but, due to the fact that I've only played in this tournament the last ten years and am usually hammered at the end of the day, I don't know many names.

"Where's Ron?" one of them asks, and Frank walks over and updates him while the other three have looks on their faces that show that they already know. They each go up and pat Frank on the back and say some encouraging words before they get in their carts and head down the fairway, following their shots. Frank opens his beer, and I sense reality again making its presence felt and weighing heavily on our minds.

A hawk cries out from down the fairway, flies out of a tree, climbs up the thermal waves, and surfs above the links. Frank and I hold the birds in high regard, and you already know that I thought the last hawk I saw was a messenger from God. Frank thinks God watches us through the eyes of little birds. He heard it in a Guadalcanal Diary song and said the song articulated what he always believed. Anyway, we watch the graceful bird, and I feel in harmony with all things. Frank watches the hawk glide beyond the trees, heading for the second and seventh tees, and then smiles at me. He walks over, gives me a hug, and kisses me on the cheek. "It's all good, my friend."

"Are you guys gay or what? Get a room. Frank, you'll lead us off after sinking that putt."

Frank and I exchange a knowing look; we've been friends for a long time and have been through a lot, but we're chronically heterosexual, and we're united in this tragedy. Frank walks over to Harley's cart. "They haven't even taken their second shot, so calm down, Harley. I'm enjoying some piss water." He takes an exaggerated drink from his light beer. "Now, give me some of that scotch!"

"Yes, sir!" Harley goes back to his bag of tricks. Out returns the silver flask. Frank takes it and drinks, "Kimo?"

I walk over and take another pull. Okay, that's tequila, vodka, and scotch, and we're only on the second hole. My mind is spirited with alcohol, humming along nicely under the hot Central Valley sun. My first hole mostly sucked, but it's Angelina's, and I'm with friends, and despite the heartbreaking surprise of this trip, I'm feeling pretty good.

"Okay, they've hit," announces Harley. "Lead us off, Franklin!" Frank tees his ball, practices, then swings and sends his ball straight down the fairway. "Nothing wrong with the fairway. Nice poke, Frankenstein. Let's see what you can do, Kimono. Remember, just give her some tongue." He sticks out his tongue and swirls it around. Yes, it's disgustingly funny to my maliferous mind.

I pull my driver out of my bag. It's a Fujiyama sold under the Jack Nicklaus Golden Bear brand. It's got a graphite shaft and oversized head, and I can hit it well with more playing time, but obviously, after that first stroke, I can also make a mess of things. I tee my ball and then set up to overcompensate for my slice, aiming at the green we've just come from. I take a deep breath; shake some of the seasickness from the alcohol in my head until I realize I'm experiencing no pain. I take my stance, and I'm feeling good. I keep my eyes on one spot and let her rip. It's a beauty! It starts out heading for the last green and then glides back toward our fairway, landing way beyond Frank's drive and rolling completely across the fairway and just into the first cut of rough.

"Nice hit!" Frank cheers.

"That's some spicy kimchi, Kimo!" adds Harley.

It felt great. Nice and smooth and free, so worth breaking out of jail for! It just takes one good swing to bring you back in golf, and there's mine for this round, and we're only on the second hole. I still might have others in me! What a great game! I thank God for getting me here safely and thank Him for the privilege of golfing with friends again. Mark Twain was credited for calling golf "a good walk spoiled," but nonetheless, it's still a good walk, a peaceful walk, outside in nature, with friends, swinging clubs, and giving each other shit. It's all good.

And then it hits me, an epiphany; the hawk, my escape, Rachel, Frank, Michelle (okay, maybe not Michelle due to her condition), Angelina's, Harley, and though I've yet to see him, Ron.

It's all good.

It's All Good is the name of Ron's boat, the boat that took Michelle to the happiest day of her life! Why not do it again? She's going to be dead in a few days anyway, and she wants to start whatever comes next from there. Why not get Ron to take the boat and let her see the Golden Gate one last time? How can it hurt? That's it! That's how I can help her! That's how I can get Ron his gravesite! Maybe Rachel was right, and this is the reason I escaped. I can get redemption. Thank you, God!

EIGHT

I wake up in pain. I can't even open my eyes because my brain feels like it's expanding like rising flood waters trying to break through the levee that is my skull and release the pressure. It's hot and stuffy here. I try to open my eyes, but my vision is impaired by an opaque film covering them. My mouth is dry, and I finally realize I'm hungover. I guess it's Tuesday, the day after Angelina's, the day I go back to jail, but where am I, and how'd I get here? If I can't remember most of the round, was it worth my escaping from prison early, or was that one of the stupidest decisions in the history of mankind? What is the last thing I remember?

I think I might have gotten closest to the pin on the sixth hole, which was right after we caught up with the cart girls. I remember Harley giving them each a twenty and promising them twenty more at the end of the round if they would make sure to resupply us at least every other hole. My swing was so relaxed by then, and I was feeling a radiant energy flowing through me, connecting me with the Divine nature in all things, or maybe it was just the alcohol, but I hit my seven iron, and the ball rose into the bright blue summer sky before dropping softly on the green within three feet of the pin. We had celebratory high fives and a congratulatory toast, and after that, the day is fuzzy, my memories lost in a fog, with just a few breaks of sunshine to faintly light my murky recollections.

I vaguely remember Harley trying to get the cart up on two wheels and me falling out when he did. Luckily, I was relaxed and just hit the fairway and rolled. Did Frank really play a hole with his shorts dropped down around his ankles? I seem to think I saw Ron and that his hair was completely silver, but that could have been in a dream. I don't remember seeing Rachel and worry that she might have gone back to Berkeley, never to be seen again. I don't remember the steak dinner or the awards ceremony after our round, but that's happened before, so I'm not too worried about that. I also don't remember if I saw Michelle again, which makes me sad. Where the hell am I? I need some fresh air and something nonalcoholic to drink.

I struggle to open my eyes, and when I finally succeed, I'm a little alarmed because I still have no idea where I am. I roll over and fall off the bed, my head hitting the floor. A kaleidoscope of colors bombards my aching brain. I rub my head and concentrate on breathing.

I feel bleary like this every Tuesday after Angelina's, but keep going back for more because I know I'll eventually recover and hear stories that bring us laughter and make it all worthwhile. But at the moment, I'm suffering, and that makes me think of Michelle. I'm pretty sure I couldn't handle the constant pain she's been enduring. Maybe what I really need is more sleep, but it's so uncomfortable where I am that I know if I can just get the inertia to blast myself up off the floor, I can find a place to get some fresh air and start feeling better.

Once again, with great effort, I open my eyes. I see that the bed I was on in this tiny room is V-shaped. I focus in the other direction and see a little hallway that leads to a small kitchen, then three steps lead up to another level, and it dawns on me that I'm on a boat. I would assume this is Ron's boat.

I fight to get to my feet, and the blood seems to drain out of my head, leaving me dizzy. I steady myself and let it pass before walking toward the kitchen, or galley as it's known in the boating world. I pass a small bathroom and see why I must have been exiled here, as not all of my vomit made it into the toilet. Seeing and smelling my post-golf feast of regurgitated bits of steak and ravioli makes me queasy and almost brings about an encore performance. I resolve to clean it later because I need fresh air quickly.

I climb the three steps to the sitting room (which I learned later is called the salon). This room has two armchairs, a couch, a small desk on my right side, and a steering wheel, or helm, on the left. There are two large windows on each side that have the curtains closed. I cross the room to a staircase. I look down and see it leads to the master bedroom (stateroom), and even though I'm in a hurry to get topside, my curiosity gets the best of me, so I go down to take a look.

It's dominated by what looks like a queen-sized bed, with a comforter colored with a beautiful sunflower design, Michelle's favorite. Two portholes on either side of the bed and a large window aft let in lots of light. There is a vanity on the port side and built-in drawers and cabinets on the starboard side. There's a large flat-screen LCD monitor hanging on a full-sized mirrored closet. It also has its own bathroom (head). No wonder Michelle was smitten on their date; hell, I probably would have accepted Ron's proposal.

I finally go back to the salon and take the six steps up to the aft deck and renew myself with crisp, clean air. It's a beautiful thing. There are two swans sitting on the dock looking at me quizzically. Last night they both looked white, but up close, I see that one is completely white with a schoolbus-yellow beak and legs, while the other has black feathers mixed in and a red face, almost like a turkey. I wonder if he was ostracized because of the color of his face. Still, he found love, which gives me hope.

"What's up?" I ask. I guess they decide I must be a nut, or maybe they get a whiff of my breath because they make a few squawks before getting up and waddling to the end of the dock where they dive into the Smith Canal.

So, was it worth whatever new penalty I have to face? I'd have to say yes. Rachel alone made these an unbelievable thirty-six hours. The sex was great and needed. Her playing the piano for Michelle is something I'll always remember. Michelle's condition is shocking and numbing, to say the least, but I got to see her again, and for that, I'm thankful. It was great to see Frank and Harley and play golf again. I wish I remembered if I had seen Ron already. I don't really want to face him now that I know he knows about Michelle and me, but I don't see a way around it.

"Good, you're awake."

Speak of the devil. I turn and see Ron coming down the stairs to the dock. His hair is silver, so I did see him last night. At last year's Angelina's, his hair was dirty blond. Stress kills. He also looks like he's put on all the weight that Michelle has lost, like some kind of cruel cosmic balance is at work.

"Morning, Ron."

He climbs aboard. "How are you feeling?"

"I've been better."

"I don't doubt that. Did you get some water?"

"Not yet."

"I told you there was water in the frig below."

"I guess I forgot."

He stands there and studies me before taking a seat. "Look,

I've thought a lot about what you said and have decided that I want to take you up on your offer."

Good God, what offer? What have I done now? Do I come clean or try to play along until my memory comes to my rescue? What if the cavalry doesn't come? Damn it; I guess honesty is the best policy. "Um, Ron, I don't remember much after the front nine yesterday. What offer?"

He nods his head. "You know, Kimo, you might want to stop drinking."

"Until two days ago, I had stopped drinking."

"I'm not sure being forced to because you're in jail counts."

"Well, I think it was Oscar Wilde who said, 'I can say no to everything but temptation.' So at least when I go back to jail today, I'll have some time away from temptation to work on being better prepared the next time I get out. Besides, isn't overindulgence the whole point of Angelina's? Isn't it a time to get together with friends and let it rip?"

"Yeah, I guess maybe it used to be. So, you don't remember our conversation last night?"

"Not at the moment."

"That's too bad. You were actually quite eloquent."

"Really? Did it have anything to do with you taking Michelle to the Golden Gate Bridge on this boat?"

"So, you do remember?"

"I remember having that idea on the golf course."

"Did you also have the idea to apologize for sleeping with my wife on the course?"

Fuck!

I drink too much. What the hell was I doing last night? I know I deserve whatever comes my way, but God, why weren't you watching out for me? "Look, Ron, I don't know what to say other than I'm sorry."

"That's it? Last night you made a case for it truly being an act of love and that it really had nothing to do with me, and to be honest with you, despite the fact that you were slurring your words and pathetically repeating yourself; I could tell it was heartfelt, and I was strangely moved by it. And as idiotic as your idea about me taking Michelle back to where I proposed to her seemed last night. After sleeping on it, I woke up this morning and had a change of heart. You're right. Why should she just stay at home in bed, giving herself morphine until she dies? With a little work, we could set her up on the boat and take her to the Golden Gate, and that just might make whatever waking moments she has left happier. Besides, it's the only way she'll allow me to bury her here."

Oh.

Well, maybe you were looking out for me after all, God. Sorry about all the doubt.

"But I can't do it alone, and last night you offered to help."

Of course, I did. Last night I was feeling no pain. Right now, I feel like crawling into a dark cave and hibernating. Then there's that little jail problem of mine. Being gone for thirty-six hours is one thing; the way I see it if I got back there today before noon, sure, there'd be a price to pay, but no harm was done, so I would hope the penalty would fit the crime. Every hour later only seems to add to my problems. And what does Michelle expect from me?

"Well, Kimo? Are you in?"

I look at Ron. He looks like he's been the president. He's aged so much since last year.

"Have you told Michelle about this?"

"No. I didn't want to get her hopes up if I don't have a crew."

"I'm not much of a crew."

"My brother and Rachel said they'd help too."

"Rachel's still here?"

"She took Frank home last night, but she said she'd come along. Michelle has really bonded with her. Have you heard her play the piano?"

"Yeah, I heard her yesterday."

"She's like Yuja Wang. I think Frank's finally found a winner."

Here we go again! My anger rises. "Frank didn't find her, I did. Besides, she's got to be at least fifteen years younger than him."

"Which makes her at least fifteen years younger than you," Ron reminds me.

"True, but my development was arrested before I was eighteen, so really she's older than me." And what the hell was she doing with Frank last night? "And if they're going, why do you need me?"

"Because I think Michelle would want you to come along."

Great, that's noble of him. The more gracious he is, the more guilt I feel. I massage my temples and eyes. "What about her parents? And your mother? Shouldn't they be there instead of me?"

"Michelle's parents are coming over Thursday, and we'll be back by then. My mom wouldn't approve of your idea in the first place, and in the second, I don't need the drama. Look, it should take us maybe five to eight hours to get there. We can dock at the Saint Francis Yacht Club in San Francisco for the night and come back tomorrow morning.

"Last night, you kept saying to live like dragonflies, whatever that means, but it was important to you. You're already looking at more time, Kimo. My wife is dying. I'm asking you to give Michelle another couple of days. She's got to be as worthy of your time as playing at Angelina's."

"You know she is, Ron." What am I thinking? Michelle is dying, and I'm here now. He's right. What difference do another couple of days make? They might throw the book at me anyway, so I've got to accept this opportunity to comfort Michelle as best as I can. "All right, I'm in. But I need something for this headache."

"Great! I've got aspirin and water below. I'll get them for you."

"Thanks."

He gets up and goes below deck. I take a couple of deep breaths. I hear windows opening below and remember that I left a bit of myself down there that Ron must have just discovered. I should have warned him, but frankly, it skipped my mind, as well as my body. Ron comes back with a bottle of water and three gels. "Dude, it reeks down there! I'm talking quite unpleasant. Luckily I've gotten used to cleaning up messes like that." He hands me the water, and I take my medicine. "You'll feel better after you take a shower and have some breakfast."

"I hope so."

"Go on up to the house and take a shower, and I'll clean up down here and get the boat ready. Come get me when the hospice nurse arrives and check on Michelle for me. Will you please?"

"Sure."

"If she's awake, why don't you tell her about the trip? After all, it's your idea."

"Okay." I get up and slowly make my way off the boat and up to the house to see Michelle. The pool looks inviting. I wouldn't mind just dropping in and sinking below all this misery above the surface. As I'm passing the pool, I'm reminded of what Michelle asked me to do yesterday and find it hard to grasp the underlying harmony in things, especially when my head feels like it's being eaten by African Assassin Bugs (Platymeris biguttata— fourth-grade boys love deadly insects) which is how I think of cancer, slowly devouring you from the inside. Of course, there are no creepy-crawlies inside me, and my headache will pass, but Michelle is certainly being consumed by the cancer cells cannibalizing her healthy ones. I don't blame her for wanting her pain and suffering to end; I'm just hoping that the trip and a morphine drip will get me off the hook.

I walk into the house, and it takes effort to make my way up the stairs. I feel like crap, and I'm worried about being alone with Michelle. Every step feels heavy, and I have a sense of foreboding like I'm climbing up the gallows to meet the hangman. I think of Jesus struggling to carry his cross up the Via Dolorosa after a long night of beatings and humiliation, and his example inspires me to face whatever comes next.

I step into the room and find Michelle sitting in the shadows, tears of pain rolling down her cheeks. It's a disheartening image that I'll never be able to forget. How about a miracle cure, God? It would be a great inspiration for the faithful and those of us on the fence. I remember when I would show *Ben-Hur* to my class every year, the kids would erupt into spontaneous applause at the end when the mother and sister are cured of leprosy. What better way to rekindle belief? All those kids she taught and their parents would be true believers and spread the word. It would be great PR! And let's face it; there have been too many fallible men standing in for you since your time on earth. Once again, the world could use a miraculous display of Divine Intervention.

"Hi." I try to sound upbeat.

"Take me to the pool."

Okay, so the hook is still set, but let's see if I can get off the line. "How about we take you to the Golden Gate instead?"

She closes her eyes and shakes her head. "I just want it to be over. I told you the pain would be back. Please help me, Kimo."

"Michelle, what if we can get something to ease the pain?"

"Nothing fucking works! I just want it to stop," she pleads.

I go over and gently take her in my arms. She's atrophied so much that she's almost nothing but bones. "I thought you had a good day yesterday."

"I did."

"Then let's have another one today."

"You got to sleep. I just suffer."

"I love you," I say.

"Then help me."

I hug her tighter. She's so frail I feel like I could break her. God, what do I do? Help! Please, heal her or take her, but just stop her suffering. "You're going to get morphine soon, which should ease your pain."

"Like Vicodin, Darvocet, and Oxycontin were supposed to? They've given me everything, and what's the point? I get to suffer a little longer and look at all your heartbroken faces? Do you think that makes it any better for me? This is not living."

She's staring at me, and those eyes that used to inspire are now filled with hopelessness and anguish. If there is a reason for all things, God, please reveal the reason for this. Otherwise it seems cruel and unmerciful to just let the cancer continue its torture. I silently pray for forgiveness and find myself tenderly lifting her out of the La-Z-Boy and carrying her down the stairs.

"Thank you. I love you too, Kimo."

I lean down and kiss her. She's burning up. At the bottom of the stairs, I stop when I notice the picture from her wedding day. She's beautiful and beaming, and Ron looks handsome and honorable. There's no foreshadowing of the calamity in their future. Who am I to take her away from him? Who am I to play God? I look down and see she's also looking at the picture.

"It's not fair," she says.

"No, it's not," I agree.

"Where is Ron?" she asks.

"Getting the boat ready for the trip," I answer. She looks from the picture of her healthy and happy back to me, and I sense a softening in her urgency to leave this world. "Can you endure one more day?"

She closes her eyes, and I feel her tremble in my arms.

Please, God, if you're not going to heal her, give her the strength to tolerate the pain until she can go peacefully, surrounded by those who love her. She takes a deep breath and then slowly nods her head. "Promise me this is the last day. When is the morphine getting here?"

"Soon. Sometime this morning."

"Okay. Take me back to my chair."

Once again, I kiss her bald head, then turn and carry her back up the stairs.

"But you promise you'll help me when the time comes?"

"Isn't this enough proof for you?"

She nods. "Thank you. And Kimo?"

"Yes?"

"You need a shower because you stink, and your breath is fucking killing me."

NINE

What the hell is wrong with me? I would have gone through with it! I would have held Michelle under until her suffering was over. I would have willingly crossed the line between right and wrong and justified it in the name of mercy. What gives me the right? Who do I think I am? I don't trust myself because ever since I've been out of jail, I've been out of control. Who am I kidding? It was being out of control that got me into jail in the first place! Maybe I don't have the self-discipline it takes for freedom. Now the memory of Kauai is beating on the dungeon door deep in the darkness of my mind. It wants out after I've suppressed it all these years, but I can't deal with that now, so I'll choose to keep it caged.

I just want to stay here in the shower where I'm safe and those around me are, too. What happened to me? Where did I get off track? Am I so far lost that I can't come back and have a normal life? If I really love Michelle, how could I be willing to end her life? And what about the way I've treated Ron?

First, I didn't respect his marriage that night in Victory Park, and now I'd take his wife's life? It would have been better if I had drowned at Mavericks. God, why'd you let me live? I don't have faith in myself, and I don't have faith in you. I need to get away from here and back to jail.

I hear a knocking on the bathroom door, it squeaks open, and I can hear Frank and Rachel singing, "Starbucks, nothing but Starbucks, saving the day!" They both start laughing, and then the shower door slides open. Both of their heads appear and find me on the floor. They both look a little too happy, and it makes me angry to imagine why. Luckily, with the water spraying down on me, they can't tell that I've been crying.

Rachel smiles, "do you always sit in the shower?"

"Whenever I can," I weakly answer.

She looks over at Frank. "Should we join him?"

Frank reaches in and turns off the water. That bastard. "I think it's time he gets out. We waited as long as we could, bro, but your mocha is getting cold."

Rachel slides the door open wider and hands me a cup. "Do I notice some shrinkage?" She teases.

Frank comes to my rescue. "That's natural with a hangover," Frank says as he tosses me a towel. "Give the guy a break."

I let the towel cover my privates and sip the mocha. Even though it's not quite hot enough for me, it still tastes good. "Thank you."

"Rough night?" asks Rachel.

I nod. "And a rough morning."

"Not as rough as Ron's," Frank counters. "The hospice nurse is here showing them how to use the IV drip. We'll all have to learn how it's calibrated in case we need to help administer it."

"Good. I hope it brings Michelle some relief."

"You look like you could use some relief," adds Rachel.

I look up at her, and although she's giving me a playfully seductive smile, I have no desire; it's as if my libido got a lobotomy brought on by my overindulgence of guilt, anger, and alcohol. I feel like lashing out.

Rachel notices my lack of reaction to her obvious innuendo. "Are you okay?"

"No! In fact, what are you doing here? Shouldn't you be in class?"

She looks puzzled and possibly hurt by my venomous tone.

The ever-gallant Frank now comes to her rescue. "Don't be a dick, Kimo, just because you're hungover."

"You asked me to come along," says Rachel.

"I did?"

"You don't even remember, do you?"

"No."

"That's too bad. You were very sweet, telling me how much my playing meant to you and Michelle, and I told you about the music thanatology class I had taken as an undergrad, and you begged me to call in and tell them I was putting into practice what I had been taught."

"Music what?"

She laughs. "That's exactly what you said last night. Basically, it's music therapy for people who are dying. It helps calm their nerves and take their minds off their pain."

"I could use some of that right now."

"You're not dying," Frank says.

"Yeah, I just feel dead."

"Man up, Kimo! Quit your fucking whining. This whole stupid thing was your idea! When I got the call from Ron this morning, I dragged myself out of bed and drove to the cemetery to borrow the keyboard from the chapel so Rachel could have something to play for Michelle on the boat. She called in and got permission to miss the next couple of days of school. Now, we got you a mocha. We'll cook you breakfast as soon as the nurse leaves, and all you need to do is get an attitude adjustment and cut out the self-pity!"

"Fuck you, Frank! It's easy to be chipper when you've probably fucked her in the ass again! But you don't know what I've been through this morning!" Damn it. What a dick. Do you ever wish you could delete what you just said, just reach out and swat the words away before they reach others' ears? I know what I said is mean-spirited and crass, and I deserve what comes next.

Frank dives on me and hits me in the face. I let him land a couple more blows in an act of flagellation before I roll him over, grab a handful of his hair, and shove him into the wall of the shower. Rachel starts screaming for us to stop, and after a few more punches, she turns on the shower and lets the cold water blast us.

"You're a fucking asshole, Kimo!" Frank says as he throws one more punch. "Haven't you noticed that Ron isn't in a good place? Then you put this stupid idea in his head? No good can come from this."

"He gets to bury Michelle in your cemetery."

The icy chill from the water and the adrenaline spike from the fight clear my head and persuade me to let him go, and I raise my hands in surrender. Rachel turns off the water.

"But you're right." I taste blood and realize I bit my lip during the struggle. It feels justified. "Rachel, I'm sorry."

She looks down at me with a mixture of humiliation, disappointment, and pity.

"What the hell is going on in here?" Ron enters and quickly shuts the door. "I've got a nurse out there with my dying wife! What do you think you're doing?"

"It's my fault, Ron. I'm sorry. I should just turn myself in."

"I'll call the cops for you," snaps Frank.

"Shut up, Frank. As for you, you started this, so you're going to see it through." Ron looks at both of us, and the disappointment on his face shames me. "Jesus Christ, will you two please grow up? Show some respect."

"I'm sorry." I'm in a downward spiral and feel like I'm sucking everyone down into my personal maelstrom.

"Frank?" his brother asks.

"What?"

"Are you going to be a problem, or are you going to help me?"

Frank looks at me with disgust before he untangles himself and starts to get up. "I'm here to help you, Ron."

Ron looks at Rachel before again addressing us. "I don't know what this is all about, but you two need to act your age. Frank, after you clean yourself up, would you please start breakfast?"

"Sure."

"Rachel, will you help him?"

"Of course," she says before turning to leave without looking back at me.

"Kimo, you have a fat lip. Are you okay?"

"I'm all right," I lie.

"It's too bad about your coffee," Ron says before he turns and leaves me alone with my smashed and empty Starbucks cup. I get up and turn the water back on, adjusting the temperature before I sit back down and let the water wash and restore me. I watch my blood and the spilled mocha blend together and flow down the drain.

I need to calm my conscious mind, so I turn to some affirmations. "God's love fills my soul and cleanses my mind. God's light shows me the way to go, and the sunshine of His love goes before me, preparing my path." I breathe deeply and try another affirmation, "I am surrounded, supported, and guided by the love, wisdom, and peace of God." I again breathe deeply and repeat the affirmations, hoping that the stormy waves of my mind will be stilled and I can somehow salvage whatever good I can get out of this day. It is essential that I quiet the selfish turbulence in my mind and focus on serving Michelle and doing whatever I can do to help, other than killing her.

***

Getting from the shower to the boat is like walking a gauntlet of negativity brought on by my choices. First, I must get past Michelle, who is now connected by a clear plastic tube to the possible lethal injection of poison that will either end her life or numb her until the cancer finishes the job. She smiles and thanks me for coming to see her. It doesn't seem like she remembers what she had asked me to do earlier, but between the disease and the drugs, who knows what's going on in her mind. She just seems to genuinely care that I'm here, which increases my feelings of guilt about what I would have done in the name of love.

Then there's breakfast in the kitchen, where Frank has made bacon and eggs and avocado toast, but neither he nor Rachel will talk or look at me. My actions have made me a leper. Rachel gets up immediately and says she's going to see Michelle, leaving me alone with Frank while I eat. The guy can hold a grudge, and I'm pretty sure he still wants a piece of me; that being said, the man can cook. I dip my buttered sourdough avocado toast into the yolks of my sunny-side-up eggs and wish that I would have eaten before I opened my mouth earlier. It's hard to spit venom on a full stomach. World Party's "Ship of Fools" is playing in my head. You're gonna pay tomorrow, you will pay tomorrow, save me, save me from tomorrow. I don't want to sail with this ship of fools. I want to run and hide, right now.

But I can't run and hide. This was my idea, and I will see it through. Besides, I'm the only fool. Ron and Michelle and Frank and Rachel are good, decent people. I'm a mess. But if Ron wants to take Michelle to the Golden Gate Bridge, I will do whatever I can to help. So, I help myself to some more bacon before I leave the frigid feelings in the kitchen and walk out to the boat.

Ron is studying his charts and looking over his operator's manual when I come aboard. "I'm glad you're here," he said. "You can help me with the safety check."

"Sure." It feels good to have something I can do to contribute in a positive way.

Ron hands me a checklist and a pen. "Read these to me and check them off when I give the word."

"Okay."

"We have three Type III PFDs and three Type V PFDs."

"PFDs?" I ask.

Ron looks at me like I'm an idiot. "Kimo, when was the last time you went boating?"

"I don't know. Frank and I went out on his boat last summer before my accident."

"I doubt you two wore life jackets or personal flotation devices."

"Oh, PFDs." It's an acronym—makes sense. "Okay, check. It says here you also need a type IV."

"Yeah, we have a horseshoe buoy just above the transom."

"Okay, check. Two B-1 type fire extinguishers."

Ron finds those and shows them to me. "We'll have one forward and one aft."

"Aye, aye, captain." Again, Ron gives me an impatient look. "Sorry."

"Look, you need to remember where this stuff is in case we have an emergency."

Great. More pressure. All I wanted to do was golf. I looked forward to it, took a big chance to make it happen, and now it's over, and I barely remember it. I read the next item on the list. "Ventilation system?"

"I checked that earlier."

I check it off the list. "Whistle or sound signaling device."

Ron picks up an air horn and presses the button, releasing a sound so loud it could bring down the walls of Jericho.

"Check. We also have an electric signal on the bridge."

I'm pretty sure my recovering head didn't need that, but I mark a check next to it. "Backfire flame arrestor?"

"Checked it earlier."

"Okay. Visual distress signals?"

Ron picks up some distress flares and reads the labels. "Still over a year until their expiration dates."

"Good." I put a check next to it. "Sniff bilges? I think that was big back in the eighties."

Ron rolls his eyes before walking to the lowest point on the interior hull. He gets down on his hands and knees and sniffs.

"What are you smelling for?"

"A fuel leak."

He gets up and walks over, and turns on the bilge blower.

"Problem?" I ask.

"SOP."

"Sop?"

"Standard Operating Procedure," he says somewhat impatiently.

"Oh. You're just TCB."

Ron looks at me, and slowly a smile builds on his face. "TCB?"

"Taking Care of Business."

"Like the Bachman Turner Overdrive song?"

"BTO, baby."

"Okay, let's TCB. What's next on the list?"

"Check first-aid kit."

Ron grabs it and opens it up. "Thermometer, tweezers, Advil, alcohol, sunscreen, various bandages, scissors, eye washing cup, hand cleaner, disposable gloves, ice packs, tiger balm, duct tape. It looks good. Remind me to get a cooler to store Michelle's morphine."

"Is that legal?"

He gives me another look. "Now you're worried about what's legal? What? Are you worried the Coast Guard might stop us and find you, an escaped convict, on a boat smuggling morphine?"

"Huh? No. I never even considered that." Fuck, that wouldn't be good now that I think about it. "Is that possible?"

"Of course. But, Kimo, they'll see Michelle, and I think they'll realize she's not a drug mule."

"They still might find me."

"True." It looks as if he's contemplating this. "I won't let that happen. By the way, I want to thank you."

"For what?"

"Last night Michelle and I had another talk. She finally said I could bury her at the cemetery."

"Oh. That's great, Ron."

"She told me that you're the reason why." Uh oh. Did she tell him what she wanted me to do? Ron comes over and hugs me, then starts sobbing on my shoulder. He slumps into my arms, and it not only surprises me but, with his added girth, it strains my lower back where I fell earlier. Luckily, I don't drop him. Good God, his pain just seems to seep out with every sob. "It just means so much to me. It kills me that I never get to visit my dad, and I thought it would be the same with Michelle." His grief erupts into a guttural moan.

"That's okay, Ron, let it out. I don't know how you've held it together. I'm so sorry about Michelle." I have no idea how long he's been holding it in, but his misery flows out of him, and it's weird. But I feel privileged to be here to support him.

"How am I going to live without her?"

How do I answer that? What could I possibly tell him? It's going to be brutally hard. With time you'll learn to live with it. Words are banal at times like these. "I don't know, but at least you'll be able to visit her grave, and she'll be there in spirit."

Ron composes himself, looks at me, and nods his head. The poor guy, he's got that same look in his eyes that Michelle had earlier, the hopelessness and fear that the end is imminent and there's nothing that's going to save her. Michelle will be gone, and we'll have to live this life without her. I have more experience with that than Ron, but it's still going to be a huge void for me and undoubtedly an abyss for him.

"You're right. Thank you, Kimo," Ron says as he sniffs and wipes at his tear-stained eyes. "Let's get Michelle to the Golden Gate Bridge. We don't have any time to take for granted."

TEN

We carry Michelle out on that La-Z-Boy like she's Cleopatra entering Rome on her throne. Rachel holds the stand with the IV drip of morphine like a staff bearer proclaiming the arrival of the queen. Yes, my back hurts carrying her to the boat like this, but it's the weight of the chair, not sweet frail Michelle. I know Ron has ice packs and Tiger Balm in the first-aid kit on board, and who knows; maybe Rachel will give me a massage later. I had a better chance of that before I made an ass out of myself earlier, but I think she's already softening up a bit; after all, she's carrying a drug that's connected to a dying woman, and that has the opportunity to change one's perspective on forgiveness.

Frank's even thawing. He saw the redness of his brother's eyes and the warmth Ron was showing me when we came in from the boat, and although I was a complete jerk in the shower, I'm hoping he's recognizing the mitigating circumstances surrounding my actions. He's probably remembering that we've all been there, done that, and might even have thrown up on a t-shirt or two.

We help Michelle out of the chair, and Rachel braces her while Ron climbs aboard the boat. Frank and I raise the La-Z-Boy up to him, and he hauls it over the rail and onto the aft deck. We then guide Michelle to the transom and give her a boost up until Ron grabs hold of his wife, gently lifts her ,and carries her to the chair. Frank follows Michelle, and we carefully hand the stand with the IV to him so we don't have to reattach it to Michelle's arm. I let Rachel board first and must admit I'm feeling better because watching her rump as she climbs aboard stimulates my primitive biological urges, and I have to agree that Ron's boat is aptly named. I willingly clamber up behind her.

"Are you okay, honey?" Ron asks his wife. Michelle nods. "Do you want to stay up here or go below?"

"Here, for now," she replies.

"Okay. We'd better secure the chair and the stand. Kimo, can you get the duct tape?"

"Of course." I move toward the stairs to go below and scoot by Rachel, putting one hand on her hip and the other on her arm to gently guide her away from my path. "Excuse me," I say as I pass, and that quick touch of her skin sends my spirit soaring. It ignites memories of caressing her, kissing her, licking her, and entering her. And that makes me think of Michelle and Victory Park; first just having her in my arms while she softly snored, then the excitement of finally kissing her, which she initiated! Now they are both just above me, and I need to get back up on deck.

As I grab the duct tape out of the first-aid kit, I'm reminded that I didn't see anyone bring out Michelle's lotion and the one thing I think I can do for her at this time that might bring any comfort is massage her feet. I quickly return to the deck and hand the duct tape to Ron. "Did anyone bring Michelle's lotion?"

Everyone looks at me. Frank and Rachel shake their heads.

"I didn't," says Ron as he takes the duct tape.

"Are you going to massage my feet?" asks Michelle.

I smile, "If you want me to."

"Yes, please."

"All right, I'll be right back. Did we forget anything else?"

"I don't know," says Ron, "but we need to get started, or the tide will keep us here."

"I'll be quick, well, as quick as a hungover old man with a bad back can be." I climb down to the dock and run back to the house. As I get closer, I can hear the doorbell ringing; maybe it's the hospice nurse. I stop and consider going back to the boat to tell Ron that someone's there, but decide that he's busy enough and I can handle this.

When I enter, I hear knocking at the front door. Thank God I look through the peephole before opening the door. I am shocked to see a police officer standing on the other side. I hold my breath and try to stay calm.

He knocks again. I silently go up the stairs to Ron and Michelle's bedroom and make my way to the window. I carefully move the drapes aside and peek down. The police officer moves away from the front door and looks at the cars in the driveway. He gets out a pad and writes down what I presume to be the license plate numbers before walking over to his squad car and getting on the radio, and typing into his computer.

What should I do? Would Frank really call the police on me? Maybe he's not looking for me at all, but why would he be checking the plates of the cars? What's he going to think when he discovers Rachel's car is parked out front? Did someone recognize me at Angelina's and turn me in? Should I walk out there and turn myself in? Maybe the tide's turning against me, both literally and figuratively. I notice the bottle of lotion on the nightstand and decide to grab it and go.

I quickly and quietly make my way back down the stairs and take another look out the peephole. I see the police officer getting out of his car. Before my heart explodes in a panic, I turn and sprint back to the boat. Do I tell them or keep it to myself? When I get to the top of the levee and the stairs leading down to the dock, I take a quick glance back at the house, half expecting to see the cop with his gun drawn and shooting at me. Thankfully the coast is clear. I frantically head down the stairs. When I get to the dock, my momentum is too much for my strained back, and it gives out, and I fall. The pain darts up my spine, and I'm left sprawled on the dock—so much for keeping it to myself.

"What's the matter with you?" asks Frank.

I grab the lotion and get up and look directly at him. "Did you call the police on me?"

"Of course not," he says.

"Well, there's a cop at the door."

Ron jumps into action. "Release the bow line, Kimo. Frank, get the two spring lines and the stern line." Frank quickly gets off the boat and starts for the stern cleat while Ron climbs up to the flybridge and fires up the twin 350 Crusader inboard motors.

"Which is the bow line?" I ask.

"The front rope," yells Frank.

"Then why don't you just call it the front rope?"

I go and untie it and throw it aboard. Frank does the same with the other three lines, and we quickly scramble back aboard.

"Frank, we need to swing the stern to port, so give the bow a push!"

Frank jumps back to the dock, runs to the front of the boat, and gives it a good shove. He then walks to the back, making sure the boat stays clear of the dock.

"Come aboard!" commands Ron. "Rachel and Kimo, steady Michelle's chair."

Rachel and I grab a side of the La-Z-Boy. I take hold of the IV stand, which is duct-taped to the right arm of the chair. Frank leaps on board as Ron powers the boat forward and away from the dock. *It's All Good* slowly heads west down Smith Canal, leaving the dock behind. I scan the levee above the dock and don't see the cop, and my heartbeat slowly calms down to a healthy rhythm. I glance over, and Rachel is smiling at me.

"This is exciting!" she says.

"It is!" agrees Michelle with more energy than she's shown since I've been back.

"Damn it; I forgot my laptop!" Ron screams down to us.

"Do we need it?" I ask.

Ron looks worried. "We don't necessarily need it. I mean, I boated before I had one, but I've gotten used to it." He looks back at their dock, then down at me. "We'll just have to go old school."

I feel a sense of relief because I don't really want to face the police at this time. Suddenly, the swans flap their wings and follow the boat.

"Look, honey, Shane and Kirsty are waving goodbye to you!" Ron yells down to us. "Kimo, come take the helm so I can show her."

"Helm?"

"The steering wheel."

"Me? Take the wheel? I'm not sure that's a good idea."

"Get up here!" he says.

So, I climb up to the bridge and take the helm.

"Look, we're barely moving. You've driven Frank's boat, so this is just a bit bigger. I'll take over when we get out of the canal."

"Okay," I say. Sounds reasonable.

"When we get to I-5, stay in the middle of the canal and don't let the tidal current push you into a pillar." He scoots down the ladder, and I watch him lift Michelle and sit next to her on the La-Z-Boy. "See them?"

Michelle struggles to lift her arm and wave. "Bye-bye, Shane! Bye-bye, Kirsty!" Tears roll down her cheek as she must realize this might likely be the final time she sees the swans.

"Watch where you're going, Kimo!" screams Frank.

I turn and see that I'm heading for a neighbor's dock. We're only going a couple of knots per hour, so I steer us back to the middle of the canal, and we're quickly out of trouble. Up ahead, I see the overpass of I-5 looming like a dark tunnel to the netherworld. If I hit a pylon, will we go down like the Titanic?

It's different driving a boat because the surface you're traveling over is moving, unlike a highway. It's more like surfing, and once I realize that, I relax. I again turn back and watch the swans flap their farewell. "Why did you name them Shane and Kirsty?" I yell down.

Ron smiles down at Michelle. "They showed up our first Christmas together. We were hungover one morning, and they came swimming up the canal. We had been listening to a lot of 'Fairytale of New York' by the Pogues. The red-faced one looked like a ruddy complexioned drunk Irishman, so we named him Shane. If he was Shane, we figured she should be Kirsty."

"Okay, I feel young. Who are you talking about?" asks Rachel.

Ron and Michelle start to teach Rachel about the wondrous musical adventures of Shane MacGowen and the lads. A movement on the southern bank of the levee catches my eye. It's a man, hidden below the levee road, sitting in a grass shelter, almost a nest, petting a tiny kitten. He looks dirty, obviously homeless, but he actually smiles at me as we pass. The north side of the canal has docks and landscaped yards or stairs leading up and over the levee to nice homes. The south side has the levee road and vegetation leading down to the water. There's a lot of trash caught up in the weeds and at least one homeless person.

"Play some Pogues for her," suggests Frank.

"When we get out in the Delta, I will, but we hate it when people blast their music passing our house, so let's wait," explains Ron.

I seem to remember that Kirsty MacColl was killed in a boating accident and decide that's not the kind of musical trivia one should bring up at the start of a boat trip, so for once, I have the good sense to keep my mouth shut. Up ahead, next to the I-5 overpass, I see a white sign going into the water with 8, 10, and 12 written in black in descending order, and I assume that's the level of clearance between the waterline and the bridge. "Ron, how high am I?"

"You'd better not be high at all; it's illegal to operate a boat while impaired," he's smiling as he says this. "The boat's height is eleven feet, nine inches. We should be okay unless I misread the tide chart."

The waterline is below the twelve by at least a foot, so as long as I keep my cool, we should be all right.

"Look!" It's Michelle; she's noticed the homeless man. "Kimo, get us close so we can give him something."

Get us close? Good God, there's a bridge for a major highway just ahead! She thinks I can just stop this thing and whip it over there? I look at the control and slow the thrust. Okay, which throttle do I push to put this bad boy in reverse? I guess, and push one forward. We jerk back to the right. The La-Z-Boy slides on the deck. Frank makes a save on the IV stand as it tips over but does not fall, thanks to the duct tape and Frank's quick action.

"Dude!" yells Frank.

"I don't know what the fuck I'm doing!" I say in my defense.

Ron looks over at Michelle. "What did you ever see in him?"

"He'll get us close."

I focus on the task at hand and figure out how to go back without crashing into a dock, a boat, or the levee. I'm also concerned about running over the swans because I'm pretty sure that would ruin the day. The homeless man has just noticed Michelle's condition. He makes the sign of the cross and then stands up in his nest, kissing the back of his kitten's neck.

"Do you want me to take over?" asks Ron.

"Ron, the last time I drove something, I crashed into a statue."

"You drove my car yesterday and didn't crash," says Rachel.

"You drove the golf cart too and were pretty stable," adds Frank. "I can't say the same of Harley!"

"Do you care if I sink your boat?" I ask Ron.

"Yes, please don't."

"Okay, well, you'll know if I need you. Feel free to speak up if you notice anything I might be doing to put our lives in danger."

"Fair enough."

I look back at the controls.

"Oh, and Kimo?"

"Yeah?"

"The tidal current is coming in, so we don't have a lot of time to get under the freeway."

"Do you want to take over, Captain?"

"Not really."

"Then will you shut up so I can focus?"

"You said to feel free to speak up if I knew something that might put our lives in danger."

"All right, anything else?"

"Keep an eye out for the cop."

Fuck! I forgot all about him. I look back at their dock and

up the stairs, but there's still no policeman. "Anything else?"

"Well, sure, but that's enough for now."

"Thank you." Okay, I've got to get a feel for this boat. I pull the left throttle back a little and slow us down so we can go in reverse and get behind the guy. I want to bring the boat in going forward. We roll back in the canal in a zigzag pattern, but at least it's not as herky-jerky as before. I swing her around and head for the southern shore.

"Do we have any food or something we can give him?" asks Michelle.

Ron looks at his brother. "Frank, what did you pack for the trip that we could spare?"

"I brought some leftover ribs and coleslaw."

"Wine?"

"Is the pope Catholic?"

"Set him up with some."

Frank goes below deck to the galley. I'm bringing *It's All Good* in close. Ron kisses his wife. "I love you." Michelle smiles. Rachel wipes a tear from her eye. It's all good.

Frank comes back carrying a bottle and some Tupperware. I maneuver the boat over adjacent to the southern side of the levee. Frank holds on to the transom ladder and leans toward the shore.

"How's he supposed to open the wine?" asks Michelle.

Frank lifts the bottle toward her. "Don't worry, it's from Berryessa Gap. They only use screw tops."

"Screw tops?" asks Rachel.

"It seems to help save the cork trees of Portugal," replies Frank.

The boat bumps up against the levee and the collision almost knocks Frank off the ladder.

"Come on, Kimo!" he screams.

"Sorry."

Frank swings over and steps off the boat. He offers the

Tupperware and the bottle of wine to the homeless man. The homeless man eyes him suspiciously, then turns and looks at Michelle, who smiles at him.

"Take it. It's good," she says.

The homeless man leaves his nest and carefully makes his way down the bank to Frank. As he reaches for the bottle, he offers Frank the kitten.

"No, that's okay," Frank tells him.

"She's for the sick lady. Her name is Joy," the homeless man says as he points with the kitten toward Michelle. "You're coming back, aren't you?" he asks.

"Yes."

"Then just bring her home to me. I'm not going anywhere. Besides, Joy's never been on a boat, and she'll be good for the lady up there. Just take good care of her; she's the runt of the litter."

Frank looks back at Michelle and Ron for guidance.

"Thank you," Michelle replies.

Ron nods his head, and Frank takes the little furry thing and hands the Tupperware to the homeless man, who opens the container and looks inside. "Ribs?"

"Yeah."

"Joy's going to be sorry she missed this meal. Thank you." He looks at Michelle, "God bless you."

All right, I'm tearing up and wiping my eyes to hide it. Michelle smiles and waves at the man. Frank comes back to the boat and hands the kitten to Rachel before climbing back aboard. I mean, really? Like we need a little kitten on board? Who knows how many diseases that tiny fur ball is carrying!

Rachel hands the little fuzzy petri dish to Michelle, and it snuggles into her armpit, and Michelle just beams, which brings a smile to Ron's face. I know what they're facing is tragic, but I yearn for what they have with each other. I also worry about Ron. I'm not sure life is long enough to get over the loss of someone so close. Sure, life goes on, but... what the hell; I push the throttles forward and head for the overpass.

The water level has risen to just below the twelve-foot mark on the sign. I don't know if we can make it. "Ron, maybe you should come up and take over."

I glance down and see Ron happily playing with the kitten, which is burrowing under Michelle's scrawny shoulder. Ron looks over at Frank. "Frank, would you help Kimo for me?"

Frank looks up at me and reluctantly joins me on the flybridge. "What's the matter?" he asks impatiently.

"Look," I point to the sign. "Ron said we were almost twelve feet above the waterline."

"Mmm. It's going to be close." He steps nearer and takes over, pushing the throttles down even more, speeding us up to the point that we're making a wake, which I don't think is legal. "You might want to get down," he says as he takes a seat in the pilot's chair.

I drop down on a knee and hold on to the windshield as we approach the overpass. Frank slows down, and we move under the freeway. If I stood up, I'd hit moldy concrete. The sound of the passing cars and trucks gets louder as we move into the echo chamber of shadows. If the freeway is like a major artery and the cars are blood cells, the boat gliding underneath feels like an undetected cancer cell. We travel under the northbound lanes, and above us, people move on with their lives, oblivious to the tragedy unfolding below. The sunlight scans us as we proceed out from the northern span and across into the shade of the southbound lanes.

"How am I doing on that side?" Frank asks.

I lean over the side and look. The boat is being pushed closer to a pillar. "You're getting close!" Frank steers away and gives us a little more thrust. "Careful of the back end!"

"You mean the stern?"

"Whatever, just look..."

The stern clips the pillar hard and rocks the boat. Rachel tumbles onto the deck, and Ron moves quickly to grab the IV stand.

"What the fuck, Kimo!" Ron yells.

"I didn't do it!"

"Sorry. My bad," admits Frank.

I climb down the ladder to help Rachel. "You okay?"

"Yeah." She takes my hand, and I help her to her feet. She's skinned her knee, and a little blood seeps out.

I turn to Ron and Michelle. "Are you both okay?"

"Honey?" Ron asks his wife.

Michelle is holding on to the kitten and has a glazed look in her eyes from the morphine. "What?"

"Are you okay?"

"I'm tired."

Ron leans over and kisses her, then looks up at me and grins. "Maybe I need some of what she's having."

"We all do."

"Can you check below and make sure we don't have a leak?"

"Sure," I say. "Rachel, why don't you come with me, and I'll doctor up that knee."

"I'm okay."

Ron throws me an assist. "You should probably put something on that so you don't get an infection. Kimo knows where the first aid kit is. It's not worth taking a chance."

"Okay," she looks from Ron back to me, and whatever anger she might have felt toward me seems to disappear because she once again smiles at me.

Oh, the divine madness! How can I think of sex when Michelle is dying? Obviously, the drive is primordial. I take Rachel's hand and lead us below deck, and all the anxiety I've felt since I woke up this morning is released, replaced with the euphoria from the simple pleasure of holding her hand. I begrudgingly let go of her so I can get the first aid kit. I find an antibacterial wipe, open the package, then get down on my knees and softly cleanse Rachel's relatively superficial wound.

I kiss it to make it better like I was taught to do when I was a child. The scuffed knee is so close to her lovely thigh that I can't help but caress the upper muscles with my free hand. Then I find myself reaching between her legs and under her shorts and massaging her gluteus maximus. That movement naturally brings my face near the joyful mysteries of her pelvic region, my lips only separated by the thin cotton wall of her shorts and bikini bottom.

"Am I forgiven?" I ask.

Rachel reaches down and runs her hands through my hair and then, without saying a word, pulls me gently into her. I want to remove her clothes so I have an unobstructed view and a clear path to a romp in her Elysian Fields, but my blissful frolic is not meant to be, for we are interrupted by Frank screaming out for someone to call 911.

Damn it, Frank. Seriously, come on, man!

Rachel rushes up, leaving me sexually frustrated in her wake.

ELEVEN

"Leave him alone! We're calling the cops!"

Frank has slowed the boat and is yelling at a guy above us on a pedestrian bridge across Smith Canal. The guy's wearing black shorts, a black t-shirt, and has a Raiders cap on backward. He is flogging another man with a car antenna. The metal whistles through the air and slices into the victim, ripping clothing, lacerating skin, and spurting blood down into the canal, reminding me of Peter Gabriel's song, "Red Rain."

"Someone call 911!" Frank yells down to us.

"I don't have a phone. Rachel?"

"Mine's dead. It hasn't been charged since my sister's wedding."

I look over at Ron and Michelle, but Ron is trying to shield Michelle, so she doesn't have to witness this random act of violence.

"Kimo, come up here and take over! I'll get my phone out

of my backpack."

I climb up and once again take control of the boat. Frank hustles down and disappears below deck. Rachel joins me on the flybridge.

"Get us away from here," she says.

I push down the throttles, and we leave the random savagery behind. Frank scrambles back with his phone. "Kimo, we can't leave the scene of the crime!"

"Just call it in and get the poor guy some help. Michelle doesn't need to stick around for this!"

"Are you thinking of Michelle or yourself?"

"I'm thinking about that poor bastard getting pummeled back there, Frank! And do you really think your brother wants that to be one of the last images Michelle sees in her life? Call it in!"

Frank angrily dials. I'm not sure if he's agitated by the attack or the fact that I was alone with Rachel.

"Yes, I want to report an assault on the pedestrian bridge over Smith Canal just west of I-5. Some guy is beating another guy with what looks like a broken car antenna. Get somebody there fast, and the dude will need an ambulance." Frank looks back at the scene of the crime. "He looks Mexican and is dressed in all black. He's also got on a Raiders hat." He frowns. "No, I'm not sure he's Mexican, but he looks Hispanic." He rolls his eyes. "Okay, Latino. Why don't you just get someone there, and they can check his fucking ID! I don't know him, and I don't care where the fuck he's from, but he's beating the shit out of the other guy, and he might kill him before you do anything!" Frank shakes his head in disbelief and disconnects the call. "Was I being racist?"

"No," Rachel says.

"This is why people don't get involved! She asked me to describe the guy, and he looked Mexican, so she asked me how I could be sure of that! What the fuck! Is that the most important detail she got out of the call? I'm not being racist; I'm trying to help!"

"You okay?" I ask.

"No, I have a 'woke' hangover! She's busy being PC while that poor guy's getting his ass kicked. I could use a stiff drink."

"Later," Ron calls out from below. "We're not even to the main channel."

"I know! I'm just saying. What the hell was that all about? Can't even take a boat ride without witnessing violence in this town?"

"What's that?" Rachel asks, pointing to a building visible above the southern bank. It has a wooden shingled roof that curves and rises like two hands in prayer, but is surrounded by a fence topped with concertina wire.

"That's Stockton's Buddhist Temple."

"Looks like a fort with that fence and barbed wire," I say.

"Well, you just saw what kind of neighborhood this is."

"But Buddhists are peaceful, aren't they?" asks Rachel.

"I don't know. Don't they have warrior monks? In all the Kung Fu movies, the monks are the ones who really kick some ass." Frank howls like Bruce Lee and makes some lame chops and a flying kick that almost sends him overboard.

"Steady there, grasshopper," I say.

"That's not really practicing what they're preaching," Rachel comments.

"Hey, Christians had the crusades and the Inquisition, Muslims have jihad, and Hindus have Gods of War. What religion practices what they preach?" I add.

"What about Rastafarians?" Frank suggests.

"That's more of a way of life than a religion, isn't it?"

"Hey, no smoking on my boat!" Ron chimes in.

"Damn it, Jim!" Frank jokes. He looks at Rachel and whispers. "You brought yours, didn't you?"

She nods.

"Okay, when we get out in the Delta, we'll stop at a beach and," he puts his hands up and gestures like quotation marks, "go searching for religion."

"You always were a seeker, Frank."

"Well, seek, and ye shall find, right?"

"Now, what's that?" Rachel is again pointing to something on the southern side of the canal.

"That's Pixie Woods," answers Frank.

"It looks like an amusement park."

"It is. Well, Stockton's version. It only has two rides unless you count the merry-go-round. It seemed so big when we were kids. We used to love playing on the pirate ship. Ron remembers when my dad used to take us, but I was too young to remember him."

"I don't think you ever told me what happened to your dad, Frank. Ron said he's not buried in your cemetery."

"His jet was shot down. We never got his body back. Officially, he's still MIA."

"MIA?" asks Rachel.

"Missing in action," replies Frank.

"Oh. I'm so sorry."

"Thanks. It is what it is. It's harder on Ron because, like I said, I don't have any memories of him, so I never really knew what I was missing."

"So, we're coming to the main channel?" I ask.

"Yeah, you'll swing right just past the Louis Park boat launch and merge into the river."

"How come we never launch from here? It's much closer to your house."

"You just saw why. This place has gone ghetto and is full of gang bangers."

"That's too bad."

"Well, that's Stockton."

"What river is this?"

"The San Joaquin. We'll take this all the way until we

merge with the Sacramento River, then we'll hit Suisun Bay, pass through the Carquinez Strait into San Pablo Bay, and finally flow into the San Francisco Bay. We're about seventy-five miles away from the Golden Gate Bridge."

"What a great way to travel! It's like a freeway of water!" Rachel's enthusiasm is charming, and I find myself involuntarily getting a hard-on. I can't believe how overwhelmingly aroused I am in her presence. It's like I'm young again.

"How many miles of water are in the Delta, Ron?" Frank asks his brother.

"Over a thousand that are navigable."

I need to focus because we're entering the deep-water channel, and a huge container ship is coming toward us. It takes up most of the space in the middle of the channel as it heads for the port of Stockton. The ship towers over us and has got to be the size of three football fields! It's a moving wall of steel. If this were a freeway, the container ship would be like a big eighteen-wheeler, and we're pedaling a tricycle.

"Good God, look at the size of that!" I say.

"Who says size doesn't matter, huh?" Rachel teases.

Frank and I fidget uncomfortably, contemplating the validity of the sexual innuendo, knowing in our hearts that we are both no more than average. I guess it's the same for women and the size of their breasts. Both genders' insecurities have created booming cottage industries which prey on our self-doubts and shame. Oh well, I suppose it's good for the economy and, therefore, a silver lining.

The wake from the massive ship heads for us. I turn and look down at Ron. "Brace yourselves! The wake is going to hit us."

"Turn into it!" Ron yells. But it's too late. The first wave hits, and we roll way over to the side before slipping back the other way. We're not even close to capsizing, but it definitely gets the adrenaline up.

"Where's it from?" I ask as the behemoth vessel moves past us.

"It's flying a Chinese flag," says Frank.

"Those Commie bastards!" I joke.

"It's the Tian Tang out of Shanghai," Frank announces.

"I wonder what that means."

"Big ass boat!" laughs Frank.

"It means heaven," says Rachel.

Frank and I look at her.

"My grandparents are from Shanghai."

"I didn't mean anything by that Commie comment. Was that racist? I just wouldn't want to come across that thing at night." I add.

"We don't travel at night, so don't worry," Frank says.

The turbulence gradually calms down as we put more space between the Tian Tang and us.

"What do you think it's carrying?" asks Rachel.

"It's probably got tainted toothpaste, counterfeit drugs, and a bunch of cheap crap that American consumers will buy, and then maybe a couple of containers of trafficked women."

"That's not funny!" Rachel scolds me and playfully slaps my arm.

I see Frank notice, and he doesn't look happy that I've escaped her doghouse. "He's the racist."

"Hey, is that a golf course?" I ask, looking over his shoulder to the near shore.

"Yeah, that's the Stockton Country Club. Ron, Michelle, we're coming up to the first tee!" Franks turns to us. "That's where they got married."

"Really?" I look down at Ron and Michelle. Ron turns the chair, so Michelle doesn't have to strain to see the shore.

"Weren't you there?" Rachel asks me.

"No. I was in L.A. or Kauai at the time."

We're passing the luxurious ballroom that sits above the

first tee with its picturesque view of the river. "That's where the reception was. The altar was over there on the tee box and when the ceremony was over, Ron and Michelle led us all straight up to the reception and a champagne toast while dancing to James Brown's "I Feel Good." It was great."

I fight the urge to correct Frank because the title is "I Got You." I don't want to be that dick, so instead I ask, "You got that on your phone?"

"Yes, I do. Should I play it?"

"Of course."

"Slow us down," Frank says as he rushes down the ladder and vanishes below deck. I pull up on the throttles and cut the engines, so we are drifting past the first tee when James Brown's exuberant, "Woo! I feel good!" pops from the boat's speakers. Frank rises from the interior carrying a bottle of champagne, which he hands to Ron before he starts dancing, shaking, and sliding around the deck. I can't see Michelle's face and have no idea if she's happy with the performance and memory being celebrated or if it just adds to her suffering, a stark reminder of what is being left behind.

To my surprise, Ron climbs out of the La-Z-Boy and joins his brother in dancing on the deck. Although they're both rhythmically challenged, it's a joyous sight. When the song is over, both brothers are covered in sweat. Rachel and I clap for them, and after taking a bow, Ron grabs the bottle from the chair and goes below deck.

"I just thought we'd toast you in front of your wedding site!" Frank calls down to his brother. He looks up at us and shrugs his shoulders. "They left from here on this boat for their honeymoon. I just wanted to celebrate it."

"Should I get us going?" I ask.

I'm answered by a new song coming over the speakers. It's John Lennon's "Grow Old With Me" from his last album, *Milk and Honey*, which came out after his murder. Ron comes back on deck and hands Frank a different bottle of champagne. "Open this while I dance with my wife," he says.

Frank takes the bottle and again looks up at Rachel and me. "This was their first dance." He looks at the bottle, "oh, and this is the really good stuff!"

Ron takes the kitten from Michelle and looks up at Rachel. "Could you hold Joy?"

"Of course," Rachel says before climbing down and taking the tiny kitten.

Ron carefully lifts Michelle up and gently sways to the music with her. He closes his eyes and puts his cheek next to hers. He slowly dances across the deck, one hand supporting the IV stand and the other tenderly holding his dying bride. They turn, and I finally see Michelle's face, which somehow looks radiant and healthy again, as it does in the wedding picture at the base of the stairs in their house. They've been transported back to one of the happiest occasions of their lives and watching them enraptured with each other, so completely in love, uplifts my soul and makes me happy to witness it instead of being locked away at the Marsh Creek Detention Center.

I flash to a different song on that album, "Borrowed Time." Unlike the song they're dancing to, they won't grow old with each other, but what they have is a blessing that I can only hope I'll experience in my life. My guilt returns as I ruminate on my actions contrary to their union. I don't seem to know anything. I thank God that I didn't kill her and take this moment away from them.

The song finishes, and there's not a dry eye on the boat. We clap for them, and they respond with a kiss. Frank pops open the bottle of champagne, and the cork shoots up like a ceremonial salute—unfortunately the loud sound scares the little kitty, who screeches and claws its way free of Rachel and flies off into the river.

"Oh my God!" screams Rachel.

"Save her!" Michelle shrieks.

Frank only hesitates to hand the bottle of champagne to Rachel before he jumps over the side after the tiny cat. Ron carefully puts Michelle back on the La-Z-Boy. He takes off his shirt, revealing a chubby stomach badly in need of some sun, then takes off his shoes and socks before joining the rescue party; fatherless sons trying to save an orphan. I don't know what to do, so I climb down and grab the horseshoe buoy, and wait to see if they catch the little critter.

"Where is it?" Ron asks.

"I've got it!" Franks announces as he comes up with it. He lifts her up to show us, and we watch as she scratches free and splashes back into the water. "Fucking cat!" Frank screams, just before he takes in a mouth full of water and sinks below the surface.

Ron starts swimming toward the spot where the cat plopped in.

"Michelle, where does Ron keep his fishing gear?" I ask.

She looks at me, trying to see through the miasmic fog in her brain. Finally, she speaks, "the guest stateroom. Under the starboard berth."

"Starboard is right?"

A weak smile sprouts on her face. "Yes."

"Rachel, take this and toss it to whoever needs it. Now, for God's sake, please don't confuse the two and throw the bottle." I hand her the buoy and go below. I hurry to the forward part of the boat, and under the bed I slept in last night, I find what I'm looking for; a net to bring in a hooked fish. I rush back on deck. "Did they get it?"

"No, she's over there!" Rachel points with the champagne bottle to the flailing animal.

I take off my shoes and shirt and jump overboard.

Good God, it's cold!

My heart protests, my muscles tighten, threatening to shut down, and I'm sure there's going to be shrinkage elsewhere, but I focus on the mission and swim as fast as I can. Of course, that's not all that fast with one hand holding the net. I struggle until I settle on the sidestroke and persevere. When I get close enough, I swing the net over the floundering little kitten, twist it under the water, and lift. I raise her out of the river to applause from *It's All Good.* I tread water and try to catch my breath.

The brothers swim back to the boat and climb aboard. Ron throws the buoy to me, and I grab on, grateful to be pulled back to solid ground. Well, solid footing.

Suddenly I stop moving and hear Ron scream Michelle's name. It's a plaintive wail that reminds me of when I was a kid and my black lab was hit by a car. The pain in that memory reverberates in my heart. I can't see what's happening on the boat, so I just hold on to the buoy and fear the inevitable worst. I feel like a lost bobber cut off from my reel by a broken line and left to drift alone on a deep ocean of woe. After what seems like an eternity, I'm again being pulled toward the boat. Frank appears and takes the net so I can pull myself back up to the aft deck.

"What's wrong?"

"Nothing," Franks says as he carefully untangles Joy from the net.

"Nothing?" I ask incredulously.

"Michelle was just asleep, and I panicked," admits Ron.

"Sorry, honey," Michelle says.

Are you fucking kidding me?

That was a lot of drama for nothing!

"You're all heroes!" Rachel exclaims as she lifts the bottle of champagne in salutation before hugging Frank and kissing him on the cheek. Frank blushes as he hands Joy to Michelle.

My heart is thumping. I didn't plan on exerting this much energy the day after Angelina's, and frankly, I'm too wiped out to be jealous.

"Let's get out of these wet clothes because we've earned a drink," Ron says as he kisses Michelle. I get up and follow him below deck. Frank joins us, and we strip.

"I hate to admit this, but I don't think any of us could get a job at Chippendales."

"Speak for yourself, Kimo. You saw us dancing earlier. We got the moves!" Franks starts dancing again while taking off his clothes. He slips on the wet floor and falls.

"Frank, quit fooling around," his brother scolds him before throwing us towels.

"Sorry."

"Frank, when you get dressed, can you get us on our way? Let's stop at our beach."

"Okay." Frank takes some dry clothes out of his bag and quickly puts them on.

"I don't have a change of clothes," I announce.

"Put on your prison pants, and I've got a shirt for you," Frank reaches back into his bag and throws me a black Berryessa Brewing Company t-shirt. "You'll have to go Hawaiian style because there's no way in hell I'm not lending you my underwear."

"No problem."

"Just don't get excited around Rachel," he says as he walks past me. He heads up for the flybridge while Ron and I finish dressing. The boat's engines come alive, and once again, we're moving. Ron takes some plastic wine glasses out of the galley, and he slips slightly as he makes his way to the aft deck.

"Kimo, could you dry up the floor for me before coming up?"

"Sure." I use the towels to mop up the floor and bring them with me to dry out on the deck.

Rachel walks over and hugs me. "You saved the day."

"Thanks." I look over at Michelle, who's once again asleep,

and somehow Rachel's claim just rings hollow. Rachel senses my sadness.

"You're not God. You can only help alleviate her suffering, which you are doing." She takes my hand, leans in, and kisses my cheek. "You're a good man, Kimo Jones."

I shiver, whether from still being cold and damp, or elation from her touch, or in reaction to her statement; I'm not quite sure. She notices, though, and rubs my arms, and it relieves my loneliness as much as it warms my body.

"Where's my beverage?" Frank yells down.

"Rachel, may I?" Ron asks as he reaches for the bottle. He notices Michelle. "She's out again?"

Rachel hands the bottle to Ron. "Between the drugs, heat, and excitement, it shouldn't be too surprising."

"True. Okay, this is a bottle of Louis Roederer Cristal Brut 2004 given to us on our wedding day. We were going to have this on our wedding night, then decided to wait and open this on our tenth anniversary, but..." Ron looks at his sleeping wife and can't finish. He pours some into a glass and hands it to Rachel. He then pours a glass for me. "Kimo, can you take this up to Frank for me?"

"Of course." I take the glass and carefully climb up to the flybridge. "Frank?"

He turns and takes the glass. "Thank you, my brother from another mother." With that I know we're good again.

I slap him on the back. "Sorry about being an ass earlier."

"Whoa, don't make me spill! You're such an ass!" he jokes.

I go back down, and Ron hands me a glass before raising his. "To my lovely wife."

We raise our glasses. In the bright light of the sun, his lovely wife's skin looks yellow and waxy and shrink-wrapped around her skull. With her eyes closed, she looks like my grandmother did in her open casket, but of course, she didn't have a wet kitten sleeping on her chest. May they both rest in peace. I take a sip of the now warm champagne, look at Ron and again notice how much he's aged in the last year. I figure the cost of living is outlasting the ones you love.

TWELVE

Mount Diablo rises in the distance as we take a westerly turn past Fourteen Mile Slough. Somewhere below its peaks, inmates at the Marsh Creek Detention Center are having lunch before their afternoon garbage detail. I thought I'd be with them today, but instead, I'm still free and looking at Lost Isle as we cruise past it.

Frank took Michelle and me to that island of wanton debauchery many summers ago before it was shut down after a murder. We played volleyball and drank Mai Tais, and I lusted after Michelle dancing in her blue bikini. This was before Ron and Michelle could party with the best of us back in those days. We almost had to fight our way out.

A hulking lothario with six-pack abs decided that Michelle should stay with him after she succumbed to her liquor libido and gave the stranger a wet kiss on the dance floor. He had an overabundance of alcohol and testosterone, so I distracted him by challenging him to a drinking contest while Frank hustled

Michelle back to his boat. After the third upside-down kamikaze, the big dude threw up and desecrated the dance floor. We were both booed and tossed out of the bar. I lugged him to the bathroom, which was disgusting on its own, and left him sitting on the floor next to a filthy toilet before making my way to Frank's boat.

The things I did for Michelle. God love her, but she was no saint.

This was in the days before social media, when good teachers could misbehave at a questionable bar without fear of it being posted online and losing their reputation or even their job. We didn't have to worry about running into someone we knew because Lost Isle is here in the middle of the Delta and only reachable by boat, plus you had to be twenty-one, and that took our students out of the equation. Michelle was a great teacher, just letting off steam after a long school year. One shouldn't be judged for the occasional naughty act.

Looking at Michelle's cadaverous body now makes it seem like it happened to different people in another lifetime. Where did the time go? What happened to us? Have I confused lust for love? I have always cared about her well-being in spite of the fact that she didn't share my sexual desire and gave me no assurance of affection other than our night in Victory Park.

Is love true only when it's reciprocated? And what do I feel about Rachel? That's got to be simple lust, right? I don't see a future for us. She's young and talented and has a bright life ahead of her. I've got more jail time. Of course, then there's Michelle, who has no future, at least not in this dimension. If the moment truly is all that matters, why do I still feel guilty about the past and worry about the future? All this questioning is making me hungry. "Ron, are we going to eat soon?"

"We're almost to our beach on Spud Island. I'll cook up a quick lunch there. Maybe you could massage Michelle's feet while I get lunch together?" he asks.

"Sure, I'd be happy to."

"I think I'd like that as well," Rachel says softly to me.

"Anytime."

The boat slows down and cuts across the channel toward the southern levee. There's a little patch of beach surrounded by overgrown Tule bulrushes, wild grape vines and rose thickets, and colorful blossoms of California's state flower, the golden poppy (Eschscholzia californica) of the family Papaveraceae.

Don't confuse it with a mafia family, even though they both have death in common. The flower has been a symbol of the dead since ancient times. It looks like somebody took a paintball gun and scattered blotches of bright orange along the levee. A Great Blue Heron flushes off the limb of a eucalyptus tree as Frank cuts the engines and glides us toward the shore.

Ron carefully starts to get out of the La-Z-Boy. Joy stirs and meows and walks over to Michelle's cheek, and starts licking with her tiny tongue. Michelle doesn't react. I walk over and touch her foot. I can see her little chest working to keep those breaths coming, but she doesn't open her eyes. I look up and meet Ron's look of concern.

"At some point she'll go into a coma," he says. "We'll have to keep her comfortable."

"Do you think she's in a coma now?"

"I don't know."

"The Smiths," whispers Michelle without opening her eyes.

"What, honey?" Ron leans down next to her. She doesn't respond. "Michelle?" He looks back at me. "What'd she say?"

"I think she said the Smiths."

"The Smiths? The group?" A mischievous smile builds across his face, and he looks back down at his wife. "Oh, you're funny, honey. God, I love you." He kisses her.

I suddenly get the joke. "Girlfriend in a Coma?" I ask.

"Michelle, that is funny, cruel, but funny."

She seems to smile, but still doesn't open her eyes.

"I'm sure it's on your iPod. I'll get it for you." Ron goes below deck as Frank climbs down from the flybridge.

"Rachel, could you please toss me a line?" Frank says as he goes over the side and climbs off the boat.

She gets up and walks to the ladder. "Which one?"

"The one on the port bow. Make sure you keep one hand on the rail!" Frank adds as Rachel carefully moves to the front of the boat and out of sight.

Ron comes back on deck, and he has a propane grill along with Michelle's iPod. He hands the iPod to me. "Could you find 'Girlfriend in a Coma' for her? And could you put together a playlist of ten or so songs that you know she loved? Maybe we can all make a playlist of songs that remind us of her."

"Sure."

I take the device and power it up. The music button is the color of the California poppy, and I press it and go to "Artists." I scroll down to the Smiths and find the song. "Do you want me to play it now or start the playlist with it?"

"Start the playlist with it, and I'll put it on the speakers while we're eating lunch."

"Okay." With that said, I get to work. I saw R.E.M. back a ways and look at what songs she has of theirs. I add "Gardening at Night," "Perfect Circle," "Letter Never Sent," "Fall on Me," "Kohoutek," and one of the final songs they did, "We All Go Back to Where We Belong." That's already six songs and only one group. "How about twenty songs?"

"Sure. Just keep it at that, or I might as well just hit shuffle. Put 'Fairytale of New York' and 'Body of an American' by the Pogues on it. We loved those songs."

Okay, that's eight out of the twenty. I'll also put on "There is a Light that Never Goes Out" and "The Boy with the Thorn in his Side" by the Smiths, and I'm already more than halfway there. Michelle turned me on to the Cure, so I go back and see what songs of theirs she has. I choose "Lovesong," "Just Like Heaven," "Inbetween Days," and "Friday I'm in Love."

I also noticed she had Ned's Atomic Dustbin. I ended up going to see them with her in San Francisco on their last tour because the guy she was seeing at the time bailed on her at the last minute. I had never heard of them. They were another of those English bands that Michelle liked at the time, but they were great in concert, so I add "Grey Cell Green" and "Premonition" to the list. That was the date I ended up like a frozen baby seal on her living room floor before waking up with my hands holding her breasts. Oh, the yin and yang of it all. Now I'm past the sweet sixteen. Who will make the last three of the final four?

"Put some Counting Crows on there too. She's been listening to them a lot lately." Ron says.

Damn it! I thought this was my playlist. It's as if Ron can read my mind, or more likely the frustration on my face, because he adds, "Make it twenty-five songs. Just make sure 'Raining in Baltimore' and 'Amy Hit the Atmosphere' are included."

Great, we get to listen to a couple of depressing Counting Crows songs. Whatever. If that's what Ron thinks Michelle wants to hear, who am I to argue? I like the Counting Crows, but if Michelle's slipping into a coma, shouldn't we try to be uplifting, or at least upbeat or humorous? I see she has some Lemonheads and add "Into Your Arms," "If I Could Talk I'd Tell You," "Paid to Smile," which she said reminded her of her days as a waitress, and "Rudderless," which she said reminded her of me.

Rachel comes back. She looks uncomfortable as she speaks. "Uh, Captain Ron, your first mate wanted me to ask you if he could pick some wild blackberries for your salad."

Ron eyes her with suspicion. "Did he bring pot?"

"What?" She sputters, surprised by his response.

"He only butters me up with Captain Ron when he wants to do something against the best practices of safe boating."

"Wasn't there a movie called 'Captain Ron'?" I ask.

"Yeah, with Kurt Russell. Michelle used to say she wished I looked like him and said she fantasized about him every time we had sex on the boat, which was a lot."

"Uh, TMI, Ron. By the way, was that the movie Goldie Hawn showed off her nice butt?"

"No, that was 'Overboard'."

"Oh."

"Rachel, did the 'first mate' set the anchor?" Ron asks.

"He tied a line to a tree on shore," she replies.

Ron looks at me and rolls his eyes. "So much for best practices." He looks back at Rachel. "Tell the 'first mate' to be quick about smoking dope. We're going to have lunch soon and won't be here long."

Rachel looks at me, and I sense she wants to know if it's the right thing to do, so I ask Ron. "Are you okay with it, Ron?"

"With my brother smoking dope? He's earned it. Do you want to join them?"

"No. I'm going to finish this playlist and then massage Michelle's feet. Do you mind if Rachel joins him?"

Ron smiles. "No, I don't. Do you?"

"No."

"Then God bless America. It's a free country. Rachel, just stay out of sight in case the police cruise by."

"Okay."

She takes off her blouse and shorts, revealing Michelle's blue bikini underneath, and now I'm having second thoughts. Good God, she has a gorgeous body!

"Isn't that Michelle's?" Ron asks.

"Yeah. She said I could wear it since I didn't have a suit."

She shrugs her shoulders and puts out her palms in a self-conscious sign of contrition.

"Oh. Of course. Okay."

Rachel grabs her little stash bag from her purse and gracefully swings herself over the deck, and disappears down the ladder into the water. After she's gone, Ron looks at me. "Michelle used to look great in that suit."

"Really?"

I know. And now Rachel does. And she's going to be alone with Frank. That bikini is going to be wet, and they're going to be getting high, out of sight and together, surrounded by all this natural beauty. I know what would be on my mind, and I know what will be on Frank's. My thoughts are exploding flak rounds sending searing shards through my unstable mind, and my spirit rapidly drops.

"Snap out of it!" Ron orders.

"What?"

"Whatever funk you're falling into."

"I can't help it. Between what I've done to you and Michelle and my stupidity and insecurity, I'm a mess."

"Open your eyes, Kimo!" Ron explodes. "This is the day God has given you! It's not to feel guilty about the mistakes you've made in the past or be consumed by lust for Rachel, though I understand that. Let it go. Enjoy the moment. Open your fucking eyes and enjoy what precious few minutes you have left with Michelle! These should be treasured moments in your life. Be here for them!"

Tears fall down Ron's face, and the enormity and importance of the occasion slap me across the face. I don't know if it is another epiphany, but my head is suddenly clear of self-pity and self-loathing.

"I didn't think you believed in God, Ron?" I ask.

"Of course, I do, just not organized religion. I don't believe some bearded dude up in the sky created the world in six days and then needed a rest. He's God. What's he, or she, or more likely it, need to rest for? And I don't believe women were made out of some guy's rib! Every religion has creation stories. I do believe that there is something greater than man, some force or energy beyond our comprehension. Call it spirit if you like, or mystery, or God, but it's not that crap you and Michelle were brainwashing your students with."

"You don't believe in Jesus?"

"What's the difference between Jesus and Confucius and Buddha and Moses and Muhammad and Gouranga?"

"Gouranga? Who's that?"

"I don't know. I heard his name in a Trevor Hall song. Must be some guy in Hinduism."

"Trevor Hall?"

"Oh, so I know some musician before you? Trevor Hall, man, he's great. You need to listen to him and expand your musical timeline beyond the eighties and nineties."

"Okay, but the difference is that Jesus was the only one who claimed to be God."

"Whatever. I believe in his message. God is love. Treat others the way you want to be treated. I'm completely on board with that. Whether Jesus was God or a prophet or just a teacher, I don't care. The virgin birth, I'm not sure about, the resurrection, okay, maybe, but it doesn't matter to me. What he said matters to me, how he lived, and the example he set matters to me.

"The institution of the church that grew out of his death is something that I just can't put my faith in. I've never met so many intolerant and judgmental people as some of those parents that you and Michelle had to deal with, and they think they're good Catholics because they go to church on Sunday. It's that old cliché that we pray together on Sunday and prey on each other the rest of the week. The fact that Michelle was worried about going to hell is enough to make me despise the teachings of your church. I don't know how you two could fill young minds with that crap."

"It's not all crap, Ron!" I'm the first to question my faith, but when others slander it, I feel compelled to stand up and defend it.

"Weren't you the one who wanted to rent buses to protest invading Iraq but was told by your principal that you needed to understand your clientele? Don't I remember Michelle telling me how upset you were that they'd let you rent busses to take all these kids to the Pro-Life March, but wouldn't let you rent those same busses to protest invading a country that never attacked us?

"The whole pro-life thing is such a joke, anyway. You Catholics aren't pro-life—you're anti-abortion! Just admit it! The thing is, nobody wants abortion! You Catholics are such hypocrites because you just care about the fetus! Once a child is born, they're on their own! Forget about social services for poor kids! Forget about medical services for all! And when these poor kids grow up and commit crimes, give them the death penalty! Or let them join the military and send them off to an unjust war! How is that pro-life?

"And what about Hell? How does anyone know if there's a hell or the devil, and why would you fill young minds with that shit unless you were trying to control them? Talk about the ultimate 'time out.'" Ron does an old woman's voice, "If you kids misbehave, you'll go to your room FOREVER! And we're going to turn up the heat! And play nothing but Celine Dion music!" Ron smiles, "how about teaching them personal responsibility?"

"We do. We also teach them to look out for those less fortunate in the community. The church is all about community. I think you're confusing us with Republicans."

"Well, most of you are Republicans! Look, I have no problem with a community that worships God, but when the institution oppresses and tries to convert others to their way of thinking, I'm out. Convert by your actions, not by words. And teaching that Catholicism is the only way to God? What about the other eighty-three percent of the world's population? They're all going to hell? How arrogant! Seriously, Kimo, what's the best thing about the Catholic Church to you?"

"The sacrament of confession, that God will forgive your sins."

"Okay, but why do you need a middleman? Why give a priest that power? Can't God hear you on your own?"

"Of course, but there's a humility in confessing to a priest that just isn't there otherwise. It takes courage and conviction to say your sins out loud to another. It's easy to forgive yourself."

"I think it's the exact opposite! I think it's hard to forgive yourself, and most people don't, but when you have some other person saying God forgives you, people tend to believe that. It's the power of suggestion. When was the last time you went to confession?"

"I don't know."

"Been a while?"

"Yes."

"Have you sinned?"

"Of course."

"Are you sorry for your sins?"

"Yes."

"Do you think God knows that?"

"Yes."

"Do you feel forgiven?"

The specter of Kauai flashes in my mind. "No."

"Neither did Michelle until we got a priest to come and talk to her."

"So, how is that a bad thing?"

"It's not bad. It just proves my point that you Catholics are indoctrinated into needing a middleman between you and your God. God is within, not outside you. Didn't Jesus say that?"

"I believe he said the kingdom of God is within."

"What's the difference, and why do you need a middleman?"

"Whatever, Ron. I don't want to argue with you about religion."

"Me neither. And I don't mean to throw stones at yours."

"Well, that's exactly what you're doing, and it's okay. I've got problems with my religion. Don't kid yourself, sure, I'm a cafeteria Catholic, but I'm not giving up my entire faith because of it."

"I don't know what that means."

"What?"

"Cafeteria Catholic."

"That's one who picks and chooses what he's going to take from the buffet. You know—I'll have a little of this and will take some of that, but there are some things I'm passing on."

"Look, I'm sorry. I'm going to the beach to get lunch started. Fire and boats don't mix. Will you watch over Michelle for me?"

"Of course. I've got two more songs to add, and then you can put on music."

"Okay. Finish that up and hand it to me, and I'll get it going while I grab the ice chest full of shrimp."

"Shrimp?"

"We're having shrimp tacos with watermelon and gorgonzola salad."

"Sounds good."

"It's going to be good. Now, how about that playlist?"

"Just a second," I say. I quickly scroll down to World Party and complete my playlist with "Sweet Soul Dream" and "Always." I hand Michelle's iPod back to Ron with twenty-five songs (all right, twenty-one of mine) to remember his wife by. It seems like an inconsequential tribute to such a beautiful human being.

THIRTEEN

Morrissey sings in his fey voice about a girlfriend in a coma, and I'm once again rubbing lotion onto Michelle's withered feet. If God is within her, he's getting his ass kicked by cancer. The temple of the soul is being overrun and destroyed. As I massage her deteriorating body, enjoying the warmth of the sun, I just can't figure out what to think about God.

Rachel returns with wild honeysuckle vines. The sweetly scented fragrance from the invasive vines blends with the faint smell of pot that lingers on her wet bikini and makes me wonder what she was doing with Frank in their own personal Eden. They weren't gone long because Ron called Frank back to help with lunch, effectively banishing them from the garden.

I don't know what to think or feel, and frankly, I'm not sure it matters, whatever they might have done, since eventually, we'll all end up like Michelle. Right now, my focus is on her. I'm asking that through the power of Jesus's name may she be healed through my touch, but with my lack of faith, I'm sure it won't work. I simply hope that she's getting something positive out of it.

"Is this song appropriate?" Rachel asks. She's holding and petting Joy.

"She picked it," I answer and then explain the sequence of events. Unfortunately, Michelle hasn't said anything since, and I'm worried that she might actually be in a coma. The expression on her face seems to show that the music and massage are soothing to her, but frankly, God only knows.

"Who is this?"

"The Smiths. They were big when you were in diapers."

"I didn't wear diapers," Rachel says with a seductive smile.

"Girlfriend in a Coma" ends and is followed by "There Is a Light That Never Goes Out." I don't know if it's the effect of the pot, but Rachel is focused on the music, and when she hears the lyrics, *And if a double-decker bus crashes into us, to die by your side is such a heavenly way to die...* she responds.

"Am I hearing this right?"

"Yeah."

"That's twisted."

"Yep. Morrissey has an interesting take on things."

"Okay, mister Jailhouse Rock, who's Morrissey?"

"He's the singer who wrote the mordant lyrics. Johnny Marr was the brilliance behind the music."

"See, that's the kind of stuff for your YouTube channel."

"Sure."

There is a light, it never goes out,

I listen to the refrain and the lovely music and can't help but feel that the light in Michelle is definitely going out. I hope and pray that she is at peace and will have an eternal life of some kind that is obviously beyond my comprehension.

"Lunch is served!" proclaims Ron as he climbs back on board. "How's my sweet Michelle?"

"She seems to be resting peacefully, but she hasn't opened her eyes or talked," I report.

He looks at his wife and smiles. "She's probably just enjoying the music." He leans over the rail. "Okay, Frank, pass it up." Ron brings up a serving tray loaded with shrimp skewers and warmed tortillas with melted cheese and lays it down on the deck. "Did I ever tell you about the time Michelle and I went to see Morrissey at the Shoreline Amphitheater?"

"No."

"It was his first American solo tour, a few years after The Smiths broke up. We had just started dating, and she really wanted to go, so to impress her, I bought tickets through a broker to get us close, spending a fortune for third-row center seats. That bastard didn't play one Smiths song! Michelle was pissed!"

"I like his solo stuff," I said.

"I like some of it too, but to ignore your legacy like that was pure arrogance, and he was killing my flow. It was Halloween, so to try to save our date, I suggested we stop in San Francisco on the way home and check out the parade in the Castro. We were totally not dressed for it. I was trying to woo her in my stylish tweed sports coat, and this guy walks up to me and says, 'Who are you supposed to be, Van Morrison?' Then this black guy in white angel's wings, and just those, walked by, and he had the biggest schlong known to man!" Ron grabs his elbow and implies that the size was from there down to his fist. "It completely blew my chance for sex that night because I was worried Michelle might think that's a normal penis size, and she was going to be extremely disappointed when we got home later. I didn't even try to pursue the matter, hoping that with time she might forget."

"Oh my God!" Rachel laughs. "He's just walking around naked?"

"Oh yeah. Just him and his donkey dick and those little white wings!"

Frank climbs up carrying a small ice chest that he hands to his brother, who puts it down next to the tray of shrimp and tortillas. "Is this the Halloween parade story?"

"Uh-huh."

"And you wonder how stereotypes get started? So, let's eat!" Frank lifts up the lid on the ice chest, revealing a bottle of tequila, cold Coronas, and small Tupperware bowls filled with diced tomatoes, shredded lettuce, thinly sliced avocado, cheese, lime wedges, chopped fresh cilantro, and another smaller Tupperware container of some kind of sauce. Ron hands us melamine plates while Frank opens and passes around bottles of beer. "Ron made this lovely lunch, and I'd like to toast him for it."

"Yes, to Ron. Though after that story, I thought you might be serving jumbo foot-long hot dogs!" Rachel teases.

"That's funny," Ron says. "But instead, we're having shrimp tacos."

"Is there a hidden metaphor there?" Rachel asks as I release Michelle's foot and sit back with the beer. Michelle suddenly lets out a disturbing wail, like that of a tortured seal. It seems to come from deep within her and shocks us all. I look over at Ron in alarm.

"I guess she doesn't want you to stop massaging her feet."

I scoot back and take her feet in my hands, and Michelle settles back down to silence. She's still with us, even though she never opened her eyes, and it seems to have taken every-thing out of her to communicate with that eerie moan. The good news is that my massage must be having a positive effect, and that brings me great joy.

"To Ron and Michelle," Frank says as he holds up his beer bottle. The three of them touch their bottles and take a drink from their beer.

"I'm thirsty. What about me?" I ask.

Rachel gets up, grabs my bottle, and puts it to my lips,

where I take a nice long drink. It goes down well in the heat. "Thank you."

Ron strokes Michelle's hair. "We're going to have lunch now, honey. Kimo will continue your foot massage, but he might take some breaks to eat, okay? He also made a playlist of some songs for you that I know you're enjoying. Rachel will play for you after lunch."

There's no reaction from his wife. He leans over and kisses her cheek and then turns back to us, his eyes wet and red. "So, take a skewer of grilled shrimp and place them on the tortilla, then add what you want from the tomatoes, lettuce, avocado, cheese, lime, and cilantro. I also recommend you put on some spicy pink mayo."

Rachel puts the kitten down in her lap so she can grab a skewer of shrimp, but Joy beats her to them and starts licking one.

"Damn it, kitty!" Rachel pulls the shrimp off the skewer and lets Joy have it. She eats one right off the stick before putting the rest on a tortilla. "Mmm, did you marinate the shrimp? It's tasty."

"Yeah, I used tequila, cumin, paprika, cayenne, garlic, lime juice, and a little olive oil. And salt and pepper, of course."

"Speaking of tequila," Frank reaches in and pulls out the bottle. "A shot of tequila all around?"

"Slow down, my brother. You've already partaken of the devil weed, and we've still got a long way to go," Ron cautions.

"But getting there is half the fun," Frank counters.

"Look, I'm still not feeling great from yesterday," I add. "If you guys want to drink, I'll stay sober."

"The hair of the dog would probably be good for you," Frank suggests. "And I know how much you love tequila, Ron. A shot of Dulce Vida Blanco? It's a hundred percent organic."

Ron smiles. "Well, if it's organic, how can I pass it up?"

"That a boy. Come on, Kimo. One shot won't kill you.

Besides, it goes great with your tacos."

"Okay. One shot."

"Bueno mi amigo! We don't have shot glasses, so just take a pull from the bottle," Frank leads the way and then passes the bottle to Rachel.

"To the chef," she says before taking a gulp. She brings it to me.

I use one of my hands to take the bottle and raise it in salutation. "Ron, this lunch looks great. Frank, dinner the other night was a beautiful thing. Rachel, you are a beautiful young lady, and Michelle, I wish you could join us, but I'm glad to be here with you. I love you all." I take a swig of the Mexican treat before handing the bottle back to Rachel, who passes it to Ron while I chase the tequila with another drink from the cold beer.

"I want to thank you all for joining me on this cruise. I love my wife very much. I'll never understand why this has happened to us, but I'm so thankful for our time together. Michelle, I love you." He takes a large drink from the bottle, then pours a little on his finger, holds it up to Michelle's mouth, and softly sticks it in. "She loved her tequila." There's no reaction whatsoever from her. He gently maneuvers himself next to her on the La-Z-Boy, then looks at me. "You're okay with staying sober?"

"Of course."

He nods his head and takes a deep breath before putting the bottle back to his mouth and taking another whopping belt. "Eat."

I follow orders, awkwardly using one hand to put all the fixings on my taco and adding a glob of the spicy pink mayo. It tastes delicious. "What's in the mayo, Ron? It's great."

"That would be a cup of Best Foods, the only mayonnaise I eat, a half cup of Mexican crema, some lime juice, agave, chipotle, and adobo sauce. I mix that bad boy up and keep it in the fridge until taco time!"

"It tastes like gochujang to me," says Rachel.

"You Rominger boys sure can cook," I say with my mouth full.

"After dad died, my mom was so busy working, we had to learn to cook or starve," Ron says.

"Mom cooked!" Frank argues.

"Pot pies and tuna casseroles maybe, but that was pretty much it," Ron replies.

"Those tuna casseroles sucked!"

"Now your memory's getting clearer little brother. The first thing I learned to make was mac and cheese. I hate it now, but we must have had that three or four nights a week. We were a couple of little fat boys there for a while."

Frank suddenly sits up straight and whispers, "cops."

"What?" My anxiety level jolts like I just jumped off the Golden Gate Bridge, my stomach trying to escape out of my throat. "They'll recognize my pants!"

"Stay cool." Ron's voice has a calming influence. "They can't even see you down there, and those just look like loud shorts. Everyone, keep your beverages down and out of sight. There's no reason to panic. It's just the San Joaquin County Sheriff's Department, and they are overworked and under-budgeted and have over seven hundred miles to patrol. They just want to make sure we're not drinking or doing drugs or are a danger to other boaters. Offer them a taco, Frank."

I'm contemplating the truth that we have been drinking, some of us have been doing drugs, one of us is most likely in a coma, and I'm a fugitive from justice wearing my orange prison pants. So why not offer them a taco? After all, we don't have any doughnuts.

Frank stands as the gray boat moves closer. "Howzit? Do you guys want a taco?"

A uniformed sheriff steps out from the cab of the patrol boat.

Ron whispers, "Rachel, could you bend over, slowly, pick up the tray of shrimp, and offer it to the officers with your biggest smile? We want them distracted."

Rachel gets up, hands Joy to me, and kisses my cheek before she slowly bends over to pick up the tray of shrimp skewers and tortillas. I don't know if the sheriffs are distracted by that view, but I sure am! Domine, ut videam. Rachel joins Frank at the rail, effectively shielding the rest of us from view. "Would you like a shrimp taco, officers?" she coos.

"No, thank you, ma'am," replies the officer. "We just want to remind you that boating under the influence is against the law, and your boat could be impounded if you were arrested."

"Thank you, officer, for keeping the Delta safe for boaters like us," Rachel answers. "Are you sure you don't want a taco? They're really good. They practically explode in your mouth with flavor."

"I'm sure they're good, but we've got to keep moving."

"What about the good-looking officer driving?"

Come on, Rachel, I'm thinking, don't push it.

"He's allergic to shellfish. His eyes will swell shut, and then I'd have to drive."

"That's too bad. I wanted jumbo hot dogs, but I didn't win the vote."

The sheriff gives Rachel a closer look. "Okay, well, you all enjoy your outing, and remember to be safe."

"We will, sir," Frank says.

Rachel rambles on, "thanks again for all you do. It must be a lonely and thankless task, patrolling all these miles of water, just the two of you, and only stopping when people misbehave."

"Yes, thanks again, officer." Frank takes Rachel by the arm and guides her back away from the railing. I release Michelle's foot and scoot back to let them pass. Michelle lets out another barking wail, and I quickly scurry back and take hold of Michelle's foot.

"Is everything okay on board?" the sheriff asks. My heart is back to *Midnight Express* mode—ba boomp, ba boomp. Oh well, if my time is up, at least I got to do something good for Michelle before she dies. This whole experience has taken its toll on me, and probably the best thing I could do right now for everyone is to stand up and turn myself in. Michelle has settled back down after I started rubbing again. I look from her poor withered foot up to her husband's gray hair. Ron gives me a look before he turns to the sheriff.

"This is my wife, officer," Ron says. "She's dying of cancer and just started hospice care, so we've brought her to her favorite beach for one last picnic. That's my brother and his girlfriend, who's also a hospice nurse, and that's my wife's brother massaging her feet."

I turn and nod my head, looking the sheriff straight in the eye and wondering if he has seen my face on a recent bulletin. His face betrays no recognition, and he quickly looks away from Michelle and me and back to Ron. I decide to be quiet and put whatever happens next in God's hands.

"Is that morphine?"

Here we go.

"Yes, it is," says Ron. "It's to help manage my wife's pain and suffering until she passes."

"Yeah, I understand, but it's a drug you shouldn't have on board your boat."

"I know. I just didn't see the harm in one last picnic. If you want, I'll turn myself in when we get back."

"No, that's okay. I'm sorry about your wife. Enjoy your picnic, but get home safely."

"Thank you, officer, we will."

I hear the motor of the patrol boat rev up and sneak a glance at it moving away. The officer goes back into the cabin, and they head toward Stockton. I look at Rachel. "Uh, you think you might have blathered on a wee bit?"

"Was I rambling? I do that when I'm stoned and nervous," she giggles.

"You did a great job distracting them, Rachel, but I was wondering if you weren't going to take no for an answer." Ron laughs. "It looked like you were going to snatch defeat from the jaws of victory!"

"Sorry," she says. "You handled that smoothly, Ron. Saying I was a hospice nurse was good."

"I thought you did a great job, Rachel," the ever-gallant Frank adds.

"You're such a kiss ass, Frank."

"Trust me; it's not a bad thing!" He looks at Rachel's butt and cracks himself up.

"Boys!" Rachel's embarrassed.

"All right, clean it up, guys. We need to finish lunch and get back on the road."

"I got to be honest, that scared the crap out of me," I admit.

"It's tough being an outlaw, Kimo, but the Delta has a history of hiding them."

"Really? Like who?" I ask Ron.

"Probably the most famous was the Yokut Indian, Estanislao. Stanislaus River and County were named after him."

"What'd he do?"

"He committed the crime of apostasy."

"Huh? Okay, I'll show my ignorance; what's that?"

"He left the church, specifically the mission in San Jose. The Spanish couldn't let Indians revert back to heathens because they weren't just saving souls; they needed labor to till the fields. I've got a coffee-table book downstairs you need to look at. It talks all about the history of the Delta Indians and does a wonderful job of explaining the spin at that time."

"What do you mean?"

"Spin, the way people use words. Spin isn't a new phenomenon. For example, when the Spanish, or Americans, or

British for that matter, won a battle against the Indians, it was called a campaign, but when the Indians won, it was called a massacre. Whenever an Indian did something like rebel, it was an outrage, and those outrages were followed by a punitive campaign in response to that outrage."

"They've always gotten the shaft in our country."

"True. If we didn't get them through a campaign, we got them through a pestilence we introduced them to. In the early 1800s, about twenty thousand Indians in the Central Valley were killed by disease. In a census taken during the gold rush, the Indian population in San Joaquin County was down to around four hundred, in 1860 that was down to forty, and in 1870 it was down to a population of five."

Frank finally stands up and throws what's left of his taco into the river. "I hate to be shallow, but this really isn't an upbeat lunch conversation. Can't we talk more about food or how great Rachel looks in Michelle's suit? And why are we listening to The Smiths? I thought the sheriff was going to arrest us for polluting the Delta with that noise!"

"This is the last Smith's song, so relax," I say in my defense.

"Why don't we let Rachel play for Michelle?"

"That'd be fine by me," I say angrily. "Ron?"

"Sure. Rachel, you ready to play?"

She finishes chewing. "I thought there was a salad to go with the tacos. Isn't that why we picked blackberries? These are really good, Ron."

Ron smiles. "The poor girl's still eating! Frank, where's the salad?"

"It's in the other ice chest still on the beach."

"What are you, stoned? How'd you forget that?"

"Because I'm an idiot. Kimo, you want to help?"

"Not really."

"That's cold. Back to being an ass, I see."

"You shouldn't have put down the music I chose."

"At least The Smiths are ending. Who's next? Depeche Mode?"

Just then, Shane MacGowan's Irish brogue sings from the boat's speakers... *It was Christmas Eve babe, in the drunk tank...*

"Oh sure, now you play the Pogues," Frank whines as he goes over the side to retrieve the ice chest with the salad.

"This is who we named the swans after, Rachel," Ron tells her.

"Okay."

"Ron, what happened to Estanislao?" I'm curious.

"After a few years of rebellion in the Delta, he returned to the mission and was pardoned."

"He returned to the mission?"

"Yeah."

"That's interesting, don't you think?"

"Why? Are you thinking of returning to the church?"

"I don't know."

"Well, just to let you know, some people say Estanislao wasn't forgiven by all at the mission and was murdered. Others say he died of a pox. Some say he simply disappeared. It's a mystery."

Mmm, just like life.

FOURTEEN

It's just after "Kahoutek" finishes when I release Michelle's foot, and she finally doesn't react. I quickly check that she's still breathing, but I don't know what to think or feel about it. The whole time I was massaging her feet, my back was killing me, and I really wanted to get up and move around, but there was something so satisfying in the way Michelle reacted when I wasn't touching her. It gave me confidence that I mattered.

Ron and Frank took Michelle below deck, and now Rachel plays Bach on the keyboard from the cemetery for her. I'm up on the flybridge, driving the boat past the windmills spinning like gigantic fans in the Montezuma Hills on the northwestern side of the river. I feel like Don Quixote chasing imaginary giants.

"Wow, we're already at the Montezuma Hills! Frank made good time," Ron says as he clumsily climbs up to the flybridge carrying the bottle of tequila.

"Did he?" I ask. I have no idea what a good time is,

considering I've never made this trip before. I do know that after lunch, Frank drove, and I couldn't keep up with all the tracts and islands Ron gave toasts to as we passed. I also know that Ron is fucked up, and Frank is below deck trying his best to catch up to his big brother.

"When did we make the Sacramento River?" Ron asks.

"It was just before I took over," I tell him.

"Did they raise the Three Mile Slough Bridge for you?"

"Yeah."

"Is that cool or what? Did you see the bridge tender's house on top? When I was a kid, I got to ride up inside it while the bridge was lifted in the fog. That's how I always pictured going to heaven, just rising up out of the fog of this life into the beautiful blue sky above."

"How'd you get to do that?"

"We were stationed at Travis Air Force Base at the time, and my dad used to love to take drives into the Delta on his days off. One time we were at the bridge and stuck in the fog. My dad started talking to the bridge tender, and he took us up. It was a great day."

"That would be cool," I say.

"My dad used to always tell me to look at the wake as we were cruising. Then he'd say that the wake was your past and there's nothing you can do about it. He told me not to fall into the trap of thinking that the wake was driving the boat; the past has nothing to do with where you're going. The only thing that mattered was how you were driving in the present moment. I don't know where he got that, but it stuck with me."

"Your dad sounds like a cool guy."

"He was. Do you think there's a heaven, Kimo?"

"I don't know, Ron. I don't know what to think anymore."

"If there is, you think Michelle will go to heaven, don't you, Kimo?" Ron asks.

"Of course!"

"She was worried. The cancer and the treatment were bad enough, but the mental torture she went through knowing she was going to die and thinking she was going to hell made it a lot worse. It wasn't until we got a Catholic priest out to talk with her that she finally calmed down."

I can see that the tequila has played with Ron's short-term memory and summoned his demons from this last year. I feel like I need to change the subject before he succumbs to the haunting. "Frank told me you went in the other direction during your honeymoon. Where was your first stop?"

"What?"

"Tell me about your honeymoon trip." I can tell his mind has switched tracks and is remembering happier times.

"Well, it's funny because the first stop almost ended our marriage. We docked in Rio Vista, and I took her to Foster's Bighorn. Have you heard of it?"

"No."

"It's a famous bar that has been there forever. All I wanted was a cold draft beer and didn't even think about the décor nor that it might set Michelle off, but hell hath no fury like my wife when she sees animal cruelty!" He takes another pull from the tequila bottle.

"Bill Foster, the original owner, was a big-game hunter back in the days when that wasn't frowned upon. I think he died back in the early sixties. Anyway, when I was a kid, my dad took me there for a bison burger, which sucked, but I remember being mesmerized just staring at all the animal heads mounted on the walls." He raises the bottle to the memory and takes a drink.

"There was everything you could possibly imagine up on those walls, a lion, a giraffe, a rhino, even a huge elephant's head with tusks! It was like a museum! So, besides wanting a cold draft, it was a way to include my dad on my wedding day.

"Michelle went fucking ballistic! She'd had a lot more to

drink at our reception because I knew I had to drive the boat, and she started screaming like a drunken sailor at me in front of everybody! Who the fuck was I? How could this be the first stop on our honeymoon! How could she have married such an insensitive prick! She had a great line, something about it being like ISIS having a bar with decapitated Westerners mounted on the walls!

"I've never admitted this because we made a pact not to talk about it, but I got no love on my wedding night. In fact, I was locked out of the master stateroom and was seriously thinking that the marriage might be over before it even started."

"Wow."

"Yeah, it was crazy." Ron takes another gulp of the Mexican spirit.

"I always thought you guys never had a fight."

He laughs so hard he spits out what he just took, "dude, we're married! Every married couple fights. What was that Kinks song, 'Marriage is a two-headed transplant, you're never alone' or something like that."

"Labour of Love."

"Huh?"

"The song is 'Labour of Love,' off the State of Confusion album," I tell him.

"Why the fuck aren't you a DJ? I mean, who else knows this shit?"

"Geeks like me, living in a rock and roll fantasy."

He smiles. "That was one of their songs too, wasn't it?"

"Yeah, that's why I said it."

"You've got a quick wit for an escaped con. So, seriously Kimo, were you raped in there?"

Good God! "No, Ron, I wasn't raped in there."

"It's okay if you were. I wouldn't tell anybody."

"Just like you kept your pact about your wedding night?"

"Well, I don't think that matters now. But touché, I get your point."

"Yeah, well, unfortunately for all of you, I was never raped in prison. It was minimum security! You know, Martha Stewart, Wall Street guys, politicians, that kind of place."

"Politicians don't go to jail! Neither do those Wall Street fuckers! That's what the problem is with this country! You get the justice you can pay for!"

"Steal a little, and they throw you in jail, steal a lot, and they make you king."

"Exactly! Who said that?"

"Dylan."

"Damn it. I was going to guess that! Isn't it funny that no straight guy wants to be fucked in the butt, but we all want to anally fuck hot chicks?"

Where the hell did that come from?

"That's insightful, Ron."

"It's the tequila talking. I'm fucked up." He takes a deep breath and swallows a burp. His eyes are glazed over, and he probably needs a nap, but I don't know where the hell I'm going, so I need to bring him back to the land of the conscious.

"So, Ron, how'd you get out of the doghouse on your honeymoon?"

It works. His eyes slowly light up like a lighthouse, and the beams shine my way. "It was the Ryde Hotel that saved my marriage."

"The Ryde Hotel? Tell me about it."

"Okay. We got a late start on the first morning of our marriage. The plan for our wedding night was for us to come back to the boat, open that bottle of champagne that we drank earlier today, and fuck our brains out. But she was so pissed at me that she locked me out of the master stateroom and passed out. I ended up drinking alone, obviously not that bottle of champagne and passing out where you slept last night.

"I didn't get us going till probably noon, and at that point,

I still hadn't seen my bride. My original plan was for us to stop in Isleton and have fresh-boiled crawdads at Isleton Joe's Bar, but after the incident at Foster's Bighorn, I didn't think she'd appreciate having to suck on the heads of crawdads, so instead, we had breakfast at the River's Edge Café. We had some great Huevos Motulenos, and that kind of put some life back into Michelle.

"So, I took her for a tour of Main Street. She was still a teacher then and found the history interesting, which it is. Isleton was founded in the late 1800s as a place to load the Delta's agriculture products onto boats and ship them down the river. The majority of the population was Chinese, who originally helped build the dikes after the intercontinental railroad was completed. In the early 1900s, laws were passed preventing the Chinese from immigrating or owning property. God love America; we historically use people then screw them.

"Anyway, soon the Japanese moved in and built a block next to the Chinese, and they worked together in the canneries with Filipinos and Portuguese and even some poor white folks. Pears and asparagus were big at that time, and Isleton boomed until World War II. Then all the Japanese were screwed, taken to internment camps, and forced to give up their property. The canneries moved to the cities because trucks had taken over for boats in moving produce. Pretty much the only businesses that thrived after that were the vice industry, gambling, liquor, and prostitution."

"Interesting history lesson, Ron, but you were talking about how the Ryde Hotel saved your marriage."

Ron starts cracking up. "I'm sorry. Just like my dad, I'm fascinated by the Delta and its history. My dad wanted to own a boat so bad, but he died before he could get one." He starts tearing up. "First, my dad, and now Michelle. I'm not sure I can survive this, Kimo." He looks over at me, and the pain behind his eyes seems like an anchor bound to him by chains and pulling him under. It depresses me. We all suffer. That's life, I get that, but why does it seem that the good get more than their fair share? I've got to pull him out of it for as long as I can.

"So, the Ryde Hotel?" I offer the question up like a buoy, and thankfully he grabs it.

"Ah, yes, the Ryde Hotel, built during prohibition as an oasis in the desert of law-enforced morality of the times. It was a first-class hotel built in the middle of a swamp, miles from anywhere, and only accessible by boat or dirt roads. The basement has a large bar and room for card tables and slot machines, and both doors, the one at the top of the stairs and the one leading to the basement itself, have peepholes. There's a trap door in the basement that leads to tunnels that go to the levee for escape or back to the two-story whorehouse built behind the hotel.

"I booked us the bridal suite, which had been remodeled and had a beautiful view of the river and a large Jacuzzi bathtub. Michelle loved the room, but I still wasn't out of the doghouse yet. I let her take a nap, and that gave me the opportunity to play a round at the executive nine-hole golf course on the grounds. Eight bucks for nine holes! Less than a buck a hole, you can't beat that! I was out there alone, swinging at my problems, contemplating marital bliss, and loving it!"

"Is that place still there?"

"Oh yeah! You'd love it."

"Okay, so you're playing golf alone on your honeymoon..."

"Kimo, it was more than me just playing golf alone. First off, I'm out in nature and had the course to myself. I was able to focus on one swing at a time and relate that to my marriage. Not every swing's going to be good, bud, just like not every moment of a marriage is going to be stellar, but I was out there playing and thinking of what a beautiful human being I had just married, and it hit me that marriage is like a round of golf! Exhilarating, frustrating, humbling, but ultimately, transcendent!"

What could I say? It sounded about right to me. At least for the golf part, I've never been married since Ron married the love of my life.

"When I was done with my round, the sun was setting, so I stopped by the boat, got the bottle of champagne, and went back to our room. Michelle didn't want to drink but had candles lit and was waiting for me in the bathtub. We consummated our marriage there as the sun set, and it was probably the most beautiful moment of my life!"

I wish I couldn't visualize it, but I can, and that makes me jealous.

"Then the next night, we took it to another level!"

All right, I've heard enough. He's had the life I wanted! He's a great guy, but do I need to hear more of what I've missed out on?

"My boss gave me a night at the Grand Island Mansion for a wedding present. This 24,000-square-foot mansion was built in 1917 as the centerpiece of an orchard empire run by some guy whose name I don't remember. Anyway, it's only open for Sunday brunch and weddings, and usually, you can only stay there if you're part of a wedding party, but my boss's money and connections got us a night to ourselves. They have an antique pool table, a one-lane bowling alley, and a swimming pool. Have you ever bowled with Michelle? She hammers the ball down the lanes, and those pins explode!"

"As a matter of fact, I have bowled with her, and you're so right. She rolls them harder than I do! We auctioned off a chance to bowl with your teacher to raise money for our school, and Michelle put me to shame." That was a fun time. The kids worshiped her as much as I did.

"She's a beast in a bowling alley, and I was afraid she'd

break the antique one there! Anyway, we stayed in the Beethoven Suite, which had a marble fireplace in the room, a double Jacuzzi tub, beautiful art on the walls, and a huge bed. It was unbelievably romantic! Hey, they have a Liszt Suite, so if you marry Rachel, you could have your reception there and spend the night!"

"Yeah, I don't see that happening."

"Listen to her! You'd be a fool to let her get away. She really likes you."

"What about your brother?"

"Look, I love him, but he's too domesticated for her in the long run."

The music she's making is definitely pleasing to the mind, senses, and spirit. "Do you really think I have a chance?"

"Why not? She's still in college, but you have some time to finish, so after that, why not?"

"What do I have to offer?"

"Now that's a good question! What do you have to offer? You don't have any money. What about your parents? Will you be inheriting any money?"

"My mom got all my dad's money in their divorce, and she and I don't talk."

"I didn't know that, Kimo. Why don't you and your mom talk?"

"It's a long story."

"Okay, if you don't want to talk about it, that's fine. So, let's recap. You're a convicted felon. You have a drinking problem. You're a failed actor, a failed teacher..."

"Actually, I was a good teacher."

"Yeah, Michelle always said that, but uh, I'm not sure even public schools hire convicted felons. Do you have any marketable skills?"

"Like what?" I ask. This is starting to depress me. What am I good for?

"Computer skills?"

"Basic."

"Look, if you were a teacher, you know you had to have good verbal and written communication skills, right? Michelle had those, and they're crucial for the job, right?"

"Okay, sure."

"You have a good work ethic. Well, you know, when you're not drinking or in jail."

"That's true."

"You've got problem-solving skills. I mean, you made it to Angelina's even though you were in prison! And, by the way, that's impressive, and I'll drink to that." He raises the bottle in salutation before taking another gulp.

"I did get lucky meeting Rachel."

"Yeah, but you took action! Action creates its own luck! And because of your action, I got lucky! Look, Kimo, you've solved my biggest problem!"

"I did?"

"Yes! Michelle's resting place. I can't tell you what that means to me. So, I tell you what, if you need a job when you get out, I'll help find one for you."

I'm touched. I've sinned against this man, and he's willing to give me another chance. "Thanks, Ron."

"Now, I'm not saying it will be a great job, but I know people, so it will be something you can start over with. It will be up to you what you do with it."

"I really appreciate you giving me that opportunity, Ron, especially considering what I did to you."

"You have to get over that, Kimo. I've forgiven you. Now you need to forgive yourself for that and whatever else is dragging you down."

"What are you talking about?" Did Michelle tell him about Kauai?

"I don't know. I can't explain it. I just get a feeling that you're full of self-loathing."

"Did Michelle tell you anything?"

"Other than about your night together in Victory Park? No. Should she have?"

"No." Should I tell him? Doesn't he have enough to deal with at this point? Don't I?

"Hey, that's Sherman Island. The confluence of this river and the San Joaquin is just beyond that in Suisun Bay. We're making good time. Just don't collide with that freighter," Ron warns me.

Sure enough, there's another gargantuan ship heading up the channel right for us, and it effectively ends the conversation. I've gotten somewhat comfortable driving this boat, but when you see sixty thousand tons heading your way, the heart starts pumping a little faster. It's time to focus. I slow *It's All Good* down and move her closer to shore, giving the big ship a wide berth.

"Remember when it passes to steer the boat head-on into the wake," he reminds me. "How are we on fuel?"

"It looks like we've got a little more than a half tank left."

"That should get us to the St. Francis Yacht Club unless we want to stop in Pittsburg to refuel and get some more refreshments." He lifts his almost empty tequila bottle.

"Pittsburgh is in Contra Costa County."

"Yeah, so?"

"I made the newspaper there yesterday. I'd rather not stop."

"Hey, aren't you the celebrity, but it's probably wise to just keep moving."

I steer the boat next to a marker buoy that has an osprey's nest built on it. The huge freighter slowly and powerfully glides past us in the center of the channel. I wonder what it would be like to cross an ocean on one of those. I think about what Rachel said earlier about having been at sea for so long and then sailing under the Golden Gate Bridge only to skip San

Francisco on your way to Stockton. Being at the Marsh Creek Detention Center is kind of like being at sea, and Stockton turned out okay for me. Although I do have to admit I'm looking forward to seeing San Francisco again.

I'm not sure where the yacht club is we're going to be docking, but if it's near the marina, I'd love to go to my favorite bar on Chestnut Street that has the "Hark, cocktails!" sign over the door. I'd also love to take Rachel to the Palace of Fine Arts to see the swans. There are plenty of secluded places there where we could have fun. Michelle used to take her class on a field trip to the Exploratorium there. God, she was a good teacher!

What I would really like is a lamb shawarma from Truly Mediterranean in the Mission. Michelle always liked Cha Cha Cha in the Height, and I have to admit they did have great sangria. It would be great to have breakfast at Bechelli's tomorrow or walk up the hill and eat some fresh sausage at Ella's. The gastronomic choices are endless. It's a great town to be a foodie.

"Okay, head into the wake!"

Ron brings me back to the moment, and I give the throttle a push, and the boat moves forward to mitigate the waves from the ship. We bounce up and down as we slice through them, but it's much smoother than earlier when we took them broadside.

"Nice!" Ron commends me.

Suddenly the music stops.

Ron and I share a look of concern, and I'm worried that the waves might have disturbed Michelle or thrown Rachel off when I hear Frank scream, "Kimo, you motherfucker!"

Jesus, what now? Once again, I silently pray, "God loves, governs, guides, and directs me in all ways."

Frank comes up from below deck and glares at me. "You fucking bastard!"

"What?" I ask.

"Calm down, Frank. Watch your language!" Ron says to his bother. "Is Michelle okay?"

"Calm down? Calm down? Rachel told me that this piece of shit is willing to kill your wife!"

Oh, fuck.

FIFTEEN

"I know," Ron says.

What?

The boat continues to rock in the wake of the passing ship.

"You know?" Frank exclaims in disbelief. "Then what the fuck is he doing here?"

"He's here to help me," Ron answers.

"What the fuck does that mean?"

"What does that mean?" I ask.

Ron turns to me. "She's my wife, Kimo. We talk. You said her soul would leave at death, not at the distribution of her ashes. She believes you."

When did I say that?

"I don't remember saying that, but ..." Wait, I think we did talk about it. Why do I open my big mouth?

"If her soul departs at the Golden Gate, I can have her remains. That's her deal. You did this. Thank you."

"Are you fucking kidding me?" Frank yells. "Not only is

that fucking insane, but it's morally wrong! I want no part in it! Besides, who's to say she's not already dead."

"She's not," Rachel says as she comes on deck.

"No thanks to that piece of shit!" he points at me.

The tempest in my mind howls. Why do I keep making major mistakes? The road to hell is paved with good intentions! I'm a decent human being, damn it! I speed the boat up and turn it back, heading west, wanting to get away or at least take flight until my legs adjust.

"Stay in control," Ron tells me. "I'm going to see my wife, and I'll take Frank and tell him what we're doing, but you need to get us there."

I slow down. This is not what I meant.

"We're doing the right thing for Michelle. She wants this. We are acting from love," her husband says to me. "If you need me, I'm below deck."

I'm exhausted. I don't usually do anything the day after Angelina's, much less something this intense. What should I do?

Ron pats me on my shoulder. "Are you good?"

That's the question, isn't it? "Ron..."

"Michelle always used to tell me how much funnier you were than me, but she knew I could provide for her, and she didn't think you could."

That sounds about right, but why is he telling me this now? "She was a good judge of character," I say.

"And she loves you, Kimo, but she married me. Help me provide this for her. Please."

Damn it, I'm not sure I can stop the tears. Ron leaves me but stumbles down the ladder. Frank rushes over to help his brother up. Ron lifts the almost empty bottle of tequila in triumph. "Look at that. I didn't spill a drop! Do we have any more tequila down there, little brother?" Ron asks.

"No! And I think you've had enough anyway," Franks responds.

"I'm the captain of this vessel, Frank, and my beloved wife is below deck dying, so I'll be the judge of whether or not I've had enough! Now why don't we go downstairs, and you can help me find something to drink. We need to talk."

Frank looks at the three of us. I can tell that he doesn't know how to handle his anger at this bombshell. Hell, I don't know how to handle it either. Why didn't I just stay and finish my time? None of this would have happened.

"My wife has been alone too long, Frank. Come have a drink with me and calm down. Please?" Ron puts a hand on his little brother's shoulder and steers him toward the stairs. Frank, shell-shocked and dazed, surrenders and is led below deck.

Rachel looks up at me. "I guess you're mad at me?"

"No, I'm mad at myself."

She climbs up the ladder to join me on the flybridge. "Kimo, I have had more fun with you in the last couple of days than I've had in a long time, maybe my entire life!"

"Great, I'm glad you're having a good time."

She quietly looks at me.

"How'd it come up?" I ask.

"Michelle told me yesterday when I was giving her a pedicure. She's in constant pain. But she said my playing sincerely made her feel better. Music thanatology works!"

"I meant you telling Frank."

"Oh. Well, he was just staring at her and wondered if it would be more humane just to give her more morphine, you know, until she OD'd? but that he couldn't do it. I told him what Michelle said about you yesterday. I promise you I had no idea he'd flip out."

This is a nightmare. "So, what do you think now that you know the truth?"

"People say the truth will set you free, but it just gets you judged. If you knew the truth about me, you wouldn't look at me the same."

"Try me."

She looks away, and when she finally turns back to face me, she has tears in her eyes. "I never once played music for my mother when she was sick. I knew she wanted me to, but I wanted her to suffer. I was happy she got cancer."

That's harsh. "I didn't realize you were so bitter. Why?"

"My mom!"

"Don't get me started on mothers."

"What's the worst thing your mother ever did?"

"Mmm, well, before I was old enough to go to school, when my mom got overwhelmed, to get some peace, she would tell me she was going to call the orphanage to come and pick me up and take me back. It terrified me. I hid under the bed for hours, not realizing it was a ploy so she could have some peace."

"You were adopted?"

"No, she just used that to scare me."

"How old were you?"

"Three or four."

"That's child abuse."

"Whatever. What about your mom?"

"I don't think she was as overtly abusive as your mother. My mom's unbearable in a different way. She's Chinese. They're not all like the stereotypical Chinese mother, but my mom was definitely a 'Tiger Mom.' She put so much pressure on me to succeed as a kid. I never got to play like the other kids because I always had to practice my piano, go to math class, or learn Chinese. She never noticed my spiraling into depression. I blamed her for everything, the divorce, my cutting. I was a bitch because that's what I thought she was. It was the chemo that got her off my back."

I don't know what to say, but what she said doesn't make me feel any better. We're passing the tip of Sherman Island, where we'll next enter Suisun Bay at the estuary of the San

Joaquin and Sacramento Rivers. There's a bit of turbulence, so I must work to keep the boat under control. I could just take a left now and follow the San Joaquin River back to Stockton, turn myself in, and end this capricious escape from reality. But that wouldn't be fair to Ron, and I have to keep in mind that this trip is not all about me.

"Why did you cut yourself?"

"I was young, and it was an unhealthy coping method. I'm guessing it's like your drinking is for you. I got over it with help, but enough about me. What's causing your suffering?"

"I would think it's obvious."

"I think it's more than Michelle."

"Think what you want," I snap back to her, causing the silence that I want, if only briefly.

"Isn't that Mount Diablo?" Rachel asks. The landmark now towers above the horizon less than fifteen miles south of us.

"Yep."

"We've come full circle, huh?"

"Not quite, but close enough."

"Boy, it's getting colder with the wind blowing the way it is."

I hadn't noticed, so I say nothing. I try to absorb nature's sublime beauty; the California sun shining in the open blue sky, the mustard-colored rolling hills, the deep flowing water, the cool wind...

"Kimo, please don't be mad at me."

...the beautiful young girl. Damn, she's cute!

"I'm not mad at you, Rachel." I'm disgusted with myself. "I do feel bad for your mom."

I look over and see tears rolling down her face. Great, tears, just what I need now. "Rachel, please, I'm not trying to make you feel bad. If anything, I feel guilty and remorseful for what I've done."

"You've done nothing wrong!"

I laugh. "I've done plenty wrong."

"I don't think so!"

"I'm glad you feel that way, but it doesn't really matter, anyway. Tomorrow I'll go back to jail, where I belong, and you'll go back to your life, which is wide open and full of potential."

"What about tonight?"

"Tonight?"

"I was hoping we could have a romantic night in San Francisco! Eat a good meal. It's such a beautiful city for lovers to get lost in each other. Can't you just be in the moment?"

I think about it, "have you ever had a lamb shawarma?"

"A what?"

"A lamb shawarma, it's like a Middle Eastern burrito. There's a place in the Mission, Truly Mediterranean, that makes a beautiful shawarma."

"Then let's go have one!"

I'd love it, but I don't know. A few hours after Michelle's soul flows toward hopeful bliss doesn't really feel like the best time to enjoy the tasteful delicacy.

"Hey, there's Port Chicago," I announce. Thank you, God, for the distraction! "I used to take my class on a field trip there during Black History Month."

"You're avoiding the subject," Rachel says.

"No, I'm just living in the moment, like you said. Tonight is hours away. Right now, we're passing Port Chicago, and I'm just pointing that out to you."

She stares at me before another smile slowly builds on her lovely face. "Okay, you coward. I'll live in the moment with you. So, what's Port Chicago?"

"That's where the Port Chicago disaster happened during World War II. Somehow the munitions detonated, and the explosion was like a small atomic bomb. Over three hundred sailors were blown to bits, and almost four hundred were wounded.

"The surviving white officers were given a month's leave to deal with the trauma, while many of the surviving black sailors had to help with the clean-up, meaning they had to pick up body parts of guys that could've been their friends. A month later, hundreds refused to continue loading ammunition, fearful that the working conditions were unsafe and there would be another explosion. The Navy charged fifty of them with mutiny, and since this was a time of war, they could have gotten the death penalty. The kangaroo court found them guilty, but they were spared the death penalty.

"Thurgood Marshall and Eleanor Roosevelt both took up their cause, and after the war, in 1946, forty-seven of the fifty were paroled back to active duty and most eventually got a general discharge from the Navy."

"Really? Over there?" Rachel says as she points to the yellow grassland on the embankment.

"Yeah, see that American flag?" I point to the flag blowing in the breeze. "That's where the memorial is."

"You'd never know something so violent and sad happened there because it's such a normal-looking place. Kind of like people, I guess."

"Yeah," I mumble. She's pretty insightful.

"I wish I had a teacher like you," Rachel says as she turns back to look at me.

"I was all right."

"Did you teach high school?"

"No, and you're a perfect example of why not."

"What do you mean?"

"I bet you were a doll in high school. Do you think I could focus on teaching with you sitting in my classroom?"

"Then you should teach college like my dad. You could take care of your distractions after class, if you know what I mean."

"Rachel, believe it or not, I'd rather have a relationship like

Ron and Michelle have than just have sex with a bunch of young college girls."

"What about me?"

"What about you?"

"It seemed to me that you enjoyed having sex with me."

"Oh, most definitely, you've been a highlight of my life. But this isn't real."

"What do you mean by that? I'm real." She grabs her breasts. "These are real. What we did yesterday morning was real. What I want to do with you tonight is real."

"Stop. Calm down. Please? I have to focus on driving this boat. These circumstances are out of the ordinary. Do you think you'd have anything to do with me if we met at a Starbucks?"

"I don't know. I do know that I met plenty of guys at my sister's wedding, but you're the one I left with. That's the reality."

"You probably just picked the biggest loser you could find to get back at your mother."

She laughs, "that might have played a part, initially, but I like you. This has been an amazing experience for me."

"Tell me about your tattoo."

"That was definitely to piss my mother off. I got it when I was sixteen."

"I thought you had to be eighteen to get one."

"Not if you get your parents' consent."

"Your parents shouldn't have consented. They should have foreseen unintended consequences, like men thinking you're older than you are."

"First off, they didn't consent. I have a friend who did it for me. And there were plenty of consequences. My mom went through the roof, grounded me for a month, took away my phone, and stopped trusting me."

"What about your dad?"

"He didn't give it much thought. I'm sure he's seen plenty of tattoos at school."

"So, why the leaves blowing off the tree?"

"We were reading Robert Frost in school, and I really liked 'Nothing Gold Can Stay' and 'Stopping by Woods on a Snowy Evening.' I liked the way he captured the melancholy and transitory nature of life. I could really relate to it with my mom's cancer and the divorce."

"So, your tattoo is inspired by poetry?"

"Yeah."

"I'll have to go back and reread him. The only one I remember is 'The Road Less Traveled.'"

"You mean 'The Road Not Taken.'"

"Is that the name of it?"

"Yes. So, Kimo, what about you?"

"What do you mean?"

"Well, you know a lot about me. Tell me something about you. Why do you have low self-esteem?"

"You think I have low self-esteem?"

"Yeah. You just called yourself a loser."

"Mmm, I don't know. Can I blame it on my parents?"

"Can't we all? What specifically did they do that you haven't come to terms with? Yes, I've been to counseling. I told you I used to be a cutter."

"You said you were young when you cut yourself. How old were you?"

"You're avoiding answering my question."

"True, but still, how old were you?"

"Thirteen, fourteen."

"Why cut?"

"It's the only way I could feel anything."

"Do you still do it?"

"No. I told you, I got help."

"So, you've come a long way in a few years, whereas I

think my development was arrested."

"When?"

"Probably when I was under the bed." I really don't want to talk about it and am thankful I see a distraction. "Look! There's the ghost fleet, or what's left of it," I point to the old ships anchored in the northwest part of the bay. "At the end of the Cold War, there were about four hundred old navy and merchant marine ships here in case we needed them for another war. Now there are about ten, and those will be gone soon. Toxic paint was flaking off from the rust and polluting the bay. That's a win for the environment."

"Why the fuck won't you be honest with me?" she explodes.

"I am being honest with you."

"Then tell me why you hate yourself so much!"

"I don't hate myself!"

"Cut the bullshit, Kimo, and be honest with me! I won't judge you."

Before I can think, it escapes.

"I killed my grandfather, okay!"

I can't believe I just told her!

Well, there it is. The truth finally escapes, flying into the air like a clay pigeon, wingless and twirling, blown to bits by a blast from a shotgun, falling back to earth in pieces.

SIXTEEN

I remember the sweet tropical fragrance of the pikake lei that the local girl seated next to me wore on the flight to Lihue. I don't know, but just that smell made me believe there had to be a heaven, even if it was simply moments on earth.

She was returning from her freshman year at a school on the mainland, and her ex-boyfriend met her at the airport in Honolulu. He put the three strands of aromatic bliss around her neck as he kissed her cheek. They were high school sweethearts in Kapaa, but her mother didn't like him because he didn't want to go to college, the mainland being too far from Kauai, so instead, he moved to Oahu, sold pakalolo, and taught surfing to tourists in Waikiki. I get why a mother would be concerned, but it sounded like fun to me.

The unwelcomed ex-boyfriend told her he would come home to visit after she had some time with her family, but she was over him, having found a nice ambitious haole on the mainland. When she asked me why I was visiting Kauai, I told her I was visiting my grandparents, though I didn't mention that my mom got a call from Sun Village saying my grandfather had taken my grandmother up to the fourth-floor outdoor walkway of the apartment building and threatened to jump. It took hours to talk them down, and the staff quickly called for us to come over and do something.

I loved my grandparents, and they inspired me. They met on a blind date one Sunday, and my grandfather proposed on the following Thursday. They stayed married until death did part them. My grandmother had to be the sweetest woman known to mankind. Even after Hurricane Iniki skinned the roof off their home and shrieking 145-mile-an-hour winds tortured her into dementia, my grandma was still a joy to be around. She slowly lost her memory and had to stop her volunteer work, and my grandparents eventually chose to leave their house because my grandfather just couldn't handle her on his own.

My mom never forgave them. She felt entitled to their home as part of her inheritance. My grandfather disagreed. He raised my mom on Oahu and moved to Kauai after she left for college. My grandmother uprooted and went with her husband to the edge of the Hawaiian Islands, which might as well have been the edge of the earth. Grandma made the most of it and was known in some circles as "Miss Kauai" for all the good things she did. As she drifted further and further away from reality, Grandma stayed sweet. Over the next couple of days, when she couldn't remember who I was, she kept asking my grandpa in the sweetest tone, "who is that nice young man visiting us?"

My grandfather was my role model growing up. He was funny, playful, and always willing to do something outrageous for a laugh. He used to ask my grandmother to sit down next to him and then pinch her butt on her way down. She would turn red and slap him on the arm and tell him to stop acting up in front of the children. He showed me that the bad boy could have a lot of fun.

My mom always complained about him, saying how mean he was, but she was a spoiled brat and couldn't be trusted. I guess the first clue that maybe she was right would have been the phone call informing me of the aborted murder/suicide. I had just lost out on a nationwide beer commercial that would have brought in a nice sum, so to numb the rejection and help my family, I told her I would fly over and investigate.

When we landed at Lihue airport, Nau, the local girl sitting next to me, welcomed me to Kauai by giving me her lei and a kiss on the cheek. She confessed the scent would fade, and the flowers would decay, and she didn't want a reminder of her ex. Plus, it would just piss off her mother, and she didn't need to start her summer break like that. I thanked her and asked if she wanted to get together, and she told me she was working at a place called Bubba's Burgers in Kapaa, and if I wanted to stop by, she'd hook me up.

We walked out into the baggage claim area, where the Hawaiian humidity smacked me upside my face. I hadn't noticed it changing terminals in Honolulu because it was raining. I realize it welcomes everyone to the islands, but sweating is not a good look for me.

Nau's mother and sisters charged her, whooping like an attacking tribe. They covered her in kisses and leis. It was beautiful and made me feel lonely. I scanned the small crowd for my grandfather, but he wasn't there. I would learn later that he had numerous post-it notes all over their apartment with my flight number and time of arrival, but he still forgot because, as I was also to learn, he too had started taking the off-ramp from reality.

I waited for a while and then decided to rent a car. I didn't have much money, and my credit card was rejected, but the guy at the counter gave me a huge break. He asked if I was a

Costco member because they had a lower rate. Unfortunately, I didn't have a membership, but when he said I didn't have to show him my membership card, he trusted me; I finally got what he meant. Because of his act of kindness, I had a car.

It wasn't far from the airport to Wilcox Hospital and Sun Village. I walked up to their second-floor apartment, noticing the beautiful birds of paradise flowers (Strelitzia reginae), red ginger, and yellow hibiscus that would have been crushed if my grandparents had followed through with their jump. I knocked, and as I waited, I leaned over the rail and looked up at the fourth floor. Yeah, I doubt they would have survived. I heard my grandfather's angry voice from the other side of his door. "Who are you, and what do you want?"

"It's me, Grandpa. Kimo."

"Who?"

"Kimo, your grandson from California. Remember I told you I was coming to visit."

I can hear my grandmother's gentle voice. "Who is it, Tom?"

He snaps at her, "Go back to your room, Anne."

"Grandpa, did you forget today was the day I was coming?"

He opened the door, and there was my grandfather in his blue cotton pajamas, a pair of Depends clearly visible under his pajama bottom shorts. "What's our relationship again?"

"I'm your grandson. Courtney's son, Kimo."

"Is Courtney with you?"

"No. She was just here."

"Good, she only wants my money." He opened the door and stepped aside. "Come in. Did you take the train?"

Okay, if the dig against his daughter, my mother, was a clue that flew right past me, this misunderstanding of reality landed. "No, you still have to fly to get here."

"Who is it, Tom?" my grandmother asks from somewhere in the apartment.

"It's me, Grandma, Kimo, your grandson."

"Come on out, Anne."

My grandmother walked out to the entryway, and I just had to smile. She was dressed the way I always remembered, a light-blue flowered print blouse over white slacks. She was a white person from the mainland, a proud mainland haole, unashamed by a history she had no part in, and the only thing she ever adapted from these islands was the Aloha Spirit. She embodied it. It illuminated her. Her hair was brushed back off her forehead, so her twinkling eyes were featured on her smiling face. "Hello," she said.

I walked over to her and gave her a bear hug, "Hi, Grandma." God, how I loved this woman! I released her so I could take the lei off me and anoint her with it. "Aloha, Tutu."

She looked a bit confused by the embrace. "Have we met?"

"Plenty of times. I'm your daughter Courtney's son, Kimo."

"Oh, okay." She had no idea who I was or who I was talking about.

"He's our grandson, Anne. You just forgot because you haven't seen him in a while." My grandfather looked at me. "Why is that?"

"I live in L.A., and it's expensive to get here."

"Oh, well, that's nice. Are you going to be coming to our house?" Grandma asked.

"We are home, Anne," my grandfather said impatiently.

"We are?"

My grandfather gave me a look that clearly displayed his impatience with her. "Where are you staying?" he asked me.

"I don't have a lot of money, Grandpa, and I was hoping I could stay here."

His frown was a cross between displeasure and panic, whether because he didn't want his routine disrupted or because he feared a witness wasn't clear at the time. "Well, I have another bed in my room, but will you be staying up late?"

It always seemed strange to me that my grandparents slept in separate bedrooms, but sleep is one thing, and sex is another. If you really want to sleep, then it makes sense to avoid the snoring, stealing of blankets, and gastrointestinal issues that can deprive it. "What's late?" I asked.

"We go to bed by seven."

"Is it even dark by then?"

"We're early to bed and early to rise."

"Well, I'll probably be up later than seven. Is that a deal-breaker? If you have a sleeping bag, I guess I could stay at the beach."

"That's against the law," he barked.

"You can come with us to our house," my grandmother offered.

"Damn it, Anne, we're home! This is it! We've lived here for seven years!"

The look on my grandmother's face broke my heart. She started to cry. I looked at my grandfather as he tried to get himself under control. "I'm sorry," he said.

I went to my grandmother and hugged her, feeling her frail body as she sobbed in my arms.

"I'm sorry, honey." My grandfather came over and cut in. I stepped back and watched my grandmother melt. "Shhhhhh, I'm sorry, Anne. You know I love you."

To be fair, Grandpa had been doing the thinking for both of them for over seven years while trying to keep up appearances to the world that all was well, and now he realized that he, too, was doomed to lose his mind. He's no Atlas and looked exhausted. What could I do to help? "Do you want me to make us lunch?"

"No, you're our guest. Sit with your grandmother, and I'll make us something."

He handed her off to me. "Anne, talk to your son, and I'll make us something to eat."

"Grandson."

"What did I say?" he asked.

"Son."

He looked closer at me. "What's our relationship again?"

"I'm Courtney's son. Kimo, your grandson."

"Yep. That's right. Kimo, sit and talk to your grandmother."

"I'd love to." I gladly took her, and we walked into the living room and sat on the couch. I never let go of her hand. "Grandma, do you remember the first time I fed the chickens?"

"No. Did you feed our chickens?"

"Well, I thought they ate eggs for breakfast, so I smashed their own eggs on the ground."

"Oh heavens! You are silly."

"I was a dumb kid."

"What happened to our chickens? I'm going to have to ask Tom what happened to our chickens. They were so cute. I loved those chickens!"

"Remember the church you used to take me to on Sundays?"

"No, I don't."

"It was kind of down in a gulch leaving Lihue and heading for Kapaa. All the old women would play their instruments and sing."

Her face brightened. "I do remember that! Immaculate Conception is the name of my church. I haven't been to mass in a long time. I don't remember the last time we went to church. I'm going to have to ask Tom why we haven't been to church. You remember how nice it was?"

"It's probably the most spiritual church I've been in. I used to love it when it rained because they had the windows open, and the sound of the rain just added a natural element to the whole experience. Those women singing the hymns in Hawaiian were full of the Aloha Spirit, and it just flowed through that place. Why don't we go tomorrow?"

"Is tomorrow Sunday?"

"No. But it won't hurt us to go even though it's not Sunday."

"That's true. Yes, let's do that. That sounds great."

"Do what?" Grandpa entered wearing a kitchen apron that says, "The Grillfather," with the logo of the puppet master from the *Godfather* movies.

"We're going to go to Immaculate Conception."

"Oh Lordy, why would you want to do that?"

"Why'd we stop going?"

"I don't know. But I did make us breakfast. Come to the table, everyone."

I helped my grandmother up, and we followed my grandfather to the dining room. "What was I going to ask him about?"

"Your chickens."

"That's right. Tom, where are our chickens?"

"What are you, a cop? What's with all the questions?"

We got to the dining room table, and three bowls were on placemats. Grandpa sat at the head of the table, and I sat across from Grandma. It looked like we were having cereal, except there were green flecks in the milk.

"Daddy, are you going to say a prayer?" my grandmother asked.

My grandfather frowned. "Oh, Lordy, didn't we stop doing that?"

"Why did we stop?" she asked.

My grandfather looked at her, then at me, but didn't answer.

"Well, can we say a prayer before we eat?" she persisted.

"Do you know one?" he answered.

My grandmother smiled. I could tell she was trying to think of a prayer, but just couldn't remember the words. My grandfather noticed, and to save her from frustration and possibly embarrassment, he jumped in with, "rub a dub dub, thanks for the grub. Yay God."

"Oh, you're silly!" my grandmother told her husband.

Yeah. He was silly, all right. Turned out we were having sour cream and chive crackers for our cereal. I told them I would take care of the meals for the rest of my trip. That first night as I was in their living room watching tv, Grandpa came out at 6:30 and asked if I was ready for bed. I told him that it was a little early for me and that I would watch the tube for a while. At 7:00, he came back in anger and loudly proclaimed, "are you going to stay up all night?" Not wanting to rock the boat, I went to the bathroom and got ready for bed. I laid awake for hours, listening to the unsteady snore of my childhood hero.

My first memory was walking back from the beach and my mom and grandma screaming when they opened the mailbox. Turned out there was a baby gecko hiding in there. My grandfather calmly got it out on an envelope and showed it to me, telling me that all of God's creatures are precious and shouldn't be harmed just because you're scared of them. This from the man who later would have hurled his wife off the fourth floor.

The next morning, I passed on another questionable breakfast and told them I was going shopping. Instead, I headed straight for Wilcox Hospital to meet with their doctor. I didn't have to wait long. The doctor was thrilled to see me so soon after the incident.

I told him about the green flakes in the milk, and he told me that the hospital sent over two meals a day, but my grandfather refused delivery because he was afraid of the cost. The doctor also told me he was about to recommend that my grandfather's driver's license be revoked. We both agreed that he wouldn't take that loss of freedom well, and I told the doctor about the post-it notes stuck all over his room and bathroom, reminding my grandfather who he was and the relationship he had with my grandmother. His brain was deteriorating, and he knew it, and that type of cognizant functioning shouldn't be behind the wheel of 3,257 pounds of Buick Skylark.

The doctor told me that soon they would both need to move to an assisted living residence, and he was especially nervous about how my grandfather would react. Obviously, he had become unstable, and the doctor had seen how families tend to terrorize the ones they love the most when they reach that state. We didn't come up with a firm plan before I left, but as soon as I walked out, I knew I needed to find a beach.

I wanted some peace, so I drove to Kalapaki. I thought that simply watching people surf would settle my mind. I parked, and on the way to the beach, I heard "Ku'u Home O Kahalu'u," by Olomana floating on the breeze. I followed the music upwind and discovered the source, speakers from a well-used pickup truck. An older man was waxing his board, and I noticed he had another board in the back of his truck.

"Howzit?" I asked, trying to sound local.

He looked me over with suspicion.

"I heard Olomana. My grandmother used to play them for me."

"You local?" he asked.

"No, but my grandparents are, and I've visited them a lot over the years."

"Oh yeah. Who are they?"

"Thomas and Anne Jones?"

"Auntie Anne?"

"Huh?"

"Auntie Anne from Immaculate Conception?"

"I don't know, but she used to go to Immaculate Conception."

He came over and held me like I was his brother, then pulled me in for a hug. Anyone's brother would feel weird by that public display from a stranger. "You look like her," he said. "Your tutu stay one saint. When did she pass?"

"She's not dead."

"For real? She never comes to church no more."

"She's got Alzheimer's, and my grandfather doesn't take her out much."

"Oh, that's too bad. Give her one hug for me, huh? Tell her it's from Kimo."

"That's my name!"

"For real? You named after me?"

"I don't know."

He broke into a big smile. "Let me tell you a story about your tutu. My daughter, Pua, was born with one cleft lip. You know what is?" I nodded, so he continued. "Your Tutu, Auntie Anne, organized one fundraiser so we could bring in one doctor from the mainland to fix 'um." He walked to the cab of his truck, pulled out his wallet from under the seat, and walked back to show me a picture. "Try look."

It appeared to be a high school graduation photo of a beautiful smiling girl covered with leis.

"Wow," I said. "She's gorgeous."

"Don't think like that about my daughter!"

"I wasn't thinking anything!" I said in a panic.

"Just kidding, bra. She stay gorgeous because of your tutu. So, haole Kimo, do you know how to surf?"

"Yeah."

"You like join me?"

"I'd love to!"

So, we waxed up both boards and paddled out. The board felt rough on my tender skin, and I realized that I wasn't in as good a shape as I thought because my shoulders and arms quickly tired. However, the warm Pacific Ocean saltwater flowing over me made me happy. I didn't care that the waves weren't huge. In fact, I was happy they were small. I respected nature and knew it was more powerful than me. Kimo led us out to the launch site, turned his board around, and sat up, a waterman comfortable in his element. Sitting on my board with another Kimo who knew and loved my grandmother was one of the best moments of my life. It was a true example of the Aloha Spirit, that love and kindness that flows through the people of the islands.

"Here comes a set, bra!"

I turned and looked around, and a reasonable-looking wave was heading our way.

"You catch dis one, and I'll get the bugga behind, huh!" Kimo said.

I started paddling long, strong strokes. The wave came, and I could feel it catch me, and suddenly I was pulled along, becoming part of it. I brought my arms down parallel to my chest and pushed up on the board, bringing my right foot up between my arms and swinging my left foot over to the center. I carefully stood up and reveled in the privilege of riding a wave. If you ever want to feel at one with nature and the mysterious energy flowing through this world, do yourself a favor and catch a wave and ride the face as long as you can. It is life.

I saw JJ's Broiler off in the distance and immediately thought of their Slavonic steak with its delicious sauce of garlic, wine, and butter. My grandfather used to take me there for their scrumptious specialty even before they moved from Lihue to the beach location. The thought distracted me from the moment, and I lost my balance and fell on my face into the wave.

Even small waves have power, and I went from being one with nature to getting pummeled by it. I was tossed around, and somehow one of my feet kicked me in the back of my head. It hurt, but more distressing was that I was out of breath. I didn't want to make it worse by panicking, so I made a mental point to relax and let the wave spit me out. Moments later, I realized that if I didn't fight to reach the surface, the wave would hold me under until I blacked out and drowned. I opened my eyes and looked for the light and then used every ounce of energy scrambling toward it! I finally broke through the surface and gratefully gasped for air.

I treaded water and took in oxygen, remembering that I didn't have insurance, and maybe the smart thing was to get back to my grandparents, the reason I was here. I saw Kimo riding the next wave coming right at me. He had a big smile on his face, and when he saw me, he gave me the shaka sign and cut back and flew out the back of the wave as I ducked under it. When I surfaced, he was back on his board and laughing.

"You okay, bra?" he asked.

"Yeah," I said. "I somehow hit the back of my head with my foot. I think I'd better get out and head back to my grand-parents."

"Okay. Just put the board in the back of the truck and give my best to Auntie!"

"Sure. Thanks, Kimo."

"No problem, haole Kimo!"

He turned and paddled back out, and I climbed onto my board and rode waves to the beach.

***

I stopped by Kentucky Fried Chicken and bought chicken pot pies, which I knew they liked because I no longer wanted soggy sour cream and chive crackers in milk. I knocked on the door, and my grandfather angrily opened it.

"Where have you been?"

"I had to wait until KFC opened," I lied.

"What?"

I slid past him, walked to the dining table, and emptied the bag. "Voila." I put the containers on the table and opened them to reveal the pot pies.

"I thought you were broke. We can't afford those."

"They're cheaper than you think. Where's Grandma?"

He focused on the food, and when he looked at me, he seemed confused.

"Grandma?" I reminded him.

"Anne, come here."

Soon she arrived in the dining room, and her eyes were red and wet as if she'd been crying. "Oh, I'm sorry. I didn't know we had company." She wiped her eyes and put out her hand. "Hello."

I ignored the hand and gave her a hug. "Are you okay, Grandma?"

"Oh my. Do I know you?"

"Yes, I'm your grandson, Kimo. I met a man who knows you also named Kimo, and he told me to tell you hello. He said you led a drive to get his daughter a surgery and that you're his hero. He knew you from Immaculate Conception."

"Well, isn't that nice?"

It was clear she had no memory of it. My grandfather had already sat down and taken a bite of his pie.

"Look what he brought us, Anne."

"What are those?"

"Oh, you know what they are," he said impatiently before looking back at me. "What are they called?"

"Chicken pot pies," I said.

"You like them, Anne."

"Of course I do, and why wouldn't I. They look good." She sat down and started eating. "Mmm, yes, I remember this."

"Grandma, I thought we'd go visit Immaculate Conception after lunch."

"Oh lordy, she doesn't need to do that," my grandfather said.

"I think it would be good for her," I replied.

"How do you know what is good for her? I said no!" He angrily took another bite from his pie. "How much longer are you planning on being here?"

"My return flight is the day after tomorrow."

"Good."

"I'd like to go to Immaculate Conception," my grandmother said.

Grandpa dropped his fork and gave me a dirty look. Why was he so angry?

"Stop being a stinker, Thomas. This nice young man cooked us a meal."

He looked from his wife to me, then back to his food. He moved some of the pot pie with his fork before looking back at me. "May I talk to you for a minute in my room?"

"Sure."

He looked at his wife. "Excuse us, Anne." Grandpa got up and led me to his bedroom. He turned around, and his head was framed by the post-it notes that he'd stuck all around the mirror over his desk; it wasn't quite a halo. "If you take her to that place, she will be recognized, and then people will know she's lost her mind."

"First off, Grandpa, it's not Sunday, so it's doubtful anyone will be there. Second, so what if people recognize her and find out about her condition? She's got an illness. It's nothing to be ashamed of."

"This is a small island, and people talk."

"It is a small island, but so far, the only talk I've heard about grandma has been great. She's loved, from what I've heard. Look, why don't you come with us and if we see someone we won't get out of the car. How's that?"

"I'm not going there!"

"Why not?"

"It's God's fault she's like this. He took my Anne away, and now he's coming for me!"

Okay. What do you say to that?

"All right, you don't have to go with us."

***

My grandmother and I finally made it to Immaculate Conception. The peace I felt there reminded me of my childhood when the weather suited my soul (thanks, Country Comfort). I didn't know when the last time my grandmother got out of the house, other than the trip up to the fourth-floor walkway for their potential leap, but she was very happy, unlike my grandfather, who silently brooded in his chair as we left.

Grandma was over-dressed in her white slacks and blue blouse, and her hair and makeup were done quite nicely, and looking at her, you'd never know she was a refugee of her embattled mind. She kept commenting on the beauty of the trees on our short drive to the church, and when she saw the chickens strutting around in the parking lot, she lit up like a little girl seeing the Easter bunny.

She was disappointed there were no people, thinking we were going to Sunday Mass and forgetting it wasn't Sunday. I sat in a pew and took in the peace that flowed through the open windows of the deserted church while my grandmother walked around like she was in a museum. "Who's that?" she asked, looking at a painting of Father Damien. I filled her in on how he sacrificed his own life in service to the banished lepers on Molokai. "Oh, isn't that nice?"

I thought about how dementia and Alzheimer's might be the new leprosy. I remembered that it wasn't the disfigurement or rotting skin that was the worst part of the disease for Hawaiians. It was being perpetually exiled to Molokai, finishing your time on earth in isolation, away from family and friends. It seemed that my grandfather had banished my grandmother to a life of exile in their apartment.

I felt sad, imagining it must torment him to have suffered through all these years with my grandmother's sickness only to realize that he had it too. What could I do to help? I only had one more day. Suddenly, the squawk of a chicken came from the back of the church.

"Awww, hi, little chicken," my grandmother cooed. She turned and gave me an effervescent smile that just lit up my soul. "Look, it's one of my chickens! Come here, dear." The chicken led my grandmother on a slow speed chase through the pews of the church before it ditched my grandmother and made an escape back out of the main door. Grandma looked weary from the physical exertion and noticed the font of holy water next to her, so she drank some to quench her thirst. I was sure God would understand.

***

We ate the leftover chicken pot pies for dinner. Grandpa was still holding on to the anger from earlier, so it was a fairly quiet meal. Grandma tried to get him to laugh at the chicken story, but he just said it was symbolic of anyone who would voluntarily step inside a church, and that hurt her feelings. I never saw this side when I was a kid—he was always encouraging or funny, and the love was unmistakable.

He sent my grandmother to bed after dinner, and while he also got ready for sleep, he allowed me to sit in his chair in the living room and turn on the tv. Everything came on earlier in Hawaii, and nothing captured my attention because I couldn't stop thinking about what I should do. Basically, my mom would have to come back and work with the doctor to get her parents the assistance they needed. It's brutal that they lived so far away, but they needed her help.

"Tom, I'm ready to go home."

I leaned over and saw my grandmother standing in front of my grandfather's bedroom door, still in the same clothes she wore to church and holding her purse. He opened his door and was already in his pajamas.

"Anne, for god's sake, we are home! Go take that makeup off, put on your pajamas, get in your bed and go to sleep!"

"We're spending the night?"

He shut his door in her face. I got out of the chair and walked over to the hall. "Hi, Grandma."

"Oh, hi. I forgot we're staying the night at your house."

"Well, is there anything I can help you with?"

"Oh no, honey. I can find what I need. I'm sorry to bother you. I get so confused sometimes."

"I had a good time with you today, Grandma. I'm glad you saw your chickens."

"Yes, aren't they sweet?"

"So are you." I went over and hugged her.

"Thank you. You're such a nice young man. Goodnight," she turned and walked back down the darkened hall.

The lullaby of reruns and the energy expended dealing with the elderly conspired with my grandfather's La-Z-Boy to entice me into a light sleep. I heard footsteps in the hall but let them pass without waking up. Finally, I was roused from my slumber by soft sobbing. In my twilight between conscious and subconscious, I couldn't quite figure out if it was coming from the tv or the apartment. Grudgingly, I forced myself awake and listened. It was coming from inside the apartment.

I got up and followed the sound. Weeping was coming from behind my grandmother's bathroom door. I put my ear to the door, and the sound broke my heart. I knocked softly. "Grandma?"

I carefully opened the door and found my grandmother on the floor in her pajamas.

"What's wrong? Are you okay?"

"Mommy got mad at me and hit me."

"Come here," I reached down and lifted her up and held her as she convulsively wept in my arms. "You're okay. I love you."

"Mommy didn't have to hit me."

Obviously.

"No, she didn't. Let me look at you." She looked so sad and vulnerable. Her cheek was red and puffy, but at least I didn't see any blood. I hugged her again. "You're going to be okay. Maybe it's a good idea to just get some sleep. It will be better in the morning."

"Okay."

I led her to her bed and gently helped her get under the covers. "I'll be right outside, okay?"

"Okay. Thank you."

I leaned down, kissed her forehead, and she said something I'll never forget but just remembered.

I spent the next few hours wide awake, once again listening to the labored breathing of my grandfather and wondering how a human being can sleep after hitting another human? I knew he was tired and afraid, but he hit my grandmother. How many other times had her skin been bruised or torn? We knew he had her up on the fourth floor, and it wasn't her idea, nor would she jump on her own.

What else had she been through that we don't know about, and what would happen to her after I left? What should I do? God help me!

I wrestled with what to do, crying in the bed, hating myself for what I was thinking, but I kept coming back to the look on my grandmother's battered face. I couldn't leave her alone to suffer through my grandfather's reign of terror. Sometime in the middle of the night, I decided that the only way I could make sure my grandmother stayed safe was to eliminate the threat. So, I took some deep breaths and asked for God's forgiveness.

I rose from my bed, took my pillow, and smothered the life out of my childhood hero.

SEVENTEEN

I wipe the tears from my eyes so I can see, knowing that I didn't tell Rachel the whole truth. Expressing what I did to my grandfather triggered a memory that I had buried and forgotten. That will have to wait until I'm in a confessional.

The engine hums, and *It's All Good* slices through the Delta, slapping the water out of its path. While I was confessing, we traveled under the Benicia Bridge, which is actually three bridges that cross the eastern edge of the Carquinez Strait connecting Solano County to Contra Costa County. The oldest bridge was built by Southern Pacific Railroad, and now the old railway bridge is between the two passenger vehicle bridges that are part of I-680.

I've crossed all three. I took the railway bridge coming back from L.A. on Amtrak's Coast Starlight, and I wish I could have left my emotional baggage at the station. It was three months after the death of my grandfather, and I was free-falling, and not in the good Tom Petty way. I was no longer interested in chasing Hollywood dreams because my nights were haunted by a succubus disguised as my good intentions. I clearly needed to retreat. Frank picked me up in Davis, and we detoured through the Delta on our drive back to Stockton. It was the second time I convalesced there, the first following our utter stupidity at Mavericks during college.

We are now approaching the Carquinez Bridge at the western edge of the strait. It connects the city of Vallejo to Crockett and is part of I-80, the connection between the Bay Area and Sacramento, the Sierra Nevada Mountains beyond the state capital, and my favorite destination, the northern shore of beautiful Lake Tahoe. Frank and I played the nine holes at Tahoe City many a Fourth of July.

Once we pass under these two bridges, we will leave the Carquinez Strait and enter San Pablo Bay. We'll then just have to flow through San Pablo Strait to enter San Francisco Bay and our destination. So far, so good.

It's been quiet since I finished my story, but Rachel breaks the silence. "No wonder you drink so much. Is that the real reason you're in jail?"

"No, I'm really in for the DUI."

"So, you were in prison before?"

"No."

"I don't understand. You killed someone."

"Nothing happened. I got my grandma out of there before she could see the body, took her to the Tip Top Café for breakfast, and called the doctor from there. I don't know if the doctor knew or suspected what really happened, but he never brought it up or did an autopsy. I think everyone just looked at it like a problem was solved. We moved my grandmother into assisted living, and life went on."

"So, you took a human life and got away with it."

"I'm not really sure I'd agree with that."

"You didn't go to jail for it."

"That is true. But I still don't think I got away with it. I know that I killed a person, and not just any person, but my own grandfather. That's hard to live with."

"How many people have you told?"

"You're the second person. Michelle was the first."

"How's your grandmother?"

"She died about a year later. Maybe we should check on Michelle. It's been quiet down there. You want to go check on them?"

"Not really. You can't just drop this on me and leave it."

"What do you mean?"

"Have you ever been to therapy?"

"No, I did AA in jail this year, well, some of the steps."

"I've been in therapy, and I don't usually admit this, but talking things out actually helps."

"Yeah. Telling you the truth did help."

"It didn't help me!"

"Oh. Sorry."

She's looking up as we flow below the first of the bridges known as the Carquinez Bridge. "Have you noticed that all these bridges are different?"

I look at the two bridges, having never thought about it before, but then quickly bring my focus back to the strait. "I never noticed that."

"Why?" She asks.

"Because I'm not the brightest?"

"Obviously, but why are they different?"

"I think they were all built at different times."

"They're like metaphors."

"Metaphors?" I ask.

"Yeah, they're different ways of doing the same thing."

"Metaphors, I thought they were symbols for something."

"Bridges! That bridge is the fifth we've seen in the last twenty minutes, and all have been different, yet they all have the same purpose."

I again glance up at the two bridges and contemplate what she said. "So, like, we're all on a journey from life to death, which is one side to the other, and the bridges are different ways to live?"

She looks at me and then back up to the bridges overhead. "Okay, I see that. I was thinking that they represent the different ways we have to solve our problems. Or, instead of life to death, maybe it's how to get from misery to happiness. Some are obviously heading in the wrong direction, and others are getting closer using intellect and feeling, heart and mind. You know who said that?"

"Liszt?"

She laughs. "That's funny. No, the Dalai Lama, dumb ass."

"Damn it. I'm 0 for two."

"One more strike, and you're out."

I don't have a comeback for this, and maybe I'm already out. We pass under the last bridge in silence.

Which direction am I heading?

She looks out to see what's in front of the boat. "I'm having a hard time with what you told me."

"I get that." I do. Some truths change things. You just have to decide how much time each conflict is worth.

"Killing a human being is a lot of baggage. I'm not sure I can deal with that," she adds.

"I know."

"I get that you were trying to help your grandmother, but..."

"There were other ways to handle it. Believe me, I know."

"And you know you can't drink your grandfather back to life."

She gives me a warm smile, once again stirring my libido, which obviously does not know nor care about timing or morality.

"Thanks."

Her smile fades, possibly reconsidering the truths she's learned about me. Rachel looks away, staring at the unknown of the approaching bay. Fear freezes her beautiful face. I look where she's looking and see we're coming upon Point Pinole, and beyond that, something that stops my heart.

One of San Francisco's famous landmarks comes into view. No, we're too far away for the Golden Gate Bridge or Alcatraz or Fisherman's Wharf.

Fog.

A wall of it, blowing like a giant sandstorm and heading our way.

"Do me a favor and ask Ron to come up and man his boat," I say, trying to hide my panic.

"Okay." She gets up and quickly climbs down the ladder. Lithe, that's what she is! I'm sure Rachel would come up with an appropriate metaphor, but the point is I loved watching her move.

Fog is often used as a metaphor to the point of cliche, the fog of war, the fog of dementia, even Dylan's "foggy ruins of time." The fog we're heading toward is the marine layer forced by the Pacific Ocean into the Central Valley. The massive difference between temperatures in the coastal waters and the inland valleys creates this moving mass of moisture. It's basically a cloud that's come to sit on the face of the earth, and I know how easy it is to get lost in that.

To the right of the fog bank and rising above it in the distance is Mount Tamalpais, a playground for many in Marin County. It isn't as tall as Mount Diablo, but it also has two peaks. The western one used to be the tallest until it was flattened for a radar dome, leaving the eastern peak with bragging rights. Speaking of radar, why doesn't this boat have it? Don't get me wrong, I love the boat, but it is so old I'm surprised it doesn't have galley slaves. I'd feel more confident if it at least had up-to-date technology. Let's face it, it's not all good.

On the Pacific side of Mount Tam are the majestic redwood trees (Sequoia sempervirens) of Muir Woods, a magical place I once took Michelle. The massive trees rise from the earth and inspire you to lift up your sight, looking beyond their crowns if you can and to the heavens, or at least the sun, or fog, depending on when you go. Putting my hands on the bark of one of these monuments to time, I could feel the energy, the life force that has flowed through them for hundreds of years, giving me a visceral connection to the past. And yes, I guess that makes me a tree hugger.

We were brought back to earth, and that moment, when we noticed a family of river otters joyfully playing in Redwood Creek. Michelle, who first was overjoyed at the sight, eventually grew melancholy and said she envied the mother. Maybe it was a premonition that she would leave this life childless. She would have been a wonderful mother. These trees, like other Native Americans, have seen their numbers butchered over time. In their lifetime of five hundred to eight hundred years, they've lost ninety-five percent of their kind. Michelle dying childless won't register on their rings, the scars of their lifetime.

Suddenly I once again hear the beginning notes of Liszt's "Hungarian Rhapsody number 2" rising from the belly of the boat. What is Rachel doing? How come Ron's not up here yet? I've slowed the boat, but the wall of fog is still heading our way. What should I do? I can't leave, I'm driving! What am I doing here? Why is Rachel playing music again? Did Michelle wake up and request it? Where is Ron, the captain of this boat? Hell, where's Frank?

I hear a low rumbling, like thunder in the distance. Just when I think I'm going to hyperventilate, I see a container ship emerge from the fog like a giant spaceship arriving to destroy planet Earth. Seeing that pushes me over the edge. Obviously, I'm no superhero. Granted, I've dealt with a couple of these goliath ships already, and I'm far enough over that the only thing I need to worry about is its wake, but why me?

The oncoming ship has effectively prevented me from turning around unless I wait for it to pass. I'd drop the anchor if I knew how, but that just makes me think of San Francisco's Anchor Steam beer, and now I'm thirsty as well as aggravated.

"Ron!"

Yeah, that's right, I'm yelling with more panic in my voice than is attractive. I'm glad Rachel isn't here to witness it.

"Frank!"

Rachel's playing of Liszt's rhapsody has reached a joyful tempo, and it's obvious to me no one below deck can hear my whining. So, without an audience, I decide to stop and just enjoy the scenery; after all, it's not every day you get consumed by a wall of fog.

I think of my grandfather. I could have done things differently. I could have protected my grandmother without killing him. I could have at least owned up to it. But I didn't. I've kept that secret buried deep within me, and even though it feels good to again let it out into the light, is it possible for me to ever find some kind of redemption for such a heinous act? The fog is cold and wet and engulfs me, closing out the outside world and leaving me alone on the bridge of *It's All Good* with the ghost of my grandfather.

Except I'm not alone. Sweet Michelle is below deck with her grieving husband. My best friend is down there too, and a lovely young girl with her whole life ahead of her is playing music to lift all our spirits. I've got to focus in order to keep us safe because I forgot about the wake of the container ship, and it blindsides the side of the boat and starts rocking us. I quickly turn the boat into the waves, and after bobbing up and down a bit, I turn back and accelerate until I feel us calm down. I slow the boat, thankful that I didn't run us into anything.

There are about ten yards of visibility, so I look for a green light to guide me in the mist. Eventually, the mist will clear, and I just need to remain patient. My senses are working overtime as I slowly move forward, the land barely visible off to my right through the fog. I can't remember if that's the port or starboard side and again question why boating needs its own terminology, though I realize it's been around for hundreds of years, and I could probably learn it with appropriate effort. I make a mental note that it's something I can do when I get back to prison if I get back. I figure we must be in San Pablo Straits when I finally see a green light! I focus on steering the boat to it, and as soon as I'm next to the buoy, I shut her down.

I hear horns in the distance blowing in a pattern. It must be a code that I'm sure Ron would understand. Rachel has finished playing Liszt's Rhapsody, so I hope that means someone is coming to relieve me. Haven't I done my time? It's hard to stay alert for so long! But, instead of getting a reprieve, I hear a crackling voice that sounds like it's coming from the great beyond. "Kimo, how's it going?"

Luckily, I don't wet my pants. After the shock-wave subsides and I realize it's not the voice of God, I can speak. "Hello?" I say meekly.

"Kimo, it's Ron. Pick up the walkie-talkie so we can talk."

I look around the cockpit and find the radio. I pick it up and speak. "Ron, do you think you could get the fuck up here and take over?"

Silence.

"Ron?"

The rhythmic blasts blow again. Obviously, they're on some sort of time management system between blasts. The answer is more silence.

"Kimo, you have to press the button on the microphone to talk. Otherwise I can't hear you."

Oh.

I find the button and push it. "Can you please come up and

take over? We're in fog, and I can't see shit!"

"Relax, Kimo. I'm at the lower helm and can see we're in fog. I'm assuming you shut off the engine because you're near a marker. That's not good. People are looking for the markers, and when they find them, that's what they'll focus on, and they sure as hell won't see us. You have to get us going again, so we don't get rammed into!"

"You know that would have been good information to have before you put your fucking boat into the hands of a rookie!"

"Okay, calm down, Kimo. Since we're drifting a bit, could you please quickly come down here?"

I look around and don't see anything in the ten-yard perimeter around the boat. "Are you sure that's a good idea?"

"If you can do it quickly, I think you'll understand," Ron says.

I look around again and then quickly make my way down the ladder, carefully, because I would hate to fall at this point. I make sure my feet are firmly on the deck before I head further down into the salon. Even though it's dark, I immediately notice that I don't see Michelle. Rachel is sitting at the makeshift keyboard, and Ron is at the lower helm. I also don't see Frank. Where are they?

"Look in our stateroom," Ron says.

I look at Rachel, who looks down at Ron and Michelle's bedroom. I walk over to the aft cabin and look in. I can see Michelle lying on the bed. I walk down into the room, and it's like descending into her crypt, and it's getting darker and creepy. I'm forced to slide around the bed to get closer for a better look at Michelle's body; only she's not dead; it's worse.

Her body convulses with tremors. It's a constant barrage of twitches, flutters, and spasms. Each propulsive force seems to spit out a bit of her remaining spirit. Michelle is about to leave this earth. Her body rejecting its beautiful host is the single most haunting image burned into my memory of lovely Michelle, and this ugly death will push itself to the front and rudely interrupt every lovely memory I have of her.

She's slipping away, and there's not a damn thing I can do about it but cry. My tears are set free, and it's a deluge. This kills me, and I can feel a part of my soul deaden, just like after my grandfather.

Ron states the obvious. "Her body is shutting down."

EIGHTEEN

"Kimo, you've got to get us moving again," Ron commands.

I turn away from Michelle and look at her husband.

"You want to keep going?"

"Of course I do. It's what she wanted, and the music actually helps!" Ron seems a little too excited, and I think the tequila might be talking. I look at Rachel, but she nods in agreement. I trust her judgment.

"Do you know what you could do to help me?" Ron says.

"What, Ron?"

"Get us to the Golden Gate Bridge."

"You realize I can't see a damn thing out there."

"Look, the light you've stopped at is most likely Point San Pablo. We're here! This is the start of San Francisco Bay! Keep going southwest until you get to the Richmond/San Rafael Bridge. Once we get there, it's due south until you pass Angel Island, then it's a straight shot west to the Golden Gate."

"You know these waters, Ron, I don't! How the hell am I

going to know which way is southwest when I can't see?"

"You were a teacher, weren't you? Didn't you teach your students how to read a compass? If I didn't think you could do this, Kimo, believe me, I wouldn't ask. I want us to live."

"Can't Frank do it?"

"Uh, my brother is passed out where you slept last night. When he comes to, I'll definitely send him up."

I look back at Michelle. I don't have a good feeling about things, but looking at my beautiful young friend suffering definitely doesn't lend itself to feeling good about anything. What's the best thing I could do for her now? "So, I just head southwest and hope I hit the bridge?"

"We'd all appreciate it if you wouldn't hit the bridge."

"What if I don't see it? How will I know if I've gone too far?"

"If you run aground on San Quentin, you've missed it."

"The prison?" I ask, conjuring a disturbing image of myself locked up there when this is over.

"That's on the other side of the peninsula. If you beach us there, then you've done some interesting work with the compass."

Before I can answer, we're interrupted by a blast of horns that sound like angels heralding Judgment Day.

"Holy fuck!" screeches Rachel.

Her reply breaks the tension, acting as comic relief because the way she said it cracks up Ron and me.

"What the hell was that, captain?" I ask Ron.

He smiles at Rachel. "That's the way we communicate in the fog, Rachel."

A wave broadsides the boat, and I knock my head on the stateroom ceiling before falling into the bed next to Michelle.

As the boat rights itself, I roll onto her. The tension's back. I don't want to smother her, so I grab her arms to push myself away, and I can feel the vibrations rolling above her bones. She's still alive, but the tube from the morphine drip has torn out of her arm. Michelle's eyes remain closed as I arrange her back onto the center of the bed. I look for Ron's guidance.

"Should I try to put that back in?"

"Do you think there's a point?"

I think there would be a point if we were going to crank it up and pull a Sigmund Freud. Maybe she's already had enough. I would like to do anything that would give her peace, but I'm not going to even try to reconnect the tube to her boney arm. I guess I'll have to go up top and do my best to get us to the Golden Gate Bridge.

"Kimo, you might want to hurry up. From how loud those horns were and the waves of the wake, I'm thinking that it was a ship passing us and heading in our direction. You could follow its lights all the way to the bridge!" Ron says.

"What about us? I know we packed an air horn. Shouldn't I be using that?"

"Yes, now you're thinking! Make one prolonged blast every two minutes."

"Let me get this straight. You want me to drive this thing, using a compass to navigate, blow the horn every two minutes, all while not being able to see diddly squat! And I'm supposed to do this alone?"

He turns to the foredeck. "Frank!"

Nothing.

Ron turns back to me. "Yeah, I guess so. He's in no condition to help right now. You can do this!"

"What about Rachel? It'd be nice to have another pair of eyes up there to help me."

"She's needed here. I'll send Frank up when he's available."

I look over at Rachel. She smiles and says, "I have faith in you. Just be careful."

How can she have faith in me? She knows I murdered my grandfather. But she also knows I love Michelle and would do anything for her, even if I'm not completely on board with this plan now that the blind are leading. If this is what I need to do, then I'll do what I can. I head for the stairs.

"Kimo?" Ron stops me.

"Yes?"

"The air horn," he hands me the tool.

"Right. What do I do with this again?"

"Give it a long blast every two minutes, so people know we are on the move."

"I don't have a watch."

"Use your phone."

"Dude, I've been in jail for a year. I don't have a phone."

"Rachel, can Kimo use your phone?"

"Mine's dead," she says.

"Look, Kimo, get up there and get us moving, and I'll send up Frank's phone. Follow the ship's lights."

So, I head back up to the bridge with a new tool to use in the darkness. And I mean darkness because there are no ship's lights to follow. I'm too late. What the hell am I doing here, anyway? My seamanship skills are nonexistent! I look around the perimeter of the boat, and at least it seems like the fog has thinned a bit. I can see about twenty to thirty yards out now. So, I guess I'll just have to use the compass and head southwest.

I give the airhorn a blast and turn the key. The engines sputter but don't start. I try again, and to my relief, they fire up. I ease the throttle and get us moving very slowly.

I know there are real dangers out there that I can't see, ships, bridges, land, and even scarier things that aren't out there but are lurking about in my own mind. I just need to go slow, keep breathing, and don't give in to fear.

"Kimo."

I scream like a little girl and almost jump out of the chair! Luckily my heart is kept in by my ribcage, or it would have broken out in wild panic. I look over and see Rachel finish climbing up to the bridge.

"Rachel, what the hell are you doing sneaking up on me like that?"

She laughs. "Relax, I wasn't sneaking up on you. I brought you Frank's phone."

"Oh. Thanks." She hands it to me. My heart still protests as it tries to regulate.

"Are you okay?"

"No, I'm not okay. I'm stressed out up here."

"This fog is intense."

"Oh, I'm tense all right. I don't know why we're doing this."

"It was your idea."

"Well, I didn't think I'd be driving this thing. And the fog was never part of it. I don't know why Ron isn't up here driving his own boat."

"Are you blind? Didn't you just see his wife? He's down there lying next to her and cradling her in his arms, trying to bring her some comfort! Stop being so selfish."

"I'm not being selfish! I want us to live. I'm being smart. I don't want to crash us into anything and sink. I could at least use another pair of eyes. Why can't he put on one of the playlists we made for her so you could help me up here?"

"That's not a bad idea. I'll suggest it, and when Frank wakes up, he can relieve me, and I'll go back and play some more."

"Good. Thank you."

She starts climbing back down the ladder.

"Oh, Rachel! Could you maybe bring me something to eat and drink, nonalcoholic, and would you ask Ron if he has another layer that I could put on? This fog is wet and really getting cold. You know what Mark Twain said?"

"Who?"

I can't tell if she's messing with me or not. I know a lot of my students didn't like to read. I'm about to enlighten her when she says, "'The coldest winter I ever spent was a summer in San Francisco.' Yeah, my dad used to say that every time we took a visitor to the city."

"Oh, good. I forgot your dad is a professor. I'm just making the point that I am getting cold."

She smiles. "I know how I could warm you up."

"Good god, girl, how can you think like that in this situation?"

"No one would be able to see us. We could go to the bow and reenact that scene from *Titanic* only we could do it naked!"

"You've got to stop. Maybe you should see if you can wake Frank up. You just might be a fatal distraction."

"You're no fun," she teases and disappears down the ladder.

I'm worried about her. Her relentless focus on sex might be a continuation of her cutting behavior. Is she using sex to distract or validate herself? Considering the circumstances, it doesn't seem like a healthy sex drive to me, even if I'm the beneficiary.

Anyway, I'll deal with that later because now I have to focus. I look at the compass and see we're heading east, and that's not good. We could run aground in Richmond or, worse, be sliced in half by a ship heading north from San Francisco or those going our way, for that matter.

So, I turn the boat around, but it's not as easy as turning a car. The water is always moving and a bit choppy, and going this slow hampers maneuverability. I keep an eye on the fog to see if anything breaks clear, then glance back at the compass and adjust until we're roughly heading southwest.

I don't know how long it's been, so I give another blast from the air horn just to warn anybody who might be close. I get nothing in return, and we haven't crashed into anything, so I feel good about things.

I'm going to be grateful for the small victories, and hopefully, that will keep me calm and the fear at bay. I remember an affirmation that may also help, "The Living Spirit Almighty flows through my thoughts, words, and deeds, and the Living Spirit Almighty is working on my behalf." It works and calms me down. It never hurts to have a power greater than oneself helping.

I hear five quick bursts coming from somewhere ahead and wonder what it means. I keep making small adjustments with the steering wheel to keep us going in a relative southeast direction, but I have no idea how far it is to the next bridge or body of land. I can no longer see land on my right, even though the fog isn't as dense as it was earlier. Did we drift too far toward the Richmond side while I was below deck? I haven't seen a red light, but I haven't seen a green one either.

I simply have no idea where we are. I strain to hear something, anything, but it's strangely silent except for the soft rumbling of our engines. I guess most boaters find out what the weather's going to be before they go out and are smart enough to stay at the dock during fog.

Once again, I hear Rachel playing music downstairs, and I think it might be "Reverie" by Debussy. A student of mine played it at a school talent show. Unless you're a parent, those concerts can be like passing a kidney stone, but this girl did a good job. She's not as good as Rachel, but it was no stone. Anyway, I guess my idea about using a playlist so I could have another pair of eyes out here for our safety slipped her mind, not to mention my hunger and thirst. That's twice she's forgotten about me.

"Holy smokes, why are we boating in this?"

I've never been happier to see Frank! "You're alive!"

Frank climbs up the ladder and hands me a cool-looking red raincoat and matching pants. "I was told you were cold." He then tosses me a plastic baggy, "And hungry."

"Thank you, my man! But is plastic good on a boat? Isn't it bad for fish if it goes into the water?"

"You don't have to eat it, just don't let it fall overboard. Move over and let me drive."

"My pleasure." I get out of the captain's chair and move behind it to slip the pants on over my shorts. It's a tight fit. I then put the raincoat on. "Much better. Thanks."

"Where are we?" Frank asks.

"I really have no idea. Ron told me to head in a southwest-erly direction and look for the San Rafael/Richmond Bridge." I open the plastic bag and pull out a handful of almonds, chocolate chips, and dried apricots, and pop them in my mouth. "Mmm, good trail mix!"

"Can I have my phone?"

"Sure." I need to put the food down and reach under the outer pants and into my shorts to fish his phone out of my pocket. Unfortunately, Ron's pants are too snug, so I shimmy them down around my ankles to get to the phone.

While I'm doing this, Frank lets out a blast from the air horn that shocks me, and I lose my balance and trip from the mess around my ankles. I hit the floor hard. Luckily, my eighth-grade judo kicks in, so I turn and break my fall by slamming my arms, hands down and exhaling when I hit the deck. Unfortunately, Frank's phone is in one of my hands when I bring it down, and, uh, I'm pretty sure it didn't survive. "Frank..."

"Quiet!" Frank snaps back.

I pick myself and as many parts of his phone as I can find up before I look at Frank. He points the airhorn again and pulls the trigger. "Hear that?" He says.

"No," I admit. "What am I listening for?"

"The echo. There's land off our starboard side."

"And just to be clear, that's the right side, right?"

"Yes. Get up to the bow and keep a lookout."

"Uh, Frank, here's your phone." I hand him what I have from his phone.

He takes it. "What the hell did you do to my phone?"

"Well, I was trying to get it out of my pocket, and you blew the horn, and I tripped over these new pants and, uh, broke my fall with your phone. Sorry."

"You fucking dumb ass! I was going to use the GPS to find out where the hell we are! That was the last connection we had to the outside world, and you fucked it up like you've fucked everything else up! Why the hell did my brother listen to you?"

"I'm sorry, Frank. I wish I had an answer to that."

"Why did I agree to come on this stupid trip?"

"Well, I think you were trying to impress Rachel."

"Shut the fuck up and get to the bow! That's the front of the boat, idiot!"

All right. It seems like Frank's still angry. I'm sure he's probably hungover, or maybe even still a little drunk, and his broken phone doesn't help. I leave the bridge only to stop at the stairs leading down into the salon to watch Rachel play.

I'm mesmerized by her amazing talent. Her music uplifts me, and I completely understand why Ron would want her to play for Michelle rather than a prerecorded playlist. I flash on the quote by Kahlil Gibran, "Music is the language of the spirit. It opens the secret of life, bringing peace, abolishing strife." Why can't I ever think of these quotes when I'm talking with Rachel?

I ponder the quote as I make my way to the bow, hoping that the music is bringing Michelle peace. I also hope it's affecting Frank. I step down onto the starboard walkway. It's larger than a balance beam in gymnastics, but not enough to give me confidence considering the ceaseless motion of water. Like a wimp, I squat down so I can put both hands on the rail and kind of duck walk slowly until I get to the bow. It's not dignified, and it's killing my thighs, but I don't want to fall overboard, especially at this point since I'm not sure Frank would even bother to stop and look for me.

Friends...

NINETEEN

"Kiss my aft, Frank!"

That's what I wish I would have said to him when he told me to come to the bow and called me an idiot. Don't you just hate it when you think of a comeback minutes after the moment you needed it. That's what happens when you're tired, and I admit it, I'm tired.

I usually spend the day after Angelina's on Frank's couch, barely moving and not thinking about much, but no, here I am, wherever we are, bouncing up and down at the bow as we chop through the water and head deeper into the fog, and I'm forced to focus because we could all die out here. But then, one of us already is.

Rachel is playing Stravinsky's "Rite of Spring." The beginning is soothing, so I hope it's bringing Michelle and Ron comfort. Suddenly the music changes and seems to mirror more the mood of angry Frank, who is looking down on me from the bridge. I know he's just worried, but his bad attitude isn't good for anybody, and the music reflects that. I don't know what Rachel is thinking, but I hope she changes the tune soon. In the meantime, I need to find a way to calm Frank down.

"Whatever happened to Joy?" I yell up to him.

"You sucked it all out when you talked my brother into killing his wife."

"Frank, you know that's not what happened. Besides, I was talking about the cat."

"What?"

"The little kitty that homeless guy gave us. Didn't he say its name was Joy?"

"Oh. The kitten. She was sleeping with me while I was passed out. She's now with Ron and Michelle."

"Do you think animals can sense death?"

"Would you please just shut up and pay attention?"

Okay, so Frank's not ready to play nice. I turn back to watch and listen. The wind has picked up, and it's a lot more turbulent up here. I wish I had a seat or some cushions or Rachel. I'm thinking about what she said about doing a naughty recreation of the scene from "Titanic." What's the matter with me? I need more control over my thoughts. I might need to suggest some kind of mindfulness class when I get back to prison, or maybe Tai Chi, some tool that integrates the mind, body, and spirit, and helps find inner peace. I need something that leads to transformation. Instead, I hear a foghorn blow. Not our little airhorn, but a loud one that seems to come from the sky. I hope it's not Gabriel.

"See anything?" I can hear the panic in Frank's voice.

I look up in the direction from where I think the sound came but only see different swirling shades of gray like rapidly changing images one sees in clouds. "I don't see anything! Hit the horn!"

Frank lets our horn blow. It is followed by another loud blast coming from the fog, only closer this time. I still can't see a thing, but I think I hear the rumblings of powerful engines and water being displaced.

"Anything?" Franks asks.

"I think I hear motors!"

"They've got to see us on radar, right? I'm going to move us over more!"

Suddenly I see it, water being thrust aside by the stem bulb of a huge steel bow slicing through the water coming toward us! "Ten o'clock, Frank! It's at ten o'clock!"

"I see it! Hold on!"

Frank pushes the throttle and whips us to the right, throwing me into the rail. As I fall, my scream is drowned out by another long blast from Gabriel's horn. I grab onto the railing, but I'm not sure I'll make it. I drop to the deck, throw my feet around one of the poles, and wrap them around it as I slide closer to the edge. I guess this is what I deserve, to be tossed overboard and sink into the murky darkness of the abyss. If there is life after death and I meet up with my grandfather, maybe I can explain why I did what I did to him.

Only, I want to live!

I don't want to die, and maybe I don't deserve life because of what I've done, but I'm not ready to leave this world or meet my maker. I don't want to account for my sins just yet, so I hold on. My arms feel like they're being pulled from their sockets like I'm being tortured on an ancient rack. God, forgive me, and please protect us!

I can no longer see the ship, but I feel the waves of its wake. Frank has us parallel to them, so when they hit us amidships, we're knocked sideways. Every time we slip down the trough, I get closer to dropping over the side, and each crest is a reprieve where I can scramble back and fix my grip.

I feel like a bug in a sink frantically trying to save itself from flowing down the drain. Up, down, knocked around like dice in the hands of a gambler on a losing streak. I'm hoping for a winning toss. My hands feel like the skin is peeling off and I'm losing my grip. Finally, the waves die down, and I no longer need to struggle to stay on deck. I've escaped the drain.

"That's it!" screams Frank. "This is stupid. What the fuck are we doing out here? I can't see shit, and that fucking ship could have run us over and never even noticed! I'm done!" He turns off the engines.

We're still alive!

I catch my breath and sit up, trying to get the circulation back to my fingers. Frank does have a point. I look around for my baggy of trail mix and come to the realization that it must have slid overboard. On top of everything else, now I'm a menace to the environment. It's time for me to go back to jail, but first, I feel it's important to tell Frank what Ron told me about staying still out here in the fog. I thank God for protecting me, then slowly get up, and my unsteady sea legs take me to the bridge.

Frank trembles in the captain's chair. "Did you see the size of that fucking ship?" Frank mumbles catatonically.

"Yeah, at the beginning, then I kind of was busy just holding on."

"What are we doing out here? I love Michelle, but I don't want to die. I think your idea is fucking stupid, and Ron's suicidal and doesn't give a shit."

"I don't think he's suicidal. He told me that in the fog, it's important to keep moving so other boats don't hit us. If he were suicidal, he wouldn't tell me that because he wouldn't care."

"But we were moving, and we almost got squashed like a grape by that fucking aircraft carrier! No, I'm done."

"So, what now?"

"I feel like grounding the boat and waiting for the fog to clear. We shouldn't be out here. If we get killed, people will say we had it coming because we're fucking stupid idiots! And they would be right!"

A fading blast from the ship echoes through the fog as if it agrees with Frank.

"Do you think that ship knows where they are?" I ask.

"Of course. They travel across oceans and have the latest technology."

"Men have been traveling across oceans since the dawn of time without technology. The Vikings made it to North America in the tenth century. The Hokulea proved that Polynesians discovered Hawaii around 500 A.D."

"What's with the history lesson, mister teacher?"

"I'm just saying it doesn't take modern technology to cross waters."

"Yeah, well, Columbus thought he was in India. He had no idea where the hell he was, and neither do we. Should we follow in his footsteps?"

"Well, he does have a holiday in his honor," I point out.

"And why the fuck is that?" Frank asks. "He never even made it to the United States."

"You can blame my religion."

"Really?"

"Yeah. Catholics wanted a holiday, so the Knights of Columbus lobbied congress, and FDR had it declared a national holiday in the late 1930s. The first Columbus Day celebration happened in San Francisco back in the 1860s, celebrating Italian Americans."

"You should get back into teaching. You know so much shit."

"I don't think a school would take me."

"You got drunk, dude. It's not like you killed anybody until this trip."

Do I tell him? I don't see how it will help considering the circumstances. It would just be more fuel for his fire, and I need to calm that down.

"You have to admit this is pretty cool. Just be quiet and listen. What do you hear?"

Frank gives me a look as if I've lost my mind. "What kind of question is that?"

"Just take a deep breath and tell me what you hear."

"I hear an idiot asking stupid questions."

"Okay, what else?"

"I hear Rachel playing."

"Yeah, isn't that beautiful? She's so talented. What else?"

"I hear water."

"Think about that. Where's that water been? Where's it going? I can also feel water because that's what fog is. Did you know that all substances can be a liquid, a solid, and a gas?"

"Are you high?" Frank says.

I laugh. "No, but my senses are heightened. Remember Mavericks?"

"Of course I do. What does that have to do with anything?"

"My senses were heightened then, too."

"Uh oh, we almost died."

"No, we were totally alive."

"We were young and stupid. And extremely fucking lucky."

"Yes, we survived."

"Not because of anything we did!"

"Is that how you remember it?"

"You know I don't remember anything after the fall! What's your point?"

"What do you remember?"

"I remember paddling out and not making it."

"Seriously, what's the last detail you remember?"

He thinks. "I remember the size of that wave."

I laugh, "Thinking about it now, didn't it seem like the size of that ship that just passed!"

He joins my laughter. "Yeah, well, fish stories."

"What was your last conscious thought, Frank?"

He looks away. Finally, he turns back to me. "Indecision."

"Indecision? That's interesting. You've never told me that before."

"You dove under, and I looked up mesmerized. I hesitated, then thought I had time to go over the top. And, as you know, I ate it. That moment when I knew I wasn't going to make it and would drop was the scariest moment of my life. Until now."

"You survived."

"You saved me."

"No, it was the waves."

"Huh?"

"The waves saved us. The same waves that got us into that mess were the ones that spit us out."

"Take some credit, Kimo. You know you did it. I don't know if I've ever thanked you enough. Thank you, bro."

He gets out of the chair, comes over and hugs me. There's no pretense. It catches me by surprise, and I'm touched. "Best thing I ever did, Frank."

He kisses me on the cheek. "You're my best friend. I missed you this year. I love you."

"I love you too, Frank. So, does this mean you forgive me?"

He releases me and looks me in the eyes. He's about to say something but instead looks down and points his ear to the joyous sound coming from below deck. "Listen to her."

I do, and her music seriously soothes my soul. If it does that for me and obviously Frank, it has to be a solace for Ron and bring comfort at some level for Michelle.

Frank says, "She's perfect."

"Nobody's perfect, Frank. She's got issues."

"Yeah, two perverted older men!"

"She had issues before us. She was a cutter."

"A what?"

"A cutter. Someone who cuts themselves to deal with the

pain in their lives."

"Rachel? That beautiful girl cuts herself?"

"I don't know if she still does, but she did when she was younger."

"Holy smokes. I can't believe that. You know, I was having such a good time with her. I never even thought about the fact that she could have pain in her life."

"Come on, Frank, everybody has pain. It's amazing what some of my students were dealing with before they even stepped into my classroom each morning, abuse of all kinds, sexual, physical, and emotional. And the masks they develop. Kids can be hard to penetrate. They look okay, but under the masks, they're suffering and terrified. That was probably the hardest part of teaching."

"How can you be a teacher and have to deal with things like that?"

"Well, I'm not a teacher anymore, Frank, remember? I'm a convict."

"Yeah, well, we're all doing time. It's going to end someday. I see it every day in my job, and business is steady."

"So, what are we going to do?" I ask.

Frank looks around. "I really don't like our situation, and I definitely don't want to be stuck out here when it gets dark."

"What time is it?"

"I don't know. You broke my fucking phone!"

"I really am sorry about that, Frank."

"You've been nothing but trouble since you showed up. This stupid, immoral trip, my phone, you're like the four horsemen of the apocalypse all in one."

"That would make me one badass rider."

"No, that makes you a pain in my ass."

"Like you were a pain in Rachel's."

"Shhhh, don't talk about that! I can't believe I did that."

"We're just a ship of fools."

"I know that's the name of a song from one of the bands you like."

"World Party."

"Whatever. It would be foolish and wrong for us to keep going," Frank states, then asks, "Who are the four horsemen of the apocalypse, anyway? One of them is death, right?"

"Yeah."

"Then what, social media?"

"That's funny, Frank, but I don't think they had that when Revelations was being written."

"They had to have something similar. Gossip, is gossip one of the riders?"

"Gossip is the Devil's Radio, according to George Harrison, but it's not one of the horsemen."

"Gluttony?"

"That's one of the seven deadly sins, Frank."

"Stupidity?"

"Well, it should be, and lord knows we've got that covered."

"You're the Catholic school teacher. What's another one?"

"War."

"War? You've already got death, isn't that redundant?"

"It's all interpretation, Frank. Different scholars have different opinions."

"Well, mine would be death, social media, politics, and global warming."

"That's as good as any I've heard. Now, what do you want to do?" I ask again.

"There really aren't any good options, are there?"

"What are our options, Frank?"

"Well, the first one I can think of is we could get squished like a bug by one of those fucking mall-sized tanker ships out here."

"I don't like that one, Frank. What else?"

"We could deliberately ground the boat, radio the Coast Guard and wait to be rescued."

"So, we'd put their lives at risk for our own stupidity."

"That's what they get paid for. It's our tax dollars at work. Besides, they're well-trained and better equipped than we are. It's their job."

"So, we run aground, wreck Ron's boat, and wait for the Coast Guard to find us. When they finally show up, they find an escaped convict, Michelle, who may or may not be dead by then, her morphine, Rachel's pot, empty tequila, champagne, and beer bottles. Mmm, how do you think that will go over on social media?"

"Obviously, if you put a negative slant on it like that, it doesn't sound good. It would probably go viral, and we'd be canceled. What do you want to do, Kimo?"

I smile at him, "Dragonfly, baby."

"What the hell does that even mean?"

"We have to live like dragonflies!"

"They have a short lifespan! I don't want a short lifespan. I want to live to be an old fucker."

"Well, you're not that far off."

"I have a long time to go unless we don't make it through this night. Why do you want to keep going? Do you have a death wish, Kimo?"

"Not at all. But it was Michelle's wish. I just want to honor that."

"That's sweet and noble of you. But look around. We can't even find the Richmond Bridge. How do you propose we find the Golden Gate?"

"Patience. Ron said to head south and then west. You did a great job figuring out where land was from the echo of the horn, and you got us out of the way of that ship! We can do this!"

"Kimo, I love my brother, and I love Michelle, but this is

not smart. We should head north, out of the fog, and go home. Look, have you seen Michelle in the last couple of hours?"

"Yes, while you were passed out."

"So, you've seen the twitching and jerking. The hospice nurse told us about that. It's one of the symptoms of active dying. She's not going to know if we made it to the Golden Gate Bridge or not, Kimo. The last thing she'll remember was we were on our way. Mission accomplished. For Christ's sake, let's chalk it up as a win and go home alive."

"What about your brother?"

"He hasn't been thinking straight in weeks! He's already won. He gets to bury her in the plot he chose for her and be able to visit her anytime he wants! We've done what we set out to do."

"Maybe you're right," I admit. Maybe I just don't want this to end because next up for me is going back to prison, only longer than the three weeks I had left before I decided to escape to play in Angelina's. "If Ron is okay with it, then I am."

Rachel's music stops mid-song. The hair on the back of my neck bolts up; something's not right.

"Michelle," Frank says her name like the inevitable has happened.

We both get up to investigate when Ron comes up quickly from below. "We're taking on water! We've got a leak!"

TWENTY

"Everybody put on a life jacket!" Ron orders us.

"Are we going to sink?" I ask.

"If we don't find and plug the leak, we will," Ron says as he heads back down. I look over at Frank, and he just shakes his head in anger.

We quickly join Ron below deck, which is a bit claustrophobic with everyone down here together. Rachel already has a life jacket on and is helping put one on Michelle. Ron tosses a couple to Frank and me. I undo the latches and slip it over my head. Unfortunately, I put it on inside out the first time, but because everyone else is busy with theirs, no one notices. I flip it over and put it on right. I fasten both the straps and tighten the lower belt so it's snug.

"Ron, this seems too big for Michelle," Rachel says.

"You're right. There's a child's vest on the fore deck. Frank, can you get that?"

Frank finishes putting his on. "Of course." He disappears

into where I slept last night, and he passed out earlier.

"How'd you discover the leak?" I ask.

"Joy," Rachel answers.

Ron takes over the story. "The kitten was snuggling with us until it jumped off the bed and started splashing and screeching. I reached over to get her, and she was struggling in about six inches of water all around our bed. Where is she, by the way?"

"Still on the bed," Rachel says.

I look over and see the soaked little kitten. With its fur slicked tight against its minuscule body, she looks like a feline replica of Michelle. Frank returns with a child's life vest, and he helps Rachel put it on Michelle. It's still too big for what's left of her.

"Ron, you don't have an infant-sized vest, do you?" Frank asks his brother.

"No. That will have to do. Get her up in her chair. Rachel, stay with her, please. Frank, radio the Coast Guard with a mayday call. Channel sixteen!"

"What do I tell them?"

"Tell them what our situation is. Where we are, how many people are on board, the name of the boat."

"We don't know where we are, Ron."

"San Francisco Bay!"

"Oh. Okay."

"Kimo, get the emergency kit and then help me find the leak."

"Ron?" Frank says timidly, tears building in his eyes.

"What?"

"I hit the bridge going under I-5 earlier. Could that have caused the leak?"

Uh oh. Ron asked me to check for a leak, and I got distracted by my libido. Why am I such a fuck up?

"Possibly. But I haven't given my boat any love since

Michelle got sick, so whatever the problem is, it's my fault. I should've checked out my boat to see if it was seaworthy, but I didn't. It's been way over a year, and that's on me. I'm sorry, Frank."

Great. Ron takes the blame. He is such an honorable guy. Good for Michelle. She picked the right man to spend what little time it turns out she had. Can I fall further from grace?

"Should I get us heading north to get out of the fog?" Frank asks.

"Not yet. Let's find the leak first. Did you hit the bridge on the starboard side?"

"Yeah, aft."

"That would make sense considering where we found the cat. Get Michelle on deck. Then you go to the bow. We need to redistribute the weight, and maybe we can keep the leak above the waterline. We have too much weight down here, and if we powered up the boat, that could possibly thrust the leak below the waterline and make things worse."

"No offense, Ron, but maybe you'd be better up at the bow. Let Kimo and I look for the leak."

"What are you saying? Are you calling me fat?"

"No," Frank is digging himself in deep.

"It's okay, you're right. I've put on a few pounds this last year. Now can you please get my wife up top?"

"Of course."

He gently lifts Michelle up and then carefully puts her over his shoulder in a fireman's carry. "Rachel, could you please make sure I'm not going to knock her head going up?"

"Sure." Rachel calmly holds Michelle's head, and they go on deck.

"Okay, Kimo, go to the refrigerator in the galley and empty a container that we can use to bail out this water." I'm about to talk when Ron puts up his hand to stop me. "Yes, the galley is the kitchen."

"You read my mind," I say.

"It's not much of a book," he replies.

"I just don't understand the need for a whole new language just because you're on a boat." I make my way to the kitchen and open the refrigerator. The first thing I see is an almost empty gallon-size plastic water container. I'm so thirsty I easily drain it. Sometimes you just can't beat water. I feel refreshed as I bring it back to Ron. "Should I chop off the top to make it easier to scoop it up?"

"Yeah, that's a good idea. Just don't chop off a finger. You might attract sharks if we have to bail out."

"That's not funny, Ron."

"It's not meant to be."

"Do you think we might have to abandon ship?"

"I hope not."

"There really are sharks in the bay, aren't there."

"Yeah, but don't worry about those. Without a wetsuit, you better hope you can breathe in the frigid water."

"You know you're not really pumping up my confidence."

"You could pump up all of our confidence if you would stop talking and start bailing the water out of the boat, Kimo."

He's got a good point. I open some drawers and find a knife block in one. I pull out a fairly big one with a serrated edge and take it to saw the bottom off of the plastic jug. Unfortunately, it slips off and cuts my index finger. "We have a bleeder!"

"Jesus, Kimo. How bad is it?" Ron snaps.

"It's your fault! The power of suggestion, you put it out there!"

"Bandage up your wound and go change places with my brother."

"I'll be okay, Ron. I can still help you."

"Damn it, we don't have time for this, Kimo. Stop the bleeding and go send my brother down here."

I feel like I've been put in a time-out. I'd rather be spanked and have it over with than to be banned in isolation. I wrap a paper towel around my cut finger and use a piece of duct tape to seal it, then I walk over and hand Ron the emergency kit as I make my walk of shame out of the belly of the whale.

I see Rachel sitting next to Michelle in the La-Z-Boy as I come on deck. The contrast between the living and the dying couldn't be starker.

"Kimo, could you bring us Joy?" Rachel asks.

"I'm not sure of that, but I can get the kitty for you," I say as I turn and go back below the deck. Ron is laying on the floor with a hatch open. He speaks without looking up, "Frank, the bilge pump is working. I'm thinking we can use one of the engines as an emergency pump if we remove the raw-water intake hose and run the throttle in the flooded water."

"It's me, Ron. Your wife wants the kitten."

He looks up quickly, his eyes alive, "She spoke?"

"Oh, no. Rachel asked me to get it for them."

He looks deflated, his energy leaking right out of him like a gashed tire. "I thought we had a miracle."

"No. Sorry." I step down into the water around the bed and reach for the tiny creature. "Come here, little girl." I grab her and step up and out of the wet bedroom. "You know, Ron, when I was down here a while ago, it wasn't wet."

"When?"

"When you called me down and told me to keep the boat moving."

Ron sits up. "So, it could be something else, or it's aggravated by our movement, which could support my theory that the leak is close to the waterline. We still need to get the water out. A gallon of water weighs about eight pounds. If we can clean up what we've already taken on and then monitor the situation, we should be able to stay afloat until help arrives."

"Think they'll find us?"

"Sooner or later. At some point, the fog will lift, and we'll

be able to be seen easily. We should be able to just drift and
stay afloat until then."

"Do you have any idea where the currents or tides will take
us?"

"It depends on where we are right now. Since the tide was
rising when we left Stockton, it should be getting closer to low
tide, which means a valley of water will be sucked out past the
Golden Gate Bridge."

"Out to sea?" I ask nervously.

"Depends, because every six hours or so, the tide changes. If we are here for high tide, we could be pushed over to
the east bay. We'll have to be vigilant, so get up there and
keep a good lookout, Kimo. And send my brother down
here."

"Okay."

"And Kimo, sorry I snapped at you. Thanks for everything.
How's the finger?"

"It's fine."

"Good. Okay, get that kitty upstairs."

"All right." I walk out into the cold, fresh air and hand the
kitten to beautiful young Rachel, and hope it brings joy on
some level to poor shivering Michelle.

"Thank you, Kimo," Rachel smiles as she takes the little
kitten and places her between Michelle's sunken cheek and the
life vest. "How are things down there?"

"We're in good hands with Ron," I say.

"I wish I were in your good hands," she coos.

"Rachel, you're too much," I say. "I've got to go to the bow
and relieve Frank. Ron needs his help. Do you need anything?
Water?"

"Just you. Until then, I'll be here with Michelle and Joy."

"Thank you for everything, Rachel."

"Are you okay, Kimo?" she asks.

"Yeah."

"You sound like you're not going to see me again."

"I do? I don't mean to sound that way. This trip is just winding down, and I won't be able to see you from the bow."

"But you'll see me again tonight in San Francisco," she winks at me.

I just smile and shake my head and boldly scoot by the chair to the narrow passage leading to the bow. This time I don't squat down like a coward, but lean into the window of the cabin and shuffle on. I really need to talk with Rachel about her innuendos because I know I'm not that sexy, and I'm concerned about her. Frank turns as he hears me approach.

"How are things going?"

"We haven't sunk yet. Your brother wants you to join him."

"Did you find the leak?"

"No, but we don't think we've been taking on water too long."

"So, what's the plan?"

"I don't know, Frank. Ask your brother," I reply. "Have you seen anything?"

"No. I think I hear a foghorn, but it could be the wind and my mind playing tricks on me." He starts to get up when he notices my finger. "What happened?"

"I cut myself."

"You don't want to be in the water with that bleeding. You know there are sharks in the bay."

"Thanks, Frank. I don't plan on getting wet."

"Good. Sharks are attracted to blood and can smell it from a quarter of a mile away."

"Okay, Frank, I saw *Jaws*. Your brother needs you."

"Sharks can also hear a heartbeat from about two football fields away."

"Would you go away, please?"

"Just saying."

"You've said enough. Your brother needs your help."

"I'm going already. Geez, lighten up. And pay attention."

"Go!"

He finally leaves, and I'm back to being alone in the fog. And so I sit, surrounded by a wet, swirling, dancing nothingness. I think of it as my subconscious mind. It's a blank canvas with endless possibilities. Huge boat-killing tanker ships, vicious sharks smelling their prey, God welcoming his followers out of a prison of their own making. It's all in there waiting to be manifested into the physical plane.

I take a deep breath of the salty sea air, and I'm happy. In this moment, I am free, just bobbing up and down, drifting on San Francisco Bay. Otis Redding would be pleased. Though, now that I think about it, I seem to remember he died in a plane crash in dense fog.

Wait!

Is that a siren's call?

I think I hear a foghorn in the distance, and when I look in that direction, I see a flash of light. Is it another ship, or is my mind playing tricks on me? I wait, watch, and listen, but am distracted by the sound of Frank coming up and throwing water overboard. I guess he made the cut without injury, and now he's made us eight pounds further away from sinking.

I hear him talking with Rachel but can't make out what they're saying. I feel a pang of jealousy which I know is unreasonable. I think it was Lavater who said the jealous are possessed by a mad devil and a dull spirit at the same time. Lord knows I need some work.

The foghorn blows again. This time I'm certain of it, though I don't see a corresponding light. The sound doesn't seem to be closing in on us, which makes me hope its origin is stationary. If so, I wonder where that might be, and if Ron knows? If he does, then maybe we could figure out where we are. Should I leave my post and ask?

I decide to wait until Frank lightens our load by my body weight so as not to be responsible for sending us down into the cold depths of the bay. Unfortunately, I do the math and figure it's a Sisyphean task for Frank. I'll wait for him to complete ten trips and then make my move. After all, the light is fading, and soon the fog will blend into the blackness of the approaching night.

Frank continues tossing water, and I continue hearing the foghorn. The blasts are in a pattern, and there seem to be two distinct tones going off from different locations with different durations of time between them. Also, every once in a while, the fog thins, and I swear I see a flash of light. Could it be a lighthouse?

I wonder how many lighthouses are spread around the bay. Between counting how many times Frank bails water and trying to get an accurate count of seconds between each blast, I feel like one of my students whose parents insisted they be in a higher math class than they were prepared for, thereby sucking any joy out of learning. I wish I had a tutor on board because my counting is all mixed up. Still, I feel like this intel is something that Ron might be able to use to help us get to shore safely. It's time for action.

I carefully make my way back to the flybridge. I look down at Rachel holding Michelle in the La-Z-Boy. She doesn't seem fazed by anything that's gone on today, or maybe it's just another example of the elaborate masks people wear. She projects poise, but I wonder how many of her teachers realized she was self-harming.

"Rachel," I say.

She looks up, and again her smile gives me a boost. "Hi."

"Have you heard a foghorn?"

"No. Have you?"

"Yes. Do you know if Frank has heard it?"

"I doubt it. He's grumbling every time he gets up to dump

water overboard. He should be up again any minute."

"How's Michelle?"

"She's still with us."

"How are you?"

"I'm good."

Frank appears and pitches another scoop of water back to where it came from. "This sucks!"

"Frank, ask your brother to come up here."

He jumps from the sound of my voice. "Holy smokes, you almost gave me a heart attack!"

"Sorry."

"He's a little busy right now. We still haven't found the leak."

"Ask him if he knows where fog horns would be?"

"So, I did hear one," Frank says proudly to Rachel.

"Yeah. I think there are two different ones. I also think there might be a lighthouse out there."

"Of course, there are lighthouses out here."

"If you know where they are, then maybe we can figure out where we are."

"I know there's one on Alcatraz, although I'm not sure it still works. Let me go get Ron."

He rushes down to get his brother.

"I'm getting hungry," Rachel says.

"There's food down in the galley. That's the kitchen for you landlubbers," I joke.

"I want a steak! I want to go to Izzy's."

Ron quickly comes on deck and interrupts, "Are you sure it sounds like a foghorn and not just a beep?"

"Yes. Listen for yourself."

Ron walks over to the starboard side, and we don't have to wait for long before the sounds float out from the mist. Ron's face burst into a smile. "It's the bridge! That's the Golden Gate Bridge! We can follow that sound, and I'm sure I can find the

St. Francis Yacht Club!"

"What about the leak?" I ask.

"We'll have to monitor it for sure, but I think this is our best bet. I heard you talking about Izzy's. Rachel, it's only a short walk from the club."

"Izzy's!" she squeals and claps her hands.

I look at Michelle's lifeless response and hope that I'm not an albatross around the neck of this boat.

TWENTY-ONE

Ron navigates from the flybridge, Frank monitors the leak below, Rachel's holding on to Michelle in the La-Z-Boy, and once again, I'm at the bow, holding on for dear life. Ron has decided to push the speed to test his theory about the waterline leak. I'm armed with the airhorn and am responsible for keeping watch for any hazards in our path though I'm taking a pounding as we plow through the waves. It's hard to keep my eyes open to look for anything with the spray from the exploding waves peppering my face like swarming gnats. I'm thinking maybe I should've kept my big mouth shut because drifting was much more peaceful.

Thankfully, Ron slows his boat down to get a report from Frank, giving my stomach a chance to settle. I lurch back on wobbly legs to hear the news. Frank comes up, and he looks no better than me. He heaves water over the side before turning back to his brother.

"You were right about the leak, Ron. It's really coming in now."

"Damn it."

"I'm going to need help down here, and we need to stop."

Ron looks back in the direction of the foghorns, which we can once again hear now that we've slowed down the engines. He seems enchanted, lured by the siren's call. He perks up and looks hard into the distance, and I follow his eyes and see the flash of light.

"That's what I thought was a lighthouse," I say.

"We're facing west, and the only lighthouse between us and the bridge is on Alcatraz. Alcatraz is about two miles from the yacht club." He looks around with manic eyes. "The sun is setting. We can do this!"

"Ron, the water is halfway to the top of your bed. We've got to get that water out and not take on any more or we're going to sink!"

"Relax, Frank. The three of us will bail out the water, and then I'll go slower. We'll get there before dark. Let's go to work." He shuts off the engines and comes down, and as he passes, I flash onto Captain Ahab and his white whale and almost ask Ron to call me Ishmael, but I think any attempt at humor would be lost on him at this point.

We work feverishly. Ron lines us up like a bucket brigade. He scoops, passes it to me, I lift it up to Frank, Frank sends it back to its source, and we do it again. Eight pounds, rep after rep, hamsters on a wheel, only we are making progress. I'm sore and tired and really need a nap, but the fear of drowning is a great motivator. Plus, I don't want my bloody finger to tempt a hungry shark, so I hold my own even though the effort starts my digit leaking again.

We finally get down to the floor just being damp. The only thing I can see adding water now is the sweat falling from the three of us. The exertion seems to have exorcized the mania out of Ron's eyes. "You guys did a great job. Thank you for all you've done for Michelle and me today."

Frank looks doubtful. "You're going to take it slow, right?"

"Yeah," he says. "Dinner's on me tonight. Rachel wants to go to Izzy's."

"What about Michelle?" I ask.

"I'll stay with her on the boat. You guys ready to do this?"

"Sure," Franks says unenthusiastically. "But if it starts flooding again down here, you better stop when I tell you."

"I'll go slow. Kimo, ready to be on lookout?"

"Of course, Ron."

I lead us up. Ron walks over and kisses his wife gently on her forehead. "How is she, Rachel?"

"She stopped."

"She's dead?" I ask.

"No, she's still breathing, but her twitching stopped."

"That's fantastic!" Ron's energy is back. He studies Michelle closely, and tears build and fall freely. "She looks peaceful. Honey, we're almost there." He kisses her again and heads to the bridge.

Michelle really does look at peace now that the disheartening tremors are gone. I don't know what that means for her overall condition, but I'm re-energized to do all I can to help Ron get her to where she wanted to be. "Rachel, you've made a huge difference today. I've got to go back to the bow, but I'll see you later."

"Okay." She smiles.

So, I'm once again at the bow. Ron has kept his word, and we're going at a slower pace, which my aching body appreciates. These last couple of days have proved to me that I really am getting old. It's time I started acting like it. So, what do I do? Do I go to the police and confess about grandpa? Well, I should go to Izzy's first. It could be my last supper as a free man. I know I had a steak after Angelina's yesterday, but I don't remember that, and a beautiful filet has me salivating like Pavlov's dog right now. Though if I am going to start acting like an adult, do

I really want to be walking around the Marina District of San Francisco with Rachel? That neighborhood is a modern-day Gethsemane, but I'm no Jesus. Maybe I ought to stay on the boat with Ron and Michelle and get takeout.

And then there is light.

The fog thins, then parts, and the north tower of the Golden Gate Bridge shimmers in glorious rays streaming from the sun setting out beyond the Marin Headlands. My whole body tingles with an ineffable, luminous joy from the view, the bridge engulfed in fog at mid-span, the light dancing on the water all the way to the silhouette of the north shore of Alcatraz. It's as if prayer and art converge, and Thomas Cole's "Old Age" has come to life.

I'm thrown back onto the deck as the boat speeds up. Ron looks transfixed by the sight, hurtling the boat toward it. I hustle to the rail and hold on. "Ron!" Either he can't hear me or simply ignores me.

I haul myself back, bouncing wildly, occasionally losing my grip, spending terrifying moments in fear before regaining it. I get to the windshield of the cabin and pull myself up. I slither my way around to the ladder leading up to the flybridge. Rachel gives me a worried look as she keeps a firm hold on Michelle. Frank frantically joins us and follows me up.

"Ron, you've got to slow down!" I plead.

"No!"

Frank joins us. "What the fuck are you doing? The water is pouring in down there! I can't keep up!"

"I've got to get there before Michelle dies!"

Frank looks at me and then lunges at his brother. As they struggle, the boat veers wildly, and I catch myself on the chair so I don't go over the side. I pull myself up and grab Frank. "Let go of him, Frank. You're making it worse!"

"We're going to sink!" He screams.

"Ron," I say calmly, "Let me drive. You go down and be

with your wife."

Ron's demented look settles as he looks down at Michelle. He eases back on the throttle. "I promised her."

"I know. I'll get us there. Go spend some quality time with your wife."

He notices his brother. "I'm sorry."

Frank is speechless as Ron surrenders the wheel and makes way for me to take over. He then climbs down and exchanges places with Rachel.

"What should we do?" I ask Frank.

"We need to get to dry land."

I look around. "Alcatraz?"

Frank scans our surroundings. "Okay. But take it slow and give me a chance to lighten our load. I'm serious. It won't take much more for us to sink."

"Why don't you ask Rachel to come up and I'll get her to drive, and I'll join you bailing."

"If she's game. I'll send her up." He starts to leave.

"Frank!"

"Yeah."

"If we start to go down, get out of there."

"Don't worry about that."

He climbs down, and I change our course and head for Alcatraz. There's a tall smokestack that I can see, but the lighthouse is still shrouded in fog, and only its light flashes through. Something's different since the last time I drove the boat. It seems sluggish. I wonder if it's the added weight from the water we've taken on. Rachel appears by my side.

"What's going on? Is Ron losing it?"

"Things seem to be catching up to him. Do you think you'd be comfortable driving the boat?"

"Me? Why? You're doing a good job."

"I'd like to help Frank bail water."

"Are we sinking?"

"No. But it's a possibility if we take on too much more water."

"I don't want to die."

"Neither do I."

She leans into me. "I was fine when I was playing music for Michelle, but to have her dying in my arms like that is so sad. She just kept shaking." Rachel is shaking in my arms, and I'm thinking about the difference.

"You've done a great job, Rachel. You've been just amazing. We'll be okay."

"I'm tired, and I'm ready to go home. This isn't fun anymore."

"I know. We'll get you home."

"I'm sorry."

"Shhh, you've got nothing to be sorry for."

"Can I just stay here next to you and do nothing for a while?"

"Of course."

"Thank you."

I glance down and see that Ron has Michelle sitting on his lap, and he's stroking her head while gazing at the setting sun. On the surface, he looks calm, but I'm glad I can't read minds. Twilight bathes Michelle's face in softening color, and knowing what's going on in her mind would be a journey worth taking. I turn back and focus on the one at hand. The fog is making a comeback. The building at the base of the smokestack is now being overrun. I'd guess we're less than a mile from the island, and I don't want to lose sight of it.

"Rachel, I want to get to Alcatraz before it disappears again in the fog. Would you tell Frank I need to pick up the speed?"

"Okay."

She heads down. I throttle up a bit just to get a feel, and it's not good. It's dragging and I have a feeling it's because we have too much added weight. It's not worth the risk, so I throttle down. Even if Alcatraz disappears back into the fog, I look at the compass and will keep going just a tad below due west. We should be fine unless we're forced to abandon ship.

"How close are we?" Frank asks as he climbs next to me.

"It's right there," I say as I point to the northern tip of the island.

"All right, I can't keep bailing. You got to ground us now."

"We're not there."

"You have to shut down the engine. We need weight on the bow and ride the ebb tide in."

I pull back on the throttle, but don't stop the engines. "We're only a hundred yards or so out. Don't you think we can make it?"

"Then you go down and bail. I'll take us in. We'll see what you think."

"Okay."

I relinquish the helm and head down.

"Kimo, send Rachel up!"

I step onto the deck. Rachel looks worried. "Rachel, Frank wants you up there."

"Where are you going?"

"To bail."

"No," the fear on her face scares me.

"It's okay. Go see what Frank wants."

I step down into the salon and understand why Frank and Rachel are scared. The stateroom is almost completely flooded. I have no idea how we're still above water. I wish I would have taught Archimedes' Principle in math. I find the discarded water jug and scoop up a gallon and head up.

"Kimo!" Frank climbs down to the deck. "Forget about that. Come with me."

I toss the water, drop the jug back down into the salon, and follow.

"Ron, are you going to help?"

"A captain goes down with his ship."

Frank looks at me with disgust. "I told you."

"Ron," I plead, "You can't give up!"

He looks at me with dead eyes. "Why not?"

"Because Michelle wouldn't want you to!"

He looks at his wife and whispers, "We're here, honey. I won't leave you until you're on your way."

"Kimo, we have to move!" Franks pleads.

"All right, what do you want me to do?"

"You grab the stern line, I'll grab a spring line, and we'll go ashore and ground her astern."

"Go on shore?" I look around. "You mean Alcatraz."

"Yes."

"We're going to pull the boat on shore?"

"We just need leverage. Wrap the lines around some rocks and let the current do the rest. It should work."

I notice that we're about ten yards from where the water meets the base of a cliff on Alcatraz that rises up to some building. "There's no beach!"

"There's plenty of places to get a grip and climb."

Has Frank lost his fucking mind? "There's a dock somewhere on this island! This is a tourist attraction!"

"We don't have time!" He walks over, unties a spring line, then moves to the stern line and unties it. He tosses that toward me before walking to the transom ladder. "Are you going to help or not? Now's the time to Dragonfly!"

Great. My own words used against me. He ties the line around his waist, climbs down, and jumps in.

"Holy smokes, it's cold!"

What the hell? I watch him flounder and wonder if he's going to drown when he finally starts swimming toward Alcatraz. Do I follow? I have a cut; what about sharks? I also haven't been swimming for a while and never in frigid water. Then the boat dips, and I have all the motivation I need. I bend over, grab the stern line, and follow Frank's lead by tying it around my waist. I make my way down the ladder, look at the water for fins, see none, then jump.

Frank was right; it's fucking freezing! I involuntarily gasp, and my muscles paralyze. I could be having a heart attack! I start to panic and breathe heavily. Thank God I'm wearing a life vest that keeps me afloat, because after about a minute, I recover from the shock and start thinking about sharks. I get control of my breathing and start to swim, my mantra being no sharks, no sharks, no sharks. I can feel the current and am worried that it could carry me away from the island. I paddle hard for three strokes, then look up to recalibrate and catch my breath. I do this until I finally reach Alcatraz's rocky shore rising up from the bay.

I grab on and pull myself out of the water. The line to the boat is pulling on my waist, and I need to secure it before I get pulled back into the bay. I try to use my legs to climb further up, but they're numb. I can't stop shivering. I look over and see Frank crawling over a rock and wrapping his line around it. He inspires me to get back to work. I massage my legs, hoping to reactivate the circulation. Slowly my legs start to work again, and I inch my way up the crag. I get to a fold in the rock where I can brace myself and hold the line. Frank gives me the hang loose sign, and I give a shaka right back.

Frank motions a thumbs up to Rachel, who starts the engines and slowly backs the boat toward us. It sputters and jerks, but she keeps steering it back. I reel in the line as it gets closer. The boat scrapes against some rocks and grinds to a stop. Rachel kills the engine. *It's All Good* is stuck sideways on the rocks, the stern low on the bay side.

I'm looking for somewhere to tie the line off when I notice Ron get up from the La-Z-Boy. He gently carries Michelle over to the transom ladder, where the water is up to the top rung. He kisses his wife tenderly and holds her face to the radiant light streaking orange, red, and pink from beyond the Golden Gate Bridge. The sun slides under the horizon, sinking into the Pacific Ocean. Ron whispers into his wife's ear before carefully lifting her over the rail.

I'm frozen and spent.

I just watch and wonder if this is how you prove your love.

Holding Michelle by her wrists, Ron lowers someone we all love into the ice-cold waters of San Francisco Bay. He keeps her head above the frigid liquid surrounding her and caressing and releasing all the pain from her body.

Michelle's eyes flutter open, and I hope she sees angels coming to lead her soul into eternal light like in Thomas Cole's painting. Her mouth opens wide as her fragile body reacts with an audible gasp. We watch as her last breath escapes its tired, cadaverous host. Michelle's suffering is over.

Ron lifts her out of the water so he can take his wife home. He's prepared a spot where she can rest in peace. And he can be there next to her, searching for some.

TWENTY-TWO

"So, what did you leave for the confessional, my son?"

My memory flashes from the boat and Michelle to the bathroom and my grandmother. That sweet human being with her face swollen and red, sheer terror in her eyes.

"I did it out of anger."

"Killing your grandfather."

"Yes, Father."

"Why?"

"She was so fragile and vulnerable. The last thing my grandmother said was that Mommy was going to call the orphanage, and they were going to come take her away."

The priest sits silently.

"That's the same thing your mom used to tell you."

"Uh-huh."

"So, your mom learned that parenting tip from her father."

"Yes. I've blamed her my entire life when it was learned behavior."

"All behavior is learned. She still behaved that way; there's always a choice. Sounds like she needs forgiveness for some of hers, but let's talk about your choices."

"They haven't been very good, I know."

"They've been sinful."

"Yes, sir."

"Okay," the priest says. "When you sin, my son, you wound your relationship with God, and you diminish yourself. You separate yourself from the God within you, and you separate yourself from your community. You're wounded by selfishness. But you need to remember that you are good, because God only creates good. By your confession, you can have your dignity restored. God loves you. Jesus thought you were worth dying for, even with your sins. There isn't one saint that didn't need forgiveness for their sins. God is happy that you've come back to confession, because it's a sign that you haven't given up on Him. What you did was wrong, especially acting from anger, but I sense it was done out of a mistaken concept of love and not malice. Led by the Spirit, we confront temptation face to face and know full well we must rely on God's redeeming Grace. You need to come out from under the bed, stand up, and take responsibility for your choices. For your penance, I'd like you to say one 'Our Father.' If you remember the Act of Contrition, you can say it now."

Huh?

That's it?

Was he listening, or is he like many of my former students? Does he have someplace to go? Oh yeah, he has a funeral. The Act of Contrition, mmm, I think I remember at least some of it. "Uh, oh my God, I am heartily sorry for having offended thee. I detest all my sins because they have offended you. I resolve with the help of your grace to sin no more."

"Well, that's close enough. You've been away for a while. God, the Father of mercies, through the death and resurrection of his Son, has reconciled the world to himself and sent the Holy Spirit among us for the forgiveness of sins; through the ministry of the Church, may God give you pardon and peace, and I absolve you from your sins in the name of the Father, the Son, and the Holy Spirit. Go in peace, my son, and do good works."

"Father?"

"Yes."

"One Our Father? Were you listening?"

He laughs. "Yes, I was. You shouldn't be surprised by God's mercy. But just know that I will be fasting for you for the next thirty days."

"What? Why?"

"Because a priest should do penance for all who come to us for confession."

"So, you're going to do more penance for my sins than me?"

"Yes. I need to follow in the footsteps of my Lord and Savior."

Wow. I didn't see that coming. How do I feel about him doing more penance than me? They're my sins! Is he laying on Catholic guilt? "What about justice, Father?"

"What would you consider just? I can't bring your grandfather back. I can't stop how he raised your mother, nor what he chose to do to your grandmother. There are plenty of victims here. It's time to move forward with love. Can you do that?"

"I'm willing to try."

"Then go in peace, my son."

Mmm. Can I do that? The priest starts to get up.

"Father, I just watched the woman I've loved since college die, and I killed my own grandfather. How do I get peace?"

He gets back down, and we sit in silence.

Finally, he says, "You want to have peace?"

"Yes, Father."

"Then have some faith. You've been forgiven. Now, I have a funeral. Go in peace."

***

I'm on my knees in a pew in front of the altar to say my Our Father. The church on Kauai with my grandmother's sweet smile, how peaceful it was, flashes through my mind. I can't remember the last time I was actually on my knees out of respect for something greater than man. "Our Father, who art in heaven, hallowed be thy name, thy kingdom come, thy will be done, on earth as it is in heaven. Give us this day our daily bread, and forgive us our trespasses, as we forgive those who trespass against us. Lead us not into temptation, but deliver us from evil. Amen."

It really is amazing how good I feel. The weight of my grandfather's death is lightened. I doubt it will ever be gone completely, but it feels like it's something I can deal with. I like the idea of doing good works.

I notice a statue of Mary holding baby Jesus and decide to say a Hail Mary even though it wasn't assigned. It can't hurt; I could use extra credit. "Hail Mary, full of grace, the Lord is with thee. Blessed are thou amongst women, and blessed is the fruit of thy womb, Jesus. Holy Mary, Mother of God, pray for us sinners, now and at the hour of our death, Amen."

I can't help but think about the hour of Michelle's death. Could I have done more? She's gone. That beautiful human being doesn't exist anymore. What happened to the energy that was her? Energy doesn't die, it just changes, right? Is her soul in heaven now? What am I doing in this church if I don't have faith in that?

And what about Mary? Was she really just fourteen when she gave birth? Did she carry Jesus for nine months and suffer the pain of childbirth without ever actually getting to enjoy the pleasure of conception, as fleeting as that might be? Then to outlive your child and suffer through his disturbing death. It doesn't seem fair. Maybe that's the point.

What about Rachel? Have I treated her with the dignity and respect she deserves?

I make the sign of the cross and walk out of the church to find Rachel's car in the parking lot. Glen Phillips's "Amnesty" plays in my head.

***

"How'd it go?" Rachel asks.

"Really good," I tell her. "I just want to thank you again for everything you've done these last couple of days. You're a special human being."

She gives me a perplexed look. "Okay. Thanks. You still want to do this?"

"Yes."

She starts the car, and we drive.

"You were in there a long time."

"Was I? I'm sorry to keep you waiting."

"It's okay; I just never really saw you as the religious type."

A quick laugh escapes. "Yeah, I can understand that. It's complicated."

She turns back and keeps her eyes on the road.

"So, what's it like? Is it like therapy?"

"I guess a little. Does your therapist absolve you of your sins?"

She laughs, "No. Does the guy you talked with?"

"That's basically the whole point of going to confession."

"So, no offense, but you killed your grandfather, and I was just a bitch to my mother, and out of the two of us, you're forgiven?"

"Do you want to be forgiven?"

"Do you feel forgiven?"

"For the most part, yes. I need to take responsibility and

practice some forgiveness myself, but yes. I'm feeling some peace with myself."

"I'd like to feel that. Inner peace would be nice. I've been in therapy for years, and I've made progress for sure, but you seem different after less than an hour."

"It's funny because it comes down to what you believe. I feel so much better because I was raised to believe that a priest could forgive my sins. I just told the priest the complete truth, unlike what I told you, and he forgave my sins. And I feel better."

"You lied to me about killing your grandfather?"

"No, I just didn't tell you that I did it out of anger."

"Why?"

"Why didn't I tell you, or why did I do it out of anger?"

"Both."

"I didn't tell you because I thought you would judge me."

"Didn't I say that about telling the truth?"

"Yes, you did, and that was on my mind."

"So the truth is you didn't kill him to save your grand-mother?"

"No, that was definitely part of it, but she told me that he was going to call the orphanage to come to get her, and I just lost it. I was enraged. It's scary for me to think about, so I buried it. It came back to me while talking to you."

I'm afraid to look at her as we drive on in silence. The scenery flies past much faster than on the boat.

Rachel breaks the silence. "You will not be punished for your anger; you will be punished by it."

I look at her, "The Dalai Lama?"

"No, Buddha. You're o for three."

"You know, I actually do know quite a few quotes."

"Okay, if you say so."

Of course, now that I need one, my mind goes blank. Silence settles back between us as we continue toward Mount

Diablo.

"What about the shammy?" Rachel asks.

"The what?"

"The shammy, the middle eastern burrito thing you talked about."

"Oh, a shawarma. What about it?"

"We didn't get the chance to enjoy San Francisco. How about now? We could grab a shammy, you could teach me golf, and then Izzy's for dinner. What's one more day?"

Here we go. I so want a shawarma from Truly Mediterranean. It's a beautiful day. We could go to Lincoln Park and play best ball so she can swing every time and we wouldn't delay anybody. It's a great way to learn golf. The walk alone would be worth it. Then a steak and beverages in the Marina, followed by a walk around the Palace of Fine Arts.

I look over at Rachel. She really is lovely. "I would love that, but I can't," I say.

"Of course you can. It's your choice."

"True. But I need to start making responsible choices. If I don't start today, right now, this moment, I could lose the inertia."

"So, you don't want to spend more time with me?"

"Come on, Rachel, you know that's not true."

Rachel looks away and keeps her eyes on the road.

***

Rachel stops just inside the gravel road to the detention center off Marsh Creek Road. Before getting out of the car, I take a long, good look at her. She hits the button releasing the lid to the trunk. I lean over and kiss her on the cheek before getting out of the car. "Thank you."

"Call me when you're free. Frank has my number."

"Sure," I say.

"It's only because you don't have a phone," she smiles,

alleviating my pang of jealousy.

"Okay. You take care."

"You too. And thank you, Kimo. It was quite a couple of days."

I walk back to get my prison uniform out of the trunk. My golf bag and clubs are in there. I forgot that she picked me up at Angelina's and took my clubs and me back to Michelle's. They call to me, looking happy to have been of use and excited to get back out on the links. I have to ignore them, so I quickly grab my uniform and shut the trunk. I walk down the road toward the Marsh Creek Detention Center. The gunfire from the range welcomes me back. I'm ready to do my time, however long that may be.

A hawk cries out from above.

It has a God's eye view of me, the shooting range, and the detention center up on the hill, out of my sight. The soaring hawk cries out again as if calling for me before banking away and heading west toward San Francisco. Toward Lincoln Park. Toward a lamb shawarma. I see myself on the seventeenth tee at Lincoln Park, looking north beyond the Golden Gate Bridge to the Marin Headlands across the bay. I could be there this day.

And it hits me.

This has to be a sign from God, don't you think?

I take a deep breath in and slowly exhale.

Michelle's funeral is tomorrow in Stockton. A beautiful young woman is ten yards behind me, and she has my golf clubs in her trunk. What's a couple of more days before facing my punishment? Shawarma from Truly Mediterranean, a hike with strokes around Lincoln Park, then an evening at the Palace of Fine Arts and the Marina.

I turn around and walk back toward Rachel's car. She starts the car up and drives away.

And just like that, I'm alone.

Maybe she really just wants to be rid of me. Maybe she just needs to get home. I had the priest and the church to help me decompress. Maybe she needs some time. And space. And solitude. Maybe she didn't even see me. I wish her well.

I inhale deeply, then slowly exhale. It's okay. She's right; I need to do my time. I have a lot to atone for, so I might as well face it and get started. I turn and walk.

It's fucking hot. I miss the coolness of the fog. I'd gladly exchange the frigid water of the bay for this oppressive dry heat. Garbage detail is going to be a bitch, if I even get to do it. As I come to the bridge across Marsh Creek, I see the baby sycamores and wonder if anyone has watered them these last few days. They look thirsty.

I stand on the bridge and look down at the trickling waters of the creek. I've come full circle. This water is just starting its journey to the sea.

Golf seems like a distant memory, but then, I can't remember half the holes, anyway. It was fun to play with Frank and Harley again. Too bad Ron couldn't join us.

I hope Ron's going to be okay. I wonder what he's doing right now. Please, God, look out for him. And please bless the soul of his wife, Michelle. I miss her.

A hawk's hoarse scream grabs my attention.

I look up and find it, surfing the thermals. And I think they're messengers from God? I need to use whatever extra time I'm given to get my act together. The great bird dives down toward the road and then rises above a trail of dust flaring up from an approaching vehicle. It's too early for the garbage detail to be returning. Besides, it doesn't look like a van. Maybe it's some sheriffs heading for the range. Whoever they are, they can drive me up the hill. This heat is wearing me out.

Wait a minute!

Is it?

Yes!

Rachel screeches her car to a stop, and her window rolls down. "We'll still do Classic Rock on YouTube when you get out, right?"

I laugh, "Sure."

"Then do your time and call me when you're released. I'm going to go play some piano for my mom."

"God love you."

"Good luck! Hope you're not some bad man's girlfriend!"

"Thanks."

She flashes a smile, waves, and drives away. I'm so happy that she came back. I feel bubbly inside. Rachel's car disappears into the dust, and I turn to climb the hill and face the music.

But before I do that, I'm going to water the trees. Water is life, and life is good.

ACKNOWLEDGEMENTS

It takes a lot of people to make a novel, and I'd like to thank some. Everyone at Atmosphere Press: Alex, Ronaldo, Kyle, Albert, Chris Knight, Chris Beale, Cameron Finch, Kevin Stone, and Hayla Alawi, thank you so much! My first reader, Ray Dinius, had faith in me in college. I was literally writing for his reaction. When I lost him I too was lost. The reason I started this novel was to work through the grief of my sister's death, God love you, Whitney. I was only half way through when Ray died. It took me a while to get back to it. Encouraged by my other reader from Loyola days, Kellee Patricia Marsh, I finally did. My cousin, Corinne Martinez, my fellow traveler on the Camino (especially after Charlie left the old slow relatives behind) has been a supporter for years. Half of this was completed at her house in Winters. Chris Cosmos was my best reader, giving me spontaneous comments as he read. My sister-in-law, Noelle, my nephews Albert, Alex, and Charlie, Andrew Steele, Carol Moxley, Jason Oiler, Linda Proano, and Dennis O'Toole also read and commented on early drafts.

Emma Borges-Scott was a tremendous help. She told me what she thought and provided a new direction. Then there's family. I couldn't have done it without them. My Dad was my greatest teacher and got me into reading early. Alistair MacLean, Ian Fleming, the Playboy Interview, and most recently, Louise Penny, were authors he shared. My Mom, God love her, unfortunately now has dementia and will miss out on this. I've known my brother my entire life. He taught me to climb out of my crib. Of course, he didn't teach me how to climb back in. Every time we escaped and wreaked havoc, I was left alone to take the fall. He was young so is forgiven. He grew up to be a phenomenal human being and an inspiration. My little sister, Whitney, was the inspiration for this book. She and her husband, Steve Clark, hosted Thanksgiving after they got married, and Steve has kept that tradition alive. I thank you all.

ABOUT ATMOSPHERE PRESS

Atmosphere Press is an independent, full-service publisher for excellent books in all genres and for all audiences. Learn more about what we do at atmospherepress.com.

We encourage you to check out some of Atmosphere's latest releases, which are available at Amazon.com and via order from your local bookstore:

Dancing with David, a novel by Siegfried Johnson

The Friendship Quilts, a novel by June Calender

My Significant Nobody, a novel by Stevie D. Parker

Nine Days, a novel by Judy Lannon

Shining New Testament: The Cloning of Jay Christ, a novel by Cliff Williamson

Shadows of Robyst, a novel by K. E. Maroudas

Home Within a Landscape, a novel by Alexey L. Kovalev

Motherhood, a novel by Siamak Vakili

Death, The Pharmacist, a novel by D. Ike Horst

Mystery of the Lost Years, a novel by Bobby J. Bixler

Bone Deep Bonds, a novel by B. G. Arnold

Terriers in the Jungle, a novel by Georja Umano

Into the Emerald Dream, a novel by Autumn Allen

His Name Was Ellis, a novel by Joseph Libonati

The Cup, a novel by D. P. Hardwick

The Empathy Academy, a novel by Dustin Grinnell

Tholocco's Wake, a novel by W. W. VanOverbeke

Dying to Live, a novel by Barbara Macpherson Reyelts

Looking for Lawson, a novel by Mark Kirby

Yosef's Path: Lessons from my Father, a novel by Jane Leclere Doyle

Surrogate Colony, a novel by Boshra Rasti

ABOUT THE AUTHOR

Dwight Jesmer grew up an army brat in a life of perpetual motion. He went to seven schools before finishing high school at Punahou in Honolulu, Hawaii. He graduated from Loyola Marymount University and then spent a decade working in the film and television industry in Los Angeles. He left the smog of Los Angeles for the fog of San Francisco to work on his Masters in Writing at USF where he got into teaching. He worked almost two decades in the trenches of education. He's written song lyrics, numerous screenplays, one play, and this is his first novel.